OPEN WOUNDS

This book is dedicated to Karen,
my partner and love of over 20 years,
And our son, Max,
for whom the sun rises and sets,
And meets all the points in between.

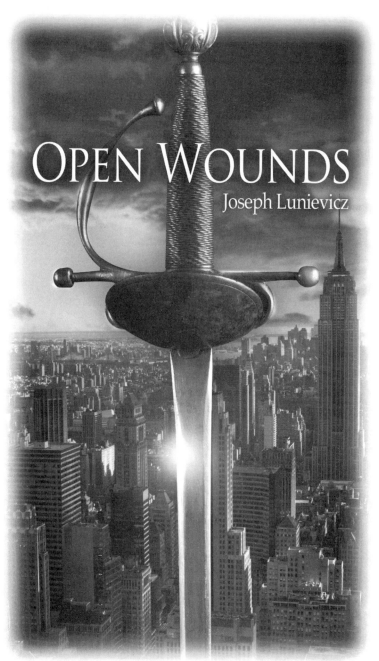

OPEN WOUNDS

Joseph Lunievicz

WestSide Books

Lodi, New Jersey

Published by WestSide Books
60 Industrial Road
Lodi, NJ 07644
973-458-0485
Fax: 973-458-5289

This is a work of fiction. All characters, places, and events
described are imaginary. Any resemblance to real people,
places, and events is entirely coincidental.

Library of Congress Cataloging-in-Publication Data
Lunievicz, Joe.
  Open wounds / by Joe Lunievicz. -- 1st ed.
    p. cm.
  ISBN 978-1-934813-51-5
  [1. Fencing--Fiction. 2. Orphans--Fiction. 3. Friendship--Fiction. 4.
Amputees--Fiction. 5. Cousins--Fiction. 6. New York
(N.Y.)--History--1898-1951--Fiction.] I. Title.
  PZ7.L9791173Ope 2011
  [Fic]--dc22

                                                          2010053732

International Standard Book Number: 978-1-934813-51-5
School ISBN: 978-1-934813-52-2
Cover design by David Lemanowicz
Interior design by David Lemanowicz

Printed in the United States of America
10 9 8 7 6 5 4 3 2 1

First Edition

OPEN WOUNDS

PART I - SUNNYSIDE

One

CAPTAIN BLOOD, 1936

It begins with blood and ends with blood.

I stared at the advertisement in the Amusements section of *The New York Times* willing it to come to life. There was a picture of a man with long hair holding a sword beneath the words, "The Seas Run Red in the Wake of Captain Blood." Everything about this man was an invitation to adventure. If I closed my eyes I could almost hear him whisper, "Come with me."

It was three days after Christmas, just before my seventh birthday. I'd stolen the paper from the pile outside my father's room. That morning, like most Saturdays, my father remained asleep. He'd been drinking heavily and I knew by the sound of his deep, long snores that he would remain asleep far into the afternoon. This was a good thing, because when he was awake, he spoke with his fists. I'd never known my mother. She'd died giving birth to me.

My grandmother stirred an hour later, then left the

house quietly, on her way to her Saturday church services. Tait Maddie Wymann believed in God above, the devil below, and hell on earth. Unlike my father, I couldn't avoid Maddie. She schooled me at home six days a week and kept me in the house doing chores the rest of the time. To keep me in line she once placed my hand over our stove burner until the skin bubbled. Other times she lashed my behind raw with a belt, and black and blued my fingers with a wooden ruler.

It was the picture of a defiant Captain Blood that made me follow Maddie–that and a curiosity about the world outside of our house that Maddie, no matter how hard she tried, couldn't beat out of me.

I opened my door and stole out into the living room, stepping carefully, trying not to make the floorboards squeak. I crept around the hard-backed chairs that served as our furniture and the small Christmas tree with a few strands of silver tinsel hanging from it that sat beneath a large crucifix with Jesus and his bloody palms by the front door.

I hesitated, staring at the doorknob, wondering if it would burn my fingers the way Maddie said it would if I ever tried to leave without her. I closed my eyes and reached forward, holding my breath. My fingers touched the brass. It was cold. I opened my eyes and exhaled, laughing, and covered my mouth with my hands. I opened the door slightly, then closed it—looking above me, then behind— to see if there were black-scaled demons waiting to drag me down into the underworld. There weren't. I couldn't believe it. No fangs or claws or long pointy tails—

just my father's snores. I thought, *Maybe they're all asleep.* I shuddered, then reached back and quickly grabbed a jacket and cap. I opened the front door and stepped outside. The air was cold and crisp. I spotted Maddie disappearing down the block and ran after her.

There hadn't been much snow that year, but there had been freezing days. My knickers covered part of my legs, but my knee socks were stretched out and hung around my ankles. The wind cut right through my jacket. I tried to keep up with Maddie as she walked quickly to the elevated station on Queens Boulevard. When I stopped to look up at the station a train passed overhead and the ground trembled beneath my feet. I shivered and swallowed hard. Maddie disappeared through the station door. I ran to the door and tried to pull it open, but it wouldn't budge. A man opened it for me and, in a panic, I ran past him, up the steps. I saw Maddie pass money to a man in a small booth, then push through a turnstile. I tried to duck under the wooden arms, but got caught by one and hit in the back of the head as it rolled around. Someone yelled, "Hey, you!" but I stumbled through and got lost in the crowd. Standing on a bench on the platform, rubbing the bump on the back of my head, I could see for miles even though the platform was crowded. At one end of the tracks I saw a tall, needle-shaped building that seemed to shoot up out of the ground. Following it into the sky, my head started to spin.

"That's the Empire State Building, son," said an old man sitting to my right.

At the other end of the tracks small patches of farmland dotted the horizon between new half-block-long apartment buildings and piles of construction. I looked back from where I'd come and saw Sunnyside Gardens—my home. I pictured my father, asleep on his bed, mouth open, pushing out and pulling in the curtains with each breath, and marveled at how big the world really was.

The train pulled up, wheels clacking on electric rails. As it stopped I jumped off the bench and ran toward where I'd seen my grandmother disappear into one of the open doors. Steeling myself, I stepped across the gap between platform and car, and entered its belly. Not far away, amid the forest of men's pants and women's wool-covered calves, I saw Maddie's sagging black socks and swollen ankles. The doors closed and the car jerked forward a few times before its ride smoothed out. I grabbed a pole and held on tight. Every time the train stopped I was thrown forward, then back, knocking into heavy coats and women's thick purses. A barking man's voice came from outside the door shouting the names of streets as the doors opened and closed, letting some people off and others on. Maddie sat down on a bench. I pressed my face against the pole and lowered myself to the floor. The windows darkened as the train went below the earth. My ears popped and the lights went out. I thought Maddie had found me out and punished me by taking me down into hell.

"Church services, church services," I repeated over and over as the train leveled out and the lights came on. The journey seemed to go on forever. Finally, we came to a screeching halt and for a moment all was still. Then the doors opened and the voice barked, "Times Square, last stop." I got up just as the crowd around me surged toward the doors.

Maddie stood and walked quickly out, passing through tunnels, around winding corridors, and up stairs. Finally I heard wind howling up ahead. A large sign above me said HOLD YOUR HAT, and all around me people grabbed for theirs with free hands. I held onto my cap as a sudden gust of wind tried to tear it free. The light of day blinded me when I reached the surface.

Giant buildings loomed over me on all sides and bright lights, lit even during these morning hours, surrounded signs for Planter's Peanuts and Wrigley Spearmint Gum. There were vendors selling a frank, kraut, and lemonade for five cents, sitting on tomato crates next to their push-carts, warming their hands at their small fires beneath giant yellow and green umbrellas. Fruit vendors yelled, "Apples, apples, apples for five cents!" and "Two peeled oranges for a nickel!" There were rattling trolley cars, honking taxis, and men yelling from doorways with posters of half-naked women behind them: "Yes, you sir, come in and see Lucinda Hellenesca whose virgin legs—as long and lithe as Eve's—lead up to the sacred temple that tempted Adam."

I couldn't believe this was where Maddie went to her church services. It was terrifying and exciting at the same time. No wonder she went every week.

I lost Maddie as the sights and smells made my stomach rumble and my eyes dart from one attraction to another. I could have forgotten her completely if I hadn't been knocked over by a kid running up the stairs.

"Watch where you're goin'!" he shouted as he passed.

Getting up, my knee scraped and bleeding, I saw Maddie standing beneath a large white sign crawling with red letters: CAPTAIN BLOOD. It was like a miracle, from straight out of the newspaper to big broad letters right in front of me, scrawled across the sky. It was a sign from God. I could see Maddie's face as she looked up at the marquee. Her wrinkled cheeks flushed bright red as she smiled, clasping her gnarled, black-gloved hands in front of her. She wore a large gray woolen overcoat that gave her figure a boxy shape and made her seem small beneath that sign—small but happy. I'd never seen her happy before—it surprised me. People were lined up alongside the building and off into the distance, puffing out frosted air in white gusts that hovered above their heads like clouds. But Maddie didn't seem to notice them as she looked up at the words in red. CAPTAIN BLOOD.

Then she turned around and spotted me. Her smile disappeared and I froze. She pulled out her pocket watch and looked at it before she looked back down at me. Then she pointed one long finger and slowly curled it in, beckoning me. I swallowed and walked toward her whispering, "Church services, church services." As soon as I was in range, she cuffed the back of my head, sending my cap flying to the ground. When I reached down to pick it up, she grabbed my hair and twisted it hard enough to make my eyes tear, then pulled my face up toward hers.

"You'll not say a word of this to anyone," she said, her lips pursed and thin. "You understand?"

"Yes," I said, not understanding at all.

She relaxed her grip and pushed me toward the box office.

"I'm cold," I said.

"Then freeze."

"What's inside the big house?"

"The face and voice of the devil, now shut your mouth."

She gave thirty-five cents to the cashier and bought two tickets, looking around quickly as if she were afraid of being seen, then led me to the back of the line. Huddled between the thick fur coats of the women surrounding us, I was at least warm. There were children, too, like me and older, with stained brown bags in their hands and dirt on their faces. They pushed and shoved each other while adults talked above them.

Inside the theatre both the cigarette smoke and the noise grew thicker. Maddie rushed me inside and we grabbed seats in the crowded back row, facing a large white wall. The seats folded down and sprang up when you got off them. I did it four or five times until Maddie smacked me to make me stop. There was an ashtray on the back of each seat in front of us. I could barely see above the people in the next row, so I folded my legs under me, sat back on my heels and, with a little shifting around, found my balance.

Then the overhead chandelier dimmed. Music swelled from everywhere. A silver beam appeared above my head and split the darkness, flooding the wall before us with light. At first I thought it was God speaking to me and I nearly peed my pants. Then I realized it wasn't God but a photoplay, a moving picture, a real talking film.

A giant antenna appeared on the wall, followed by men in uniforms marching, bombs dropping, and airplanes soaring. Then the wall went black and the music stopped. In the darkness I couldn't breathe. Then a different kind of music came on that grabbed me around the chest and wouldn't let go. Trumpets blared. Crossed cutlasses and ships painted on stretched canvas filled the wall. Words splashed onto the ships in what seemed to be letters that stood hundreds of feet high, so tall I thought they would fall off the wall and on top of me. Then the light disappeared and left the world in shadows. A horseman appeared, galloping through cannon fire, searching for Doctor Peter Blood. And then came Captain Blood in the flesh and handsome as the devil. I forgot about my grandmother. I forgot about my father. I forgot about church services. I forgot about everything but the giants above me, their crashing cannons, their heaving ships, and their clashing swords.

I emerged from the theatre rubbing my eyes as I tried to adjust them to the light of the lobby. My grandmother left me there, whispering, "Don't move till I come back."

I stood on the marble floor beneath the crystal chandelier that marked the beautiful entrance. Through squinted eyes I stared at the winking lights above me. There was a commotion by the front doors and a group of men and women entered, the men in tight-fitting suits—dapper black tuxedos with tails—smoking cigars as big as zeppelins. The crowd parted in front of them and they walked up to me. One man in particular—black-haired, clean-shaven, dark-eyed, with a thin, athletic look—seemed to be the center of attention. He had a woman on each arm. Each wore a low-cut dress that shimmered like stars as she moved. The man puffed on a stogie that wreathed his head in smoke. I was in their way and unable to move. The man looked at me and released the two women. He bent down on one knee and withdrew his cigar from his mouth.

"Do you know who I am?" he asked with an accent I'd never heard before. His hair was oiled and slicked back perfectly. His teeth gleamed.

I shook my head.

"Someday, when you are bigger, you will come to know who I am. This man, Flynn"—he pointed with his cigar at the life-size poster of Captain Blood above the popcorn stand—"they say he is a great swordsman. He uses his sword up there, on screen. Not here, in—in flesh." He took my hand and placed it in his. "See?" he said. "This is flesh, not screen. *Flesh*."

I nodded and shook his hand. He shook back, laughing. It was a strong grip for such a thin man.

A flash of light blinded me.

"Great shot, Flanagan," someone said.

I smelled something burning. When my eyes cleared, the man, and the crowd of people around him, were gone.

"Do you know who that was?" a man in a worn doorman's tuxedo asked me from behind.

I turned around and saw a man, younger than my father, flexed in the same position Captain Blood had been when he swung his sword—knees bent, right arm forward, left arm curled up toward his ear. I shook my head.

The doorman lunged forward and I dodged. He laughed and pretended to swing an imaginary sword from side to side. "That," he said between cuts and thrusts, "was . . . Aldo . . . Nadi!"

"Fesniv!" the manager yelled from the box office.

The doorman froze, sweat dotting his forehead.

"Fesniv!" yelled the voice again.

The doorman winked at me. "He just gave a fencing exhibition with Santelli and Costello at the Plaza Hotel. They say he's the greatest swordsman who ever lived."

"Greater than Captain Blood?" I asked.

I never heard him answer because Mad Maddie Wymann grabbed my ear and dragged me out into the cold.

"A villain at heart, and nothing but trouble," she said. "You're just like your father."

I hoped that wasn't true, because even then I hated my father more than anyone else in the world.

Two

THE BLACK PIRATE

The following Saturday Maddie left for her church services as usual, only she made sure my father was awake when she left so I couldn't follow her.

That afternoon, sitting by the front door beneath the crucifix, I heard the boy who lived next door, Tomik Kopecky, playing with another boy on the other side of the wall. I knew Mr. Kopecky was a limousine driver because I'd seen him in uniform in front of our house, getting into his long black car that seemed to stretch on forever. Tomik had four sisters I never saw, but sometimes I heard them laughing from the room next to mine.

"You shall not take her while I live," Tomik said.

"Then I'll take her when you're dead!" the other boy said. Then there was the clack and clatter of wood hitting wood.

I pressed my ear to the wall to hear them better.

"Now I want to be Captain Blood," Tomik said.

"But I was the Frenchie all day yesterday," said the other.

"Siggy, you've got to play Lava-sour!" Tomik shouted.

"Cedric!" my father's voice called from the kitchen, and I jumped away from the wall. "Get away from the front door and do your chores." He held a white dishtowel with ice in it against his forehead as he sat at the table. "And stay the fuck out of my way today. I've got work to do and I need quiet."

My father had worked as an illustrator for an advertising company in Manhattan but had lost his job a few years after I was born. Now he worked freelance out of the back room across from me.

I spent the rest of the afternoon cleaning the windows before going back to my room. Staring out my window into the empty garden, I saw Tomik and his friend, Siggy, run past, swords poking through their belts at rakish angles.

My father's snoring interrupted me. I crept out to the kitchen, found my father's copy of *The Times*, and took it back into my bedroom. Usually I would only look at the papers he'd finished reading so I wouldn't get caught, but that day I had to look. I scanned the Amusements section, searching through the titles of the photoplays that were listed until I found the one I was looking for: "Held over for one more week! *Captain Blood*."

That evening, the moment Maddie came through the front door, my father left. "He's in there," he said, and pointed at my room with a toss of his head.

"Where are you going?" she asked.

"Out," he said.

I waited until Maddie had gone into the kitchen and I could hear her running water into the kettle for tea. When she turned around, saucer and teacup in hand, I was standing next to my chair, hands folded in front of me. I pictured myself as Jeremy Pitt, Captain Blood's navigator, tied up and ready to be lashed by the slave overseer, but knowing that, no matter how badly they hurt him, he would never give up the Captain and crew's plans for escape.

"You don't go to church services on Saturdays, do you?" I asked.

Maddie dropped her tea, the saucer shattering as it hit the floor. The cup bounced three times, spilling all its contents, before it broke.

"Why do you go to see photoplays if they're the voice of the de—" Maddie slapped me hard across the face before I could finish. I didn't move, even though my cheek was on fire.

"Why do you go to see photoplays on Saturday—" I began again.

Maddie stopped me with a backhand that left my ear ringing.

I felt blood roll down my chin. "Why do you go—" The sound of her hands hitting my cheeks punctuated each of my attempts to speak. I kept hearing Jeremy Pitt's voice: *I didn't tell them a thing, Peter Blood. I didn't tell them a thing.*

And then it stopped.

Maddie's hands were spotted with blood, hers and mine mixed together, and she held them at her partially opened mouth.

"Why," I began slowly, barely able to stand, "do you go . . . to see photoplays . . . on Saturdays . . . if they're the voice . . . of the devil?"

"You will not speak of this again," she whispered.

"Then, take me . . . with you. If you don't, I'll tell."

Her eyes opened wide, then narrowed to slits. "This is the lying Jew in you speaking. Just like your mother—conniving to hook my son—"

"I'll tell . . . ," I repeated.

"You wouldn't."

"Take me with you," I said, then fell to the floor.

I woke up sometime later, on my bed with a wet towel over my face, breathing the strong smell of camphor. Maddie was in her room. Light leaked out from underneath her closed door. I washed myself slowly and cleaned my cuts.

I stayed in bed for three days. Each afternoon and evening, Maddie left me soup on my nightstand. My father was gone the whole time. By the fourth day, when he came back, the swelling had gone down. He looked at me closely for a moment, as if for the first time he could actually see my face.

"Looks like you got the shit beat out of you." He grabbed my hands and examined them. The smile disappeared. "Didn't throw a punch at all, did you."

The next Saturday, Maddie stepped into my bedroom. "Stay out of my way, and don't speak to anyone," she said.

"Where you going with the boy?" my father yelled from his bedroom.

"I'm taking him to church services," she said.

I followed her, and the outside world opened up.

✛

We saw *Captain Blood* again and for me it was almost better than the first time. I think Maddie had seen it the previous week, too, because she mouthed the words as Levasseur, Jeremy Pitt, and Peter Blood said them on the screen.

After that there was *The Informer, Ceiling Zero, The Professional Soldier*—with one of Maddie's favorites, "Mister" Victor McLaglen—and *Yellow Dust*. In a notebook I told Maddie I'd lost, I wrote each of their titles down along with my favorite line or scene and pasted the different-colored ticket stubs next to each title. I kept the book hidden beneath my mattress.

The newsreels like Movietone and Paramount News gave me *The Times* photos come to life. German Nazi soldiers in black uniforms saluted a man called Hitler with arms that shot straight up into the air like switchblades. And we all laughed at the Italian leader, Mussolini, who puffed his chest out and waved his hands like a clown—even though the map that lay across the screen showed a place called Abyssinia in Africa under attack from his troops.

We went to all the theatres around Broadway, like the Strand, the Rivoli, and The Capitol. We always went in the morning and never stuck around for the live shows that came on in the evenings.

On my journey to the train, I also saw Tomik Kopecky and sometimes his friend, Siggy Braun, though usually it was just Tomik, alone. At first they were only faces pressed up against the glass of Tomik's front door, staring at us as we walked past them—Siggy with wire-rimmed glasses that covered his small face like goggles. I stared back. But if I stared too long, I'd lose Maddie and miss the movie, so I didn't dawdle.

Then one day Tomik nodded and I nodded back.

A week later he asked, "Where you goin'?" His knickers were worn and stained, his coat frayed at the sleeves, his gloves fingerless. He stood with his head cocked to one side, his curly brown hair unruly beneath his cap.

"Church services," I replied before Maddie could chase him away, grab my ear, and pull me along behind her.

After that, Tomik would trail us, like a lone secret agent, all the way up to the elevated line. When Siggy was with him, they seemed like each other's shadow. Maddie didn't notice them, but I did.

The first Saturday in April, we saw Douglas Fairbanks's silent film *The Black Pirate*. On our way home that afternoon, Maddie came to an abrupt stop one block away from our house. Lost in imagining myself to be swimming under water beneath the hull of a ship, knife between my teeth, side by side with the Black Pirate, I wasn't looking where I was going, so I bumped into Maddie's legs from behind. Normally she would have cuffed me for being so clumsy, but this time she did nothing. Across the street were several policemen in dark blue and a sheriff with a megaphone, standing on the sidewalk in front of the houses. Their windows were boarded up from the inside, and where there wasn't wood, there was furniture pushed up against the glass in what looked like a barricade. The roof was lined with odd pieces of rusted barbed wire, and the top of the fence, to either side, was ridged with broken glass.

"What's—," I began, but Maddie's hand lifted away from her side in warning and I closed my mouth.

"This is the last notice of eviction," the sheriff said, raising the megaphone to his lips. He had a slight Irish brogue. "Now, you haven't paid your mortgage and you've been warned, so come on out or I'll have to send my men in to get you." The four men in blue behind the sheriff stood stamping their feet, pacing back and forth in the cold.

We all waited, but nothing happened. A hand pushed a front curtain aside and I saw a man's haggard face peer out before the curtain closed sharply again.

"Now, Cap?" one of the men in blue asked.

The sheriff crossed his arms on his chest and nodded.

"Let's get 'em out," the man in blue said, darting forward. Three of them filed up the short front steps. The two with billy clubs stepped to either side of the man with the axe, while the fourth man in blue stood in front of the large bay window, but back far enough to cover the others. The man with the axe spit into his hands, grabbed the axe's haft, and swung. It crashed into the wood of the front door and split it.

"We've had a notice, too," Tomik whispered in my ear. I jumped, but he closed his hand quickly around my mouth and put his other finger to his lips. Siggy Braun stood next to him with a tentative smile on his face. I nodded.

Two more blows and the policeman reached in to pull

out a large piece of splintered wood. Sand spilled out in a small waterfall from the opening.

"They've sandbagged the door, Cap!" the man in blue yelled back at the sheriff.

"You know what to do, then!" the sheriff yelled back.

Tomik pointed up to the shallow-sloped roof. I saw a hand appear at the edge, holding on to a small package.

"Look out!" the policeman by the window shouted, looking up at the same time.

The three men in blue looked up. They hesitated for a second, just long enough for the shower of white flour and black pepper to cover them.

"My eyes!" the man with the axe yelled, dropping to his knees while the other two retreated. "My eyes!" More flour fell and covered his head. He sneezed and staggered down the steps, leaving his axe behind.

"My father says," Tomik whispered in my ear, "if we miss another payment, we'll be like them, fightin' with pepper and flour against the coppers."

"My father sells hats," Siggy added in my other ear.

"You folks over there," the sheriff yelled, noticing us for the first time. And it wasn't just us. We were now a small crowd of about ten, watching from the other side of the street.

"He says," Tomik continued, "he's gonna get a job from a man named Farthings, some Joe from the docks with new money."

"You folks over there," the sheriff interrupted, "go on home. This is none of your affair. Go on home."

Maddie turned away, her face ashen, and left.

I looked at Tomik and Siggy. They both smiled at me.

"Tomik Kopecky," he said, putting out his hand, as if we were adults.

"Cedric Wymann," I said, and looked down at it.

He kept his hand out, waiting.

I put out my hand slowly.

He took it, never losing his smile, and we shook.

"I'll call you Cid," he said.

"I'm Sigfried but everyone calls me Siggy," the other boy said, and we shook hands, too.

I looked over my shoulder at Maddie's retreating figure. "I gotta go."

"See you when I see you," Tomik said.

I nodded and turned toward Maddie.

"Let's go at it again," the sheriff's voice boomed out of his megaphone. "Keep your hats low over your eyes and drag the devils out."

I turned back toward Tomik and Siggy, but they were gone. The police charged the front door, and flour and pepper filled the air a second time.

I'll see you when I see you, Tomik had said.

"Not if you know Maddie Wymann," I said to myself.

Three

LAST OF THE MOHICANS

Several weeks later, a note written in pencil appeared under our door. Maddie tore it up. I hunted for it in the garbage and pieced it together later, after she was asleep.

"Come out and play," it read.

The notes appeared each Saturday morning and afternoon thereafter, either beneath the front door or tacked to it, sometimes in a scrawl and other times in a neat print. Then the notes started to appear beneath the back door, too. We never used the back door. It only led out to a stained concrete patio and a garden that, in our section, was overrun with weeds. Maddie took all the notes and burned them.

Then, late one night as summer began, Maddie and my father had a fight. I didn't hear it or see it—I must have slept through it—but in the morning Maddie wouldn't come out of her room, my father's door was closed, and there was broken glass on the kitchen floor. Later that morning, when I knocked on Maddie's door, a hoarse voice like sandpaper answered, "Leave me alone."

The rest of the week, Maddie went out of her way not to say anything to me unless it was absolutely necessary, and when she did, she put her hand against her throat, as if it pained her to speak. I could see there were purple bruises circling her neck.

She avoided my father. So did I.

Then Saturday came and we saw *The Last of the Mohicans*. The names Chingachgook, Uncas, and Hawkeye were magical, taking me to green forests where Indians and soldiers fought each other with tomahawks and rifles. They were exactly the way three friends ought to be—ready to die for each other. Just as we reached our front door, Maddie turned to me and placed her hands on her hips. I lifted my gaze to hers and stared back. Tacked to the door was another note, fluttering gently in the early summer breeze.

"Come out and play," the note said.

"Go," Maddie said, the word almost a whisper.

"Where?" I asked.

She closed her eyes to slits. I ran.

Two houses away, Tomik and Siggy stepped out from behind a bush to intercept me. I was looking behind me, to see if Maddie was following, so I didn't see them and crashed into both. We went down together in a tangle of arms and legs.

Uncas and Hawkeye, I thought.

Tomik propped himself up on an elbow. His lip was bleeding. "Cid," he said.

"Cid," Siggy repeated, adjusting his eyeglasses.

I remember noticing how dirty the two of them were and how clean I was. I got up slowly. Tomik threw a punch at my shoulder. I blocked it automatically and drew back to give him one.

"Wait," Siggy said, raising his hands. "That was for fun, Cid. Tomik did it just for fun. We always do that to each other." Siggy punched Tomik lightly on the shoulder and Tomik replied with a quicker, harder one on Siggy's. Siggy rubbed his shoulder and looked at me. "See?"

"That's right, Cid," Tomik said. "Come on."

"Where?" I asked.

"There." Tomik pushed both Siggy and me to the ground and ran off down the block shouting, "Catch me if you can!"

Siggy got up and ran a few feet, then stopped when he saw I hadn't moved. "Come on," he repeated.

I followed.

When we got to the corner Tomik was waiting for us, sitting beneath the street lamp. "What took you so long?" he asked.

That first night of freedom, I came home in the dark, my knickers torn at the knees, my socks hanging down below my ankles, my shirt untucked and covered with dirt stains. I grabbed the front door and yanked it open like a returning king, a huge smile splitting my face from ear to ear.

My father was waiting for me. He swayed from the drink and held a belt loosely in his hand. "You don't get something for nothing in this world," he said, breathing heavily. I watched the buckle of the belt circle slowly near the floor.

"I got you out, boy—yes, I did. Nobody did that for me . . . nobody. So here's the price of freedom . . ." He raised the belt to strike me and I leapt at him, fists swinging, but one swing of his belt sent me crashing to the floor.

When he was done, he leaned against the wall and slid down next to me. I lay on the floor, unable to move, my shirt in tatters and my back laid open. "You killed your mother, boy," he said. "I can't forgive that. But I give you this, you got some fight in you."

I swore then and there that when I was older, I'd make my father cry out in pain, I'd leave him on the floor, torn and bleeding, and I'd throw salt onto his open wounds.

In the morning I woke up and my father was gone.

It was two weeks before I could see Tomik and Siggy again.

Four

ANTHONY ADVERSE

Two weeks later, Maddie and I were walking back toward the house after seeing *Anthony Adverse*, Maddie walking five paces in front of me, when Siggy ran up from behind. He only stopped for a second to grab my shoulder and catch his breath.

"Scarps," he said, pointing back toward Skillman Avenue. "Run!"

I looked where he pointed. Three large boys were running toward us.

"Who's Scarps?" I asked.

"Rick Scarpetto, now come on!" Siggy gasped. His hair was a mess. Blood ran out of his mouth and over his lip. He held his glasses in his hand. The black frames were broken in the middle and the glass in one was badly cracked.

"Who's that with him?"

"The Smith brothers!"

"They did this to you?"

Maddie had already disappeared into our house up the street so I was alone with him.

"We have to go!" Siggy tugged at my arm; then, with a final glance over his shoulder, gave up and ran.

I turned to face the three boys who were approaching. They stopped in front of me, also breathing hard. Rick Scarpetto, or Scarps as Siggy had called him, looked to be almost twice our size, with a mop of thick black hair and small black eyes. Billy and Arnold Smith were older, too, and looked exactly alike, short and pudgy, but wide across the shoulders. They had crew cuts and their hair was blond. They all wore long pants with holes at the knees. I'd seen them before at a distance on my travels with Maddie, but I didn't know them.

"Billy, who's this kid?" Scarps asked between breaths, his hands on his hips.

I stared at them in response.

"Dat's da Wymann kid," the boy named Billy said.

"Da Wymann kid," Billy's twin said.

"So you're the one that lives with the old witch and the drunk," Scarps said.

I ran into him, butting him with my head, and tackled him to the ground. He recovered himself in a second and easily threw me to the side. Then he stood up and rubbed his chest where I'd hit him.

"Just like your old man," he said. "Dumb as a doorknob and twice as stupid."

I ran at him again, only this time he was waiting for me and punched me squarely in the side of the head before I could hit him. I landed on the ground but pushed myself up to stand. They circled me.

"Did yah see his faddah fightin' at Kilkarney's?" Billy

asked. "Drunk, with pee all down his pants, hah! Cryin' about some broad named Abigail."

I swung my fists in the direction of the boy's voice.

"Look out, Billy," the other twin shouted.

I connected with some part of Billy Smith's stomach and I heard him grunt in pain. Then fists punched me in the side and back. I swung in all directions before someone clipped me on the side of the head again and I passed out. I felt them kicking me in the back and sides as I lay on the ground, coming to.

"Make 'im pay for dat," Billy said. "Make 'im pay for dat good."

"Cid!" I heard Siggy shout from far off.

"Rick Scarpetto," a woman's voice yelled, a little closer, "you leave that boy alone!"

Scarps leaned down close to my ear and whispered, "Just like your father. Another stupid Limey. Listen to me, stupid Wymann. I saw you runnin' with the Braun kid and Kopecky. You do that and you'll get in it deep with me. This neighborhood is mine and you'll pay to be in it. You understand?" Then he spit on my face and ran away laughing, with Siggy and a woman shouting after him.

I tried to sit up but my head and ribs were sore. Blood ran down the side of my face. A strong arm reached around my back and helped lift me into a seated position.

"Cid, oh no," Siggy said. "You got all busted up." He was pacing back and forth in front of me, mumbling, "I'm sorry, I'm sorry."

"I'm Siggy's mother," the woman said to me, looking into my face. My eyes focused and I saw a beautiful woman, short and thin, her brown hair tied up in a bun and held in place by a rag. She smelled of lavender. I fell in love with her immediately. "You must be the Cid Wymann my son's been talking about so much."

I nodded.

"You look bad," she said, glancing at my face and head, "but I think you'll be okay. Cuts to the head bleed a lot, that's all. Here," she said, pressing a cloth into my palm, "apply pressure with your hand." She guided the cloth to my forehead. "You want to come back to our house and I'll see if I can take care of these?"

I nodded again.

"Come on, Siggy," she said, "help me get him up."

Mrs. Braun took me back to her home with Siggy, sat me down in her kitchen, and cleaned my cuts, putting iodine on each of them. It stung, but I didn't flinch. Their kitchen was so different from Maddie's. There were ceramic figures of dancing men and women standing on shelves, and bright yellow tile painted with red flowers on the counters. In the living room there was a soft-looking sofa against one wall, a leather chair next to it, a round carpet on the floor, and a large radio on top of a mantle in the corner.

"I'm going to tell your father to speak to Rick Scarpetto's and the Smiths' parents when he gets home," Mrs. Braun said.

"You can't do that," Siggy said.

Mrs. Braun folded her arms across her chest and eyed her son. "Well, when your father comes home, we'll talk about this. In the meantime, both of you stay close the rest of the day. I'll go over to your house, Cid," she looked at me, "and tell your mother."

"My mother's dead," I said around my fat lip.

Her mouth formed a large O. "I'm sorry, Cid. I mean I'll speak to your—"

"My father's gone."

"Then your—"

"Grandmother, Maddie Wymann," I said.

"Your grandmother, then."

Siggy wouldn't look at me. When his mother left us alone in the living room, he kept his eyes downcast. "I came back as fast as I could."

I looked past him at the house-shaped clock above his head.

"If I'd stayed, they'd've beat us both up. You should have run with me."

"Why'd they beat you up?" I asked.

"They're bullies, that's why. They don't need no other reason. Tomik and I are always running from them. You gotta learn to run, too." Above me a small bird emerged from behind a door in the clock. It cuckooed twice, for two o'clock. Siggy opened his mouth again and then shut it.

"I hit Scarps," I said, watching the cuckoo retreat back into its magical home.

Siggy stepped back from me. "You hit him?"

"And one of those other boys, I don't know which one. They look too much alike."

"You hit one of the Smith twins?" Tomik Kopecky asked, throwing the kitchen door open and entering like a Roman gladiator.

"Once," I said.

"Cid's met Scarps and the Smith brothers," Siggy said.

"Had to happen sooner or later." Tomik came in and sat down next to us, giving us both the once-over to see how bad we were hurt. "I wish I'd've been there," he said, his mouth curling downward into a frown.

"Why?" Siggy said. "So all three of us coulda been busted up?"

"No," said Tomik, "'cause we're friends, and friends should stick together, right, Cid?"

"We're friends," I repeated, not quite sure how the words felt coming out of my mouth. Then I gave them a lopsided smile. "Friends."

Siggy filled Tomik in on what had happened, then turned toward me. "Where'd you get Scarps?"

I pointed to my chest.

"Once?"

"Once each, I think."

"What'd you hit 'em with?"

I pointed to the top of my head and then to my fist.

Siggy and Tomik laughed. I joined them. My head and ribs hurt when I laughed, but I didn't care.

"I'm sorry I ran," Siggy said quietly when we stopped laughing.

"It was two against three, right?" Tomik asked.

Siggy nodded.

"Then you got nothing to be sorry for. Two against three is bad odds. You gotta run when it's two against three. But Siggy, we're not running anymore . . ."

Siggy nodded, looking like he felt better. I nodded, too.

Then Siggy's frown returned. "What if I'm alone?"

"Then you gotta run," Tomik said. "'Cause one kid against three is just like two against three—it's bad odds. But now we got Cid, everything's changed, and Scarps and the Smiths gonna learn that, too."

I listened to them talk back and forth for a while. It didn't really matter what they said, because in my mind I kept hearing one word over and over again: "Friends."

Mrs. Braun returned quietly a little while later, with a dark expression on her face. She saw the three of us sitting on the circular rug in the living room, laughing.

"Tomik Kopecky," she said, "I should have known you'd be here by now."

"What did Cid's—" Siggy began, but Tomik touched his arm and Siggy stopped talking.

Mrs. Braun walked over to me and touched my cheek with the tips of her fingers. She held them there a moment and I felt warmth spread out to my ears, up to my scalp, and down into my throat. She lowered herself to one knee and looked into my eyes.

"I spoke to your grandmother," she said.

She's not going to let me see Siggy anymore, I thought. *And if I can't see Siggy, then I can't see Tomik. And if I can't see either of them . . .* I lowered my eyes from hers and braced myself to be hit.

"She said"—she cleared her throat and smiled at me—"after a little discussion, that you could have dinner here tonight with us—if you wanted."

Siggy clapped his hands.

"Do you want to do that?" she asked.

I lost myself in her brown eyes and nodded.

"What about Tomik?" Siggy asked.

Mrs. Braun turned around and looked at her son. "Of course Tomik can stay, as long as his mother and father say it's all right."

"They do," Tomik said.

"Tomik Kopecky," Mrs. Braun said, shaking her head slowly.

"Yes, Mrs. Braun?" Tomik replied, a huge smile splitting his face.

"Stay around the house until dinner, okay, boys? I've got laundry to do out back and I don't want any more injuries to patch up."

That night Siggy's father was held up late at work so we ate without him. There was roast beef with gravy, mashed potatoes, peas, and fresh-baked biscuits. When I smelled them, my stomach growled and my mouth watered.

Five

THE LIVES OF A BENGAL LANCER

Another week passed without my father returning. Maddie starting searching for him at bars late at night. I could tell because she came home smelling of cigar and cigarette smoke. On Saturday, she took me to the Strand to see *The Lives of a Bengal Lancer* with Gary Cooper. She slept through most of it. On the way home, with the rain drumming down on our backs sounding like horses' hooves, the thunder like cannon, I repeated over and over the lines from the trailer: "One thousand seven hundred fifty to one! Always outnumbered! Never outfought! These are the Bengal Lancers . . . heroes all."

At Siggy's house the weather kept us in. Seated on their living room rug, Tomik waited until Mrs. Braun went into the kitchen before he whispered, "Siggy, let's show Cid the schlager."

"What's a schla-ger?" I whispered back.

"My father was a schlager fighter in Germany." Siggy whispered, too.

"They fight each other with swords and try to cut each other's faces," Tomik added. "He sells hats at Knox the Hatter's on Madison, but he's a real fighter. And he's got"—using his index finger he traced a line from the corner of his eye down to his chin and from the bridge of his nose across to his ear—"scars. Two of them."

"Has he ever killed anyone?" I asked.

Siggy opened his mouth but Tomik spoke for him. "Sure. Lots of people. Especially those who gave him the scars. He probably fought over a woman."

"He did not," Siggy said. "It was because he bumped into—"

"A woman," Tomik said. "All men fight over women, right, Cid?"

I shrugged, not sure of the answer.

"Right," Tomik said. "He cut off their ears—"

"The women's ears?"

"No," said Tomik, "the guys he beat in the sword fight. And he gave their ears to his girl as a gift—like a trophy. That's what they do with bulls in Spain."

"They cut off their ears?" Siggy asked.

"Yup."

"Why?"

"Because that's what girls like."

"That's not what girls that I know like," Siggy said. "The girls that I know, they just call me four-eyes or throw rocks at me. I gave Cindy O'Reilly a frog and she threw it at me."

"Ain't you learned nothing yet?" Tomik asked. "Girls don't like frogs, boys do."

"Then why would girls like an ear that's been cut off?"

"Well—these girls are different," Tomik said, pushing out his chest. "They're women."

Joseph Lunievicz

"Like our moms?" Siggy asked.

"No, not like our moms. These are real women, real . . . tomatoes."

"Broads?" Siggy asked.

"That's right," Tomik said, "dames. Now, let's show him the sword!"

"The schlager," Siggy said indignantly.

"The schlager," Tomik repeated.

"Well," Siggy said, hesitating a moment, "okay."

Siggy went ahead, checking the hallway to make sure it was empty. Then he waved us into his parents' bedroom. I entered the room and stopped, struck by the sight before me. There, hanging on the wall, was a sword maybe four feet in length, with a large metal basket hilt and a gleaming edge.

"It's sharp," Tomik said. "Like a razor."

"No, it isn't," Siggy said.

"'Course it is," Tomik said, reaching toward it with his index finger.

"My mother said it was too dangerous so she made my dad get rid of the edge."

Tomik pulled his finger quickly away from the blade as if he'd been cut, and dropped to the floor cradling his hand.

"What happened?" Siggy yelled.

"Shhh," Tomik said, and we all looked down at his hidden finger. "It's cut off."

"But it's not sharp," Siggy said, with less certainty.

Tomik pushed his finger into our faces and Siggy jumped back. I didn't move.

Tomik smiled. "He filed it down."

"Filed it down," Siggy repeated, grabbing his chest near his heart as if he'd had a heart attack.

"Filed it down," another voice, a deeper voice, said from behind us.

We all turned slowly around. There, standing in the entrance to Siggy's parents' bedroom, was a short man wearing a sharp black porkpie hat with two large scars marking his face like raised pink tracks. Siggy and Tomik jumped, knocking the blade to the floor. I turned around to look at the man I knew must be Mr. Braun.

The man looked down at me and smiled. It turned his face from that of a monster into that of a man. "You must be Cid," he said with a German accent.

"You look like Anthony Adverse," I said, "except for the scars."

Mr. Braun laughed. "My son has told me about you." He gazed down at me a moment and touched the scars on his face with his fingers. "You are not afraid of these." It was a statement, not a question.

I shook my head slowly.

"Nothing much scares you then, does it?" His smile disappeared and his hand dropped to his side.

I shook my head again.

"Did you like the schlager?"

I nodded.

"Come back again and I will show you how it is used." Mr. Braun leaned forward, pointing to the scar on his cheek. "Perhaps I will show you how to make these cuts?"

I swallowed hard.

"Abel, why are you frightening the boy?" Mrs. Braun

asked from behind me. Her voice broke the spell we were all under, and Tomik and Siggy ran forward to Mr. Braun, Siggy circling his arms around his father's hips and hugging him tightly.

"You're not mad, are you, Dad?" Siggy asked.

"Not at all, Sigfried. Now you boys wash your hands because your mother tells me dinner is ready."

Tomik and Siggy ran past him, but I stood staring at Mr. Braun a moment longer.

"Nice to meet you, Mr. Cid Wymann," he said.

"Likewise," I said.

Sitting at the dining room table moments later, Tomik and I drank Coca-Colas and stuffed ourselves from plates filled with corned beef, green beans, and beets that were lined up in front of us.

Mr. Braun sat down with us and quickly made us laugh as he described a Mr. Edelman who came in each week to try on new hats and complain about the food his wife made for him, then farted—clearing the counter of customers— as if to say, "See what she does to me!"

"Abel Braun!" Mrs. Braun scolded him, hiding her own grin behind her napkin.

"Wait," he said, his eyes widening, leaning toward his wife. "I almost forgot! Today I met Aldo Nadi."

"Aldo Nadi?" I said, unable to stop myself.

"You know who Aldo Nadi is?" Mr. Braun asked in surprise, turning to face me.

I nodded.

"Tell me, then," Mr. Braun said, "who he is?"

"The greatest fencer in the world," I said.

"Is he?" Siggy asked.

"If Cid says he is, then he must be," Tomik added.

Mr. Braun sat back in his chair. "How do you know this?"

"I met him at the Strand last year."

"The Strand?"

"He came to see *Captain Blood*."

"*Captain Blood*," he said, smiling. "Yes. Rafael Sabatini."

"Sabatinidini," Siggy echoed.

"Who's that?" I asked.

"The author of the book, Cid. When you can read better, I will show it to you and you can read it."

"I can read," I said.

"I'm sure you can," Mr. Braun said, smiling. "So can Siggy and Tomik. But this book is for adults."

"I read *The Times*," I said.

"Why do you read that?" Siggy asked.

Tomik shushed him, watching what was happening.

"*The Times*?" Mr. Braun asked, leaning forward. "Tell me something from *The Times*."

"Hugh Allesandroni is best in foil here," I said, "Heiss in épée, and Armitage in sabre. John Huff is also one of the best and he fenced against Aldo Nadi last year at the Plaza Hotel."

Mr. Braun looked at me. He shook his head slightly, and let out a short laugh.

"Can we listen to *The Shadow* tonight?" Siggy broke in.

"No, Siggy," his mother said.

"But Mom—"

"No, your mother is right," Mr. Braun said, reaching over to ruffle his son's hair. "Some music and a snack, and then it is off to bed for all of you. I shall walk these two home tonight when we're finished."

✝

It was a warm night and the three of us walked home quietly, watching lightning bugs flash in front of us.

When we rounded the corner to our block we saw a black limousine parked in front of our houses. A man in a gray uniform leaned against the hood, smoking a cigarette. When we reached Tomik's open door, we could see Mr. Kopecky inside standing next to a man in an expensive blue suit holding a thick cigar between his fingers. As Mr. Kopecky listened to the man, he stooped forward, his large hands clasped uncomfortably in front of him, his head bowed. Mr. Kopecky was a big man, but the man with the cigar, although shorter and narrower, seemed larger. The two men shook hands and the man with the cigar walked out, followed by two other men in dockworker's clothes we hadn't noticed before. The man with the cigar stopped at the door in front of us and placed the stogie between his teeth. His cold green eyes gave me the chills, even though he smiled from behind his smoke ring.

"This your boy?" he asked, taking the cigar out of his mouth.

Mr. Kopecky was right behind him. "Yes, Mr. Farthings," he said, grasping Tomik's shoulder as if he didn't want Mr. Farthings to mistake me for him.

"I've got a boy about his age, too," Farthings said, his smile disappearing as he dropped his cigar to the ground next to us and crushed it with his foot.

"This is my friend, Cid," Tomik said, and I saw his father's hand squeeze his shoulder, trying to keep him quiet.

Mr. Farthings looked at Tomik, then at me. "What's your last name, boy?"

"Wymann," I said.

He nodded and turned away. "I'll see you in the morning, Kopecky."

"Yes, Mr. Farthings. Thank you."

We all watched as Mr. Farthings got into his car along with the other men and drove off into the night.

"Looks like we're staying for a while," Tomik whispered to me.

Mr. Braun and Mr. Kopecky exchanged a few pleasantries, then Tomik disappeared as the door closed behind him. Mr. Braun looked down at me and then up at my front door, only a few feet away. It was still closed. I reached to open it.

"You are welcome in our house anytime," Mr. Braun said.

I looked up at his face. The moonlight caught the smooth, raised skin of his scars and made them glisten.

"Good night, Cid."

I turned away from him and opened the front door.

Six

THE CHARGE OF THE LIGHT BRIGADE

A running battle with Scarps and the Smith twins continued through the fall. Between each row of gardens in our neighborhood ran a north-south lane bordered by fences and bushes, and overgrown with green ivy at least as tall as our heads. We played cat and mouse between these hedgerows, hiding when we could, taking a beating when we were caught. But we got our licks in, too.

Over the course of the season, Siggy went through two more pairs of glasses and Tomik's nose was broken. My hands became calloused, and my clothes took on the worn look of Siggy's and Tomik's. But Scarps and the Smith twins became more cautious when the three of us were together. Tomik said it was because of my hard-as-rock head. "It's an anvil of justice," he said one day.

"An anvil of what?" Siggy asked.

"Of justice. Like *The Shadow* or *The Spider*. They use guns to get the bad guys. Cid uses his head."

My father still hadn't returned. A man in a gray suit came by our front door one morning smoking cigarettes and holding a white envelope. I watched him through the window from behind the curtain. Maddie refused to answer the door. She stood in the doorway to her room and waited until the man slipped the envelope under the door and left. There was a red stamp on the front stating boldly PAYMENT OVER-DUE. Maddie's hair, gray before, had turned white.

Then, on an October evening, Mr. Braun came home early and swept us out the door together just as it was getting dark, shouting over his shoulder to Mrs. Braun that we'd all be home in time for dinner.

"Where are you taking the boys?" she asked.

"We have delivery to make," he said, tapping a hatbox he held under his arm.

"Where we going?" Siggy asked.

"It is business and I need the help of you boys."

"What help?"

"Keep quiet, Siggy," Tomik said. "Your pop will tell us when he tells us. Right, Mr. Braun?"

"Right, Tomik."

We ran up to the station, our leg muscles burning from the final flight of stairs, and dove into the train, poking each other and play fighting as the train jerked forward toward Manhattan.

It was strange taking the train with someone other than Maddie—strange and wonderful. Tomik and Siggy traded baseball cards they'd brought with them while Mr. Braun commented on each one.

"Camilli had thirteen triples and tied Averill in homers," he said.

Siggy looked at Camilli from Phili's card and hesitated with it halfway between himself and Tomik.

"And Fox was three thirty-eight with forty-one homers—the home run king, if you ask me."

Tomik stopped with his card meeting Siggy's. They both looked up at Mr. Braun and he shrugged.

"You did not bring cards?" Mr. Braun asked me.

I shook my head.

"Why not?"

"He can't keep 'em," Tomik said, grabbing Siggy's card and leaving his on Siggy's lap.

"Dad," Siggy said, putting his cards in his back pocket, "tell us about the schlagers. Cid's never heard the story and Mom's not around to say you can't."

Mr. Braun smiled. "Perhaps. But"—he leaned toward us—"you must not tell Mrs. Braun."

We all nodded as the train rattled from station to station and the lights in the car flickered.

"I went to a university called Tübingen—in Germany. The fraternity houses dueled with schlagers. One day an upperclassman bumped into me and fell. I apologized. He said he would meet me at The Bloody One."

We all leaned in closer and Mr. Braun lowered his voice slightly.

"'You must have a second and two witnesses,' he said. 'We will bring the referee and the surgeon.' I thought it was a joke, but I was wrong.

"The Bloody One was crowded. The walls were white and there were no windows. We wore thick leather armor and gloves, with iron goggles over our eyes. There were two lines painted on the floor. We each placed our right foot on the line. They gave us swords."

"Schlagers!" Siggy said and his father raised his hand for silence.

"'Do not move off the line,' they told me. 'If you move off the line you are a coward and will lose.'" Mr. Braun held his arm out and wind-milled it in a cut, first to Tomik's head, then to Siggy's and my cheeks. All three of us ducked and dodged as if it held a sword.

"Tell Cid why you can't move," Siggy said.

"Because the duel is about courage, not skill. It is about standing in your place and taking the strike on your head and not crying out. Then watching as they sew your head back together, without saying a word."

"But it hurt, right?" Siggy asked.

"Yes," his father replied. "The boy gave me this." He pointed to the scar beneath his eye.

"But you won other fights, right, Mr. Braun?" Tomik asked.

"'Course he did," Siggy said defensively.

"I fought four times. The third and fourth times I won. The second time I got this." He pointed to his other scar.

"Did you kill anyone?" Tomik asked.

Abel Braun laughed but did not answer.

We got off at the Fifth Avenue stop in Manhattan. Cold air buffeted our faces and pushed our chins against our chests before we were even up the stairs. Mr. Braun pulled his hat down and his coat tighter around his neck.

"Are you boys with me?" he asked, looking down at us.

We nodded and ran up past him. At a newsstand Mr. Braun bought Tomik and Siggy copies of *New Fun Comics* and *Detective Comics* and he bought me the latest issue of *Screen Stories*. It had a picture of Errol Flynn as Major Vickers from *The Charge of the Light Brigade*, lance held high, charger snorting beneath him, hair tousled by the wind in the valley beneath Balaclava. In that moment, the wind still tugging at our cheeks, it was as if we were all mounted on powerful horses waiting behind Mr. Braun, our lances high, ready to follow him into the Valley of Death.

"Where are we going, Dad?" Siggy asked.

"Patience," Mr. Braun said.

I looked around and realized I was in a different city from the daytime one I'd visited nearly every Saturday for the past nine months. It was still crowded but now, even though the sun had set, the streets were lit by lights of all kinds—so many that it almost seemed to be day. Running along the sides of Grand Army Plaza from Fifty-eighth to Sixtieth Streets were beautiful hotels. Doormen in long, deep green or dark red coats, wearing white gloves and black hats, waited in front of their polished brass-plated doors to greet customers, open the door for them, call for a cab, or whistle for a bellhop to carry luggage.

"We go to the Savoy Plaza," Mr. Braun said, pointing to a stout building with arched columns where three large flags flew above the entrance.

Screen Stories clutched tightly in my hand, I crossed with the others to the entrance. Mr. Braun tapped his hatbox as we approached the doorman. "Delivery," he said, but the doorman held out his arms.

"You can go in. The kids can't."

Mr. Braun leaned in close and whispered some words to him.

The doorman smiled and looked around as if checking to see who was watching, then opened the door and motioned for us to pass.

"Quickly now," Mr. Braun said.

The polished dark wood interior and crystal chandelier flashed by me like images from a photoplay. Mr. Braun stopped at the desk a moment, then shepherded us toward the elevators. The doors opened on a hall with a spotless red carpet running its length, shaded lights above each door, and polished brass door numbers and knobs. We walked down the hall to 321. Mr. Braun knocked and we all pressed our ears against the door. Through the wood we faintly heard the sound of steel tapping, then sliding against steel.

The door opened and a tall man stood blocking the light. He was thin but he filled the doorway. I recognized him immediately as the man I'd met at the Strand over a year before, only he seemed larger now and somehow more . . . dangerous. He wore a thick black canvas plastron coat, black knickers, and black tennis shoes, and he carried a metal mesh mask under his arm. In his gloved right hand was a foil that appeared to grow out of his fingers. His black hair was combed slickly back and to the side.

"Yes?" he said.

"Signore Nadi," Mr. Braun said, bowing at the waist. Tomik slapped Siggy and me on the back and we followed suit, bowing low together.

Mr. Nadi smiled at the gesture, then bowed slightly in return.

"Mr. Nadi, I have come to deliver the hat you ordered last month at Knox the Hatters."

Mr. Nadi looked at the box that Mr. Braun was presenting. "I remember you," he said. "You fenced schlager at Tübingen. It is a butcher's sport."

"Yes," Mr. Braun said, not meeting the man's gaze. "Well . . . I brought my son and his friends to meet you. So they can meet the world champion."

"Ah."

"I . . . I hope that you do not mind. They are fans of the movie sword fights and I wanted them to meet a real swordsman, to, to see what the real thing is."

"They want to learn to fence?" For a moment Mr. Nadi's face lit up, his eyes sparkled.

"I don't know," Mr. Braun said, hesitating, "but I thought if they could see—"

"I do," I interrupted.

"And who are you?" Mr. Nadi asked.

"Cid Wymann," I said. "I met you at the opening of *Captain Blood* one year ago. You were with two women and there were photographers. You said to come see you sometime."

Mr. Nadi scanned my face as if trying to remember who I was. "Mr. Cid Wymann," he said finally, "I think you cannot afford me."

Tomik, Siggy, and Mr. Braun turned to look at me.

Mr. Nadi placed his mask and foil down on a small table near the door. He picked up a silver cigarette case, snapped it open, and took out a cigarette. He lit it and blew smoke into the hall above our heads, seeming to think something over. "You want to see the real thing," he said finally, "then you come in to see the real thing."

He stepped out of the way, and we entered. The room was large, with a high ceiling and a long strip of bare wooden floor. There was a partially open door that led to an adjoining room, its interior cloaked in darkness. A man stood at the far end of the room with his mask under his arm and his foil in his gloved hand. His brown hair was wet and lay flat against his head. His forehead glistened. He wore white from head to toe, but the outfit was marred by sweat stains at the armpits and neck.

"This is John," Mr. Nadi said, finishing his cigarette and putting it out in an ashtray. "He is a student." He pointed to a space along the wall at the center of the room between some hard-backed chairs. "There, you may watch."

We stood between the chairs, no one daring to sit.

"In Europe they pay me one thousand dollars to fence in public. Three bouts, fifteen touches. They arrange all and invite me to compete against champions. The room filled with signores and signorinas to watch, men and women who know *doublé* from counter-beat. When they give *applauso*, they cheer for the artist and they cheer for *forza*, power shown by one over another. Here . . . I am reduced to this." He placed his mask on his face and stepped in front of his opponent. The man in white saluted and put on his mask, too.

First Nadi gave his student a lesson, a pattern of drills they played out for us. Each completed maneuver finished with Nadi's blade striking the underside of his student's blade and holding it in a curve, the foil bent in a semi-circle because its tip was pressed against Nadi's chest. After fifteen minutes, his student struggling for breath, Nadi said something in Italian and they stopped, stepped back, and saluted. The student retreated some more until they were five paces apart. Then they saluted each other again and dropped into en guarde positions. Neither fencer moved for what seemed forever, but when they did move, it was like lightning. Nadi flew forward with his arm extended as his blade reached toward his student's chest. The student ran backward as he attempted to parry and get away from the point. The moves were so quick my eyes couldn't follow. One moment Nadi stood en garde, the next his blade had struck his student's chest and his own mask was coming off.

"Seen enough?" he asked, as he shook hands with his student and turned back to look at me.

I nodded.

"Still want to fence?"

I nodded again.

"Save your money and come back when you are older." His eyes moved toward the door.

"Yes," Mr. Braun said, shaking himself as if from a dream. "Yes."

"You will leave the hat?" Mr. Nadi asked, pointing to the hatbox Mr. Braun was still carrying under his arm as we headed toward the door.

"Yes, of course," Mr. Braun said, and placed the hat on one of the chairs. "Of course."

Seven

ROMEO AND JULIET

A battle was coming and we all knew it. By the first of December there were less than two dozen families left in the Gardens and the kids from each side were ready. Then the temperature rose to sixty and we mobilized for war.

Scarps and the Smith twins were West Siders, as were the four Czech Divis and the three German Breits. We were East Siders and allied with the three Micks—Frank, Mike, and Patrick, whom everyone called the Shaughnessy brothers—and Feliks Chudzik, a skinny Pole who had four sisters with round white faces that Tomik called "the moon maids" after a book by Edgar Rice Burroughs his father had read to him.

On our Saturdays together, Tomik and Siggy kept me mostly to themselves, so I knew our friends and enemies mostly by the stories Tomik and Siggy told me about them. But on the Saturday of the battle for Sunnyside Gardens, all hands were needed and my hands were ready. Maddie and I had seen *Romeo and Juliet* starring Leslie Howard and Norma Shearer that morning, so I thought of us all as a bunch of Montagues and Capulets looking to test our courage.

The day of battle began with questions—Siggy's questions. "You've seen so many movies," Siggy said. "When do you go to see them? Do you see them on Saturday before you come to play with us?"

"I go to church services on Saturdays," I lied.

"But then when do you see movies?"

Tomik looked up from the wooden peach basket he was turning into a shield. We were in the back of Siggy's garden, making shields to go with our wooden swords.

"During the week," I said.

"We never see you out during the week," Siggy said. "You stay in a lot."

I nodded.

"Well, what do you do inside all the time?"

"My chores and schoolwork."

"But you don't go to school."

"I have school every day but Saturday," I said. "And chores, too."

"So do we, but we don't have school on Sundays. My mom says your grandmother is too strict."

"She's a battle-ax," Tomik said.

"She's scary," Siggy said. "But Sister Annie uses a ruler on your knuckles so hard your fingers are like to fall off when she hits them. She's worse than scary. Hey, we go to the movies on Fridays. We should all go together."

"Cid can't," Tomik said, looking over at me. "He's got schoolwork, ain't that right, Cid?"

I nodded.

Mrs. Braun poked her head out of Siggy's back door. Shaking her head at our shenanigans, she said, "I'm going to the store on Queens Boulevard. Stay out of trouble for a while, please."

"'Course, Mom," Siggy said, and his mother's head disappeared.

"Cid's got Saturdays with us," Tomik said. He slapped the palm of his hand against the rim of the peach basket. "Anyway, today we're going to war!"

"War!" Siggy echoed. He picked up a battered pot that had lost its handle and placed it on his head. It sat crookedly and partially covered his eyes, so he tilted it back and drew the string he was using as a chin strap down under his chin. Tomik had a colander for a helmet, while my head was bare. But we all had the wooden swords Siggy's father had made for us, and peach baskets from Trundlemeyers Grocers, looped with rope inside so that we could grip them as shields.

Tomik raised his arms into the air and gave out a high-pitched Tarzan yell. Siggy and I followed suit. A few moments later we heard other yells to the west and north.

We carefully entered the hedgerow, looked both ways, and headed north. Two houses up, we met the Shaughnessey brothers and Feliks.

"Are you sure Scarps—," Feliks began.

"He ain't coming," Tomik said. "I told you all, him and the Smiths are gone today. My mother saw them walking toward the El this morning with Scarps's mother. For once, it'll be an even fight between us and them."

Feliks looked down. He was a small boy almost Siggy's size with blond hair and freckles.

"Besides," Tomik said. "Look here." He pointed at me. "Cid's the anvil of justice. He's taken on Scarps all by himself. Ain't that right, Cid?"

I nodded.

"And this is for the kingdom of Sunnyside." He slapped the flat of his sword against his shield.

Feliks looked at me. He was scared. I saw it in his eyes.

"We need you, Feliks," Tomik said.

Feliks swallowed, then nodded.

"Good."

We moved down to Thirty-ninth Avenue and crossed it to the small woods near the rail yard, across from the Phipps apartment complex. There was a clearing in its center that some hobos had used for a camp but was now deserted. The grass was as tall as my head, and dry. It stabbed my cheeks as we cut our way through it.

We reached the clearing before the West Siders. There were boulders and rocks in a circle at the clearing's center with a pile of blackened logs from the long-dead remains of a fire. Tomik climbed on top of the largest boulder and stood over us. He gazed out toward the west.

"Here they come," he said, almost to himself.

We shifted from one foot to the other. Feliks shivered and his sword rattled against his shield.

Tomik jumped down off the boulder and shouted, "Missiles!" He placed his shield above his head and everyone else copied him. I hesitated a second and was clipped on my forehead by a small rock as the air around us filled with pebbles. They clattered off our shields and landed on the ground like bouncing hailstones.

There was yelling from all sides and the West Siders charged. Sword and shield clashed. Then Siggy was knocked to the ground by a heavy blow from Josef Breit's sword. Josef raised his sword to strike downward and I ran at him. Our shields hit. I felt him lose his balance and kept driving with my legs until he came up hard against a rock. I heard the air whoosh out of him as he hit it and sank to the ground. There were tears in his eyes.

The fighting stopped.

The Divis and Josef's brothers gathered around him. There was blood on the stone from where Josef's head had hit it.

Tomik looked at me, his eyes blazing. Siggy stood up shakily. The Shaughnessy brothers clenched their swords tighter. Feliks was gone.

"Why'd you do that?" Josef's brother Manny asked.

"He hurt Siggy," Tomik said. "Ain't that right, Cid?"

I nodded. I was still seeing the world through a red curtain. Then we heard the rattling of chains and turned toward the north. It seemed that Scarps and the Smith brothers were not gone for the day after all. The three of them emerged from the tall grass, Scarps with a doubled length of thick chain in his hands and the Smiths with shields and crowbars.

Tomik turned to Siggy and said, "Get some help."

"But—," Siggy began.

"Go," Tomik said, and pushed him in the direction of home.

"You want to play war?" Scarps yelled as he came closer.

"War," Billy and Arnold echoed.

"My father said your dad was fired from the docks last week," Tomik shouted back. "Maybe you should go back to Italy where you came from!"

Scarps's face contorted in anger and he swung the chain like a lariat over his head. Billy and Arnold ducked and circled to each side to flank us.

The Breits and Divis backed away, as did the Shaughnessy brothers.

Tomik looked over at me. His eyes asked me if I was going to stay or run. Before I could answer, he turned back to Scarps and raised his shield in defense. I stepped up next to him.

"I've waited a long time for this," Scarps said, his words accented by the sound of the chain cutting through the air above his head. "There's no mama to stop us this time. No house to hide in. No papa to hide behind. You're going to get what's coming to you, Kopecky. And when I'm done with you, I'm going to do the same to Limey Jew-boy Wymann."

"He ain't a Jew-boy and you're still a Wop," Tomik said, and launched himself forward just as Scarps struck with his chain.

The links hit Tomik's shield and shredded it, stopping him in his tracks. A second swing glanced off his helmet, and a third struck his arm and threw him to the ground. He shouted in pain and grabbed his arm. It was bleeding and hung to his side at an awkward angle.

Scarps's chain began its circling motion again. He smiled and looked down at me.

"Now's your turn, Wiii-man," he said.

Having seen how the chain had worked against Tomik, I was ready when Scarps struck. I ducked and pressed myself against the nearest rock, and the chain ricocheted off the stone above my head. It came around again and shards of rock showered onto me. I ran forward then, staying low under the chain, and forced Scarps to take a few steps back. His chain angled further up and I might have been able to reach him had it not been for the Smiths. Arnold threw his crowbar at me and it struck my side, sending me to my knees. This gave Scarps a moment to regain his balance and lower the swinging chain back down to my level. I reached for the crowbar that had dropped nearby but the chain hit me before I could grab it. The links destroyed my shield and gashed my forearm.

I rolled away, back up against the stone, pressing my face into its cold surface. I looked to my right and saw Tomik throwing rocks at Arnold with his good arm, trying to keep him from closing in. Then I felt something pressed into my palm, something wire-handled and heavy. Siggy had placed his father's schlager blade into my hand. It was too big for me by half, but it felt right in a way the wooden sword had not. It felt real. Siggy looked into my eyes but before I could say anything, the chain stopped whirling and I yelled at him to get down. Billy had come up behind Siggy, ready to take Siggy's head off with his crowbar.

"Get 'em, Billy," Scarps yelled.

Siggy threw himself to the ground and the crowbar hit the rock. Not able to lift the blade with one hand, I swung the schlager two-handed and clipped Billy on the side of his head. A small flap of skin flew off and a spray of blood covered us with red. Siggy kicked Billy's knee and Billy, screaming and grabbing at his head, dropped his crowbar and shield and fell to the ground. I couldn't stop the schlager blade. It skipped off the stone and continued, making me spin completely around. Then I heard the chain start to circle again.

I'd been lucky hitting Billy and knew I couldn't count on being lucky again. But the blade made my arms longer and maybe that was something Scarps hadn't counted on. I stepped away from the stone and Scarps attacked.

"Wiii-man," he yelled and his chain hit the rock where my head had been, scattering more stone chips into the air. I ducked, extended my blade—now held with both hands—and lunged. My point caught Scarps in the chest and knocked him back, perhaps more from surprise than because it pierced his skin, for the tip was not sharp. I lost contact with him and lunged forward again, aiming higher and catching him in the throat. The chain, which had still been circling overhead, crashed into my side and knocked me to the ground—but not before I saw Scarps paw at his throat that was now bubbling with blood.

I stood up as best I could as Scarps looked down at the blood on his hands and then up at me. I raised the blade high above my head and held it there, unable to balance its weight.

"Scarps, I'm bleedin'," Billy Smith yelled. "Da Jew-boy chopped my head in two!"

Scarps saw my blade ready to descend, then turned and fled, the weaponless Smith brothers close behind him, Billy holding his head with both hands. Overbalanced, I fell backward. The world swam for a moment, then I saw Siggy's and Tomik's faces above me. Tomik was smiling.

"My mom was at the store," Siggy said quickly. "I didn't know what else to do. . . ."

They helped me up, Tomik's face alternating between pain and pleasure as Siggy went on and on.

Then we heard sirens and all three of us ran. We ran back to Siggy's home with our arms around each other, holding the sword between us.

We cleaned and placed the schlager back where it belonged. Siggy's mother bandaged our wounds that evening when she came home and swore we would never be allowed out of her sight again.

"What will your mothers think of me?" she asked.

My mother's dead, I thought.

"'Tank God my son got all his limb,'" Tomik said, in his best imitation of his mother.

We all laughed, even Mrs. Braun.

Later that night, Mr. Scarpetto and Mr. Smith came by Tomik's and my houses with some of their friends. They were drunk. I heard them shouting from my room.

"Kopecky! Wymann! Come on out, you sons a-bitches. Give your boys knives to fight with, do yah?"

"Who gonna pay for the stitches to my boy's head? Who gonna pay the doctor—"

I heard a door open and the men grew quiet.

I looked out my bedroom. Maddie's door was closed and the light off. I ran to the front window.

Mr. Kopecky's broad back was in silhouette. He held a shotgun at his side. "Who gonna be da first?" he asked.

The men on the street swayed back and forth. Mr. Scarpetto stepped forward. "You not always gonna have a gun, Kopecky."

Mr. Kopecky thumbed back the two hammers, clicking them into place.

The line behind Scarpetto wavered, then dispersed. Mr. Scarpetto waved his fist, then turned tail and headed up the block toward the bars on Skillman.

Eight

THE KING OF THE DAMNED

Cold weather drove us all indoors and our neighborhood became less of a battleground and more of a ghost town. Tomik heard that Mr. Scarpetto had gotten his job back on the docks, and there were no more nighttime visits from angry fathers. Christmas came and we didn't put up a tree. Maddie and I saw only one film that month—*King of the Damned*, a movie about a rebellion in a prison colony. The rest of the Saturdays, Maddie slept in.

Tomik and Siggy each got me gifts. Tomik gave me his Van Lingle Mungo and Frenchy Bordagaray cards and Siggy gave me three small metal knights. "They're us, see?" he said.

I didn't have anything for them.

Maddie had taken to drinking from a bottle of whiskey she hid in the kitchen cabinet. By nightfall most evenings she was unconscious. She left me alone more and more during the day. The man in the gray suit returned the first week of each month and waited on our front porch, smoking cigarettes and throwing them on the sidewalk when he was finished, taping our payment notice to the front door.

One night before she retreated into her room, I asked her, "Where's my father?"

"I don't know," she answered. "I don't know." I heard her snoring later. When I knew she wouldn't stir, I walked over to my father's room and opened his door. I'd never been allowed inside before. The stale smell of tobacco was everywhere. There was a drafting table in the corner by the window. I could tell Maddie had cleaned up because there wasn't any dust.

On the table were logos for MILLIONS NOW "TAKE IT EASY" ON WASHDAY USING RINSO SUDS; GIVE A MAN A SNIDER'S CATSUP; BEST COFFEE I EVER TASTED, WITH OR WITHOUT CAFFEINE—KELLOGG'S KAFFEE-HAG COFFEE. There were also logos for cigars with names like Partagas and Ramon Allones, along with sketches of old men, roosters smoking cigars, and the faces of young women.

When I looked closer I noticed there were other, smaller drawings hidden in the corners and sheltered beneath these drawings. They were of men in black hats and capes with guns in their hands, and women in dresses that revealed everything, their backs arched and mouths open as if screaming. A partially finished Partagas logo with the number 4 on it fell to the floor next to a box overflowing with magazines. I grabbed a magazine and read its cover. It was a copy of *The Spider, Master of Men*. The box was filled with copies of others like *Argosy* and *The Shadow*. I went back to my father's drawings and recognized the man in the black hat and cape as my father's drawing of The Spider. I took one and folded it in half. When I got back to my room I placed it in my now-filled movie log book under my mattress.

The next day Maddie went into his room and packaged up his things. She cried while she did this, and cursed my father to the seven layers of hell. I'd never seen her cry before. She burned his drawings and left the room empty of everything that spoke of its life before.

January began. Siggy asked me about my father while we were listening to *The Shadow* on the radio, lying down on his living room floor. "Where is he?" he asked.

I answered the same way Maddie did. "I don't know."

"Don't you miss him?"

I shook my head slowly.

"Why not? I mean I'd be crying if my dad—"

"Shut up, Siggy," Tomik cut in.

"I don't understand."

"Not every father is like yours, Siggy," Tomik said.

Maddie woke up early the following Saturday and told me to get dressed. Our front door had a notice of eviction on it. Maddie tore it off and threw it to the ground. Thirty minutes later we stood on the elevated tracks above Queens Boulevard at the Lincoln Avenue Station, waiting for the train to arrive the same way we had so many times before. It was early February, my birthday month. The wind poked holes through our coats as we leaned into it. We saw a train arriving on the horizon and Maddie stepped up toward the edge of the platform. There were only a few people out that morning. Maddie was silent. The wind blew harder. She shifted forward then back.

I looked up at her, and then burrowed my neck further into my collar. I pulled my cap down lower over my ears. Her gaze was steady, locked upon the oncoming train. Then her head twitched once to the left as if a string were attached to her earlobe and someone had tugged down on it. She withdrew her left hand from her pocket and flexed her fingers, holding them out in their fingerless black gloves. The train approached the platform, brakes squealing, and her fingers closed into a fist. She leaned forward again, too far forward, and thrust her hand back toward me, fingers splayed once more. She disappeared as the train passed and took her with it. Her hand stayed in front of me a moment, fingers twitching, as if annoyed that they'd been left behind. Then they disappeared too.

The lead car shuddered to a halt and a single scream followed the squealing brakes. I didn't realize until later that my throat was raw because I was the one who'd been screaming.

When the police came they asked me questions. I stared back at them, unable either to answer or to believe that Maddie was gone. Finally, two Irish cops with red and brown hair took me home—only there was nobody to take me home to.

I didn't have a key so they had to break down the door. One of Tomik's sisters opened their door while the police were kicking mine in. Behind her, in their living room, I saw Scarps sitting on a worn sofa, dressed smartly and scrubbed clean, his hair slicked down, with a boy on one side and Mrs. Kopecky on the other. The boy next to Scarps was dressed well, too, in pants and a clean shirt with a sweater. He was somewhere in age between me and Scarps. His face reminded me of someone but I couldn't place whom.

"So, Eddie," Scarps was saying to the boy, "you want to play some cards or somethin' 'til your dad gets back?" Then the police hit my door again and they all looked toward me. Scarps smiled as our eyes met.

"What's going on out dere, Otka?" Mrs. Kopecky asked. "Is that your brodder?"

"No," Tomik's sister said, then turned away from me and closed the door just as mine crashed open.

I packed a bag of clothes.

"Where can we take yah, kid?" the policeman asked. "You got any relatives or friends you could stay with?"

I asked them to take me to Siggy's.

Mrs. Braun was there with Siggy and Tomik when I arrived. They were just having lunch, jelly sandwiches and oatmeal cookies. Siggy answered the door and his face lit up. "It's Cid, Mom," he yelled over his shoulder. When he looked back, he saw the two policemen behind me.

"Can we speak to your mother, son?" the officer near me asked.

Mrs. Braun came up behind Siggy in the hall. "Cid, this is a nice surprise—" She stopped when she saw the police. "What's happened?"

They took off their hats. "Can we come in, ma'am?"

Mrs. Braun said yes, but never took her eyes off me. Siggy and I went to the kitchen, where Tomik was stuffing his face full of sandwich, while she sat in the living room with the police. We overheard them from the table where we sat.

"Did that happen, Cid?" Siggy whispered, his jaw dropping.

I didn't say anything.

Tomik stopped eating and pushed the remains of his sandwich in front of me. I picked it up and slowly ate.

"Where you going to live?" Siggy asked, then stopped himself in mid-thought. His lips stretched into a large smile. "Hey. Maybe you can live here?"

Mrs. Braun came into the kitchen behind me. I felt her hands on my shoulders.

"I'm sorry about your grandmother, Cid. It's just, just horrible."

I heard the words, but they were like dry leaves floating around my head. I felt the warmth of her hands through my clothes. She kissed the top of my head. I closed my eyes and cried. Like *The King of the Damned* I'd broken free of my prison, only it hurt in a way I'd never dreamed it would.

After a while Mrs. Braun whispered, "You'll stay with us for a while, okay?" And they were the warmest, kindest words I'd ever heard.

Nine

THE PRISONER OF ZENDA

Snow came down and covered the ground that night, leaving the earth white. Siggy and I roomed together, sharing his bed like two brothers. Over the next week there was a simple funeral for Maddie, and I was placed in temporary custody of the Brauns while the court searched for my father or any other relatives. I told them my father was gone and there were no other relatives. The bank took our house.

I told neither Siggy nor Tomik about seeing Scarps at Tomik's house.

I became part of the Braun family. They fit me in easily, including me in everything they did. We listened to *Dick Tracy*, *The Shadow*, and the news together. Mr. Braun gave me his copy of *The Times* after he finished with it, and I could read it in any room of the house I wanted. We ate meals together and Mrs. Braun washed my clothes for me, mending them when they needed it. Yet even with all this attention, I missed Maddie. It surprised me how much I missed her at night, after Siggy had gone to sleep.

Because I didn't go to school, I attached myself to Mrs. Braun during the day, following her around the house, fold-ing clothes, dusting, sweeping, and washing dishes. I was used to the work so it was easy. She said, "Thank you, Cid," whenever I finished a task, and I burned with pride when she told Mr. Braun how much of a help I'd been. During the day I stayed close to their home and away from other kids, but when school was over, Siggy, Tomik, and I were inseparable.

We all went to see *The Prisoner of Zenda* on a Friday evening at the Strand and took turns pretending to be Douglas Fairbanks and Ronald Colman all the way home, our imaginary swords clashing in the night and echoing in the subway cars.

"Do you think twins really look exactly alike?" Siggy asked on our way back from the subway.

"'Course they do," said Tomik, "else they wouldn't be twins. Look at the Smiths."

Siggy nodded.

"My father had two friends when he was a kid who was twins," Tomik said, "and he said you couldn't tell 'em apart for nothing until one got his hair all cut off because he got lice and they couldn't get rid of it otherwise."

"What would you do if you had a twin?" Siggy asked him.

"I'd send mine to school for me," Tomik said quickly, "have him take all my punishments when I got in trouble, and hide him in the closet when I didn't need him."

"What would you do, Cid?" Siggy asked.

"Me?" I said. "I'd keep him close, be his best friend."

"Just like us," Siggy said. "That's what I'd do, too."

"We'd have double anvils of justice," Tomik said, raising one fist into the air.

"And," Siggy continued, "I guess it wouldn't hurt too much if my mom got mad at my twin once in a while for something I did."

"Only," Tomik added, "your mom, Siggy, would be able to tell."

Walking back with them I couldn't believe how happy I was.

A few weeks passed. Then one evening, Mr. Braun came home early. He arrived with his hat between his hands, his cheeks pink from the wind, and his eyes downcast. He stood in the kitchen, puddles of water expanding outward from his rubber boots. Tomik, Siggy, and I sat at the kitchen table, drinking milk, eating cookies, and trading baseball cards. Mrs. Braun wore a new red dress as if she were getting ready to go out. When the back door opened and Mr. Braun stepped under the arch, we all stopped what we were doing and turned to face him.

"Abel?" Mrs. Braun asked, frozen in her place.

"I have lost my job," he said, unable to look up.

"What—"

"They let five of us go today. We were allowed to leave early. They gave me a week's pay."

"A week's pay? Abel, what shall we do?"

He looked up. Sadness marked his face with shadowed lines. "I do not know."

They stood, unmoving for a while. The wind blew against the storm door behind him and made it rattle.

"Come in," she said finally, moving toward him with her arms outstretched.

Mr. Braun left each morning to look for work, and

returned each evening with nothing to show for his efforts. The tension in the house rose as the days passed and no work was found.

When Mr. Braun finally came to speak to me, I knew it was coming because I'd heard him argue with Mrs. Braun the night before. It had been late and Siggy had been asleep. I lay listening to their muffled voices.

"We can't leave him here, Abel."

"We can't take him with us."

"Why not?"

"You know how my family feels about . . ."

"About what? About Jews? My grandmother and grandfather were Jews. I am a Jew. Our son is a Jew."

"And my family does not know that."

There was a long silence. Mrs. Braun broke it. "Abel Braun. This is the United States, not Germany. That is one of the reasons why we came here."

"This world is as it is, Rosamund. These are not my rules. I do not want to leave the boy either, but you and Sigfried must come first. We have no place else to go."

They were leaving and they were not taking me with them. They were not taking me because I was a Jew. Being a Jew meant nothing to me, other than a name Maddie had called my mother. I didn't even know what a Jew was, but it was about to cast me away from a family that I loved and that I thought loved me.

"We cannot keep you with us, Cid," Mr. Braun said the following morning. "I do not have the work and the bills must be paid. We may have to leave soon ourselves—perhaps go to Baltimore." He looked up at me furtively, then away. "I have family there. They can take us in, make room for us. But the space they have is small."

"I'm small," I said.

"Yes."

"I can work."

"Yes."

"Then take me with you. Please."

"I am sorry, Cid. But you must stay."

My hands started to tremble so I made them into fists and pressed them into my thighs. It was unfair. I wished I could rip the Jew out of me and leave it behind, but it seemed no matter what I did or where I went, it followed me. *"You killed your mother,"* my father's voice echoed, *"and that I can't forgive."*

"I have talked to a woman at St. Agnes in Manhattan," Mr. Braun said. "They will take you in and care for you while they continue to look for a relative."

"I have none," I said softly.

"Of course you have," he said, looking past me. "They will find them." His hands settled in his lap and he looked down. "And if no one comes for you . . . we will come back and take you. I promise."

I looked up at Mr. Braun and nodded. I believed him because he'd been kind to me. I believed him because I had nothing else to believe in.

"St. Agnes will be a way station for you," Mr. Braun said, "a long sleepover. This I promise to you," he repeated. "I promise."

✝

The morning I was to leave Tomik did not appear. Siggy buried his head in his mother's arms. Mrs. Braun kissed me goodbye in her kitchen, the tiles framing her brown hair with shining yellow. Her nails were bitten down to nubs and two of them were bleeding. There were dark circles under her eyes. She grasped Siggy protectively as if to say to the world, *This one you can't have*.

"We're sorry, Cid," Mrs. Braun whispered over and over as the door closed behind me.

Mr. Braun and I walked to the train station. I carried a small bag with some clothes that Mrs. Braun had packed for me, my three knights, my film notebook, and the two baseball cards that Tomik had given me—the Dodgers' Van Lingle Mungo and Frenchy Bordagaray. Near Skillman I saw Tomik with Scarps and the Smith twins, only he wasn't running from them. They all stood around a boy, the same well-dressed boy I'd seen sitting on the couch in Tomik's living room. The well-dressed boy was talking and the rest were listening. Tomik saw me but didn't wave. Scarps hit him in the shoulder and Tomik lowered his gaze, away from me.

Mr. Braun didn't speak during the trip. We didn't touch until, in front of St. Agnes's, he offered me his hand. After we shook, he gave me a package wrapped with a piece of red ribbon I recognized as the one Mrs. Braun had used to tie her hair. I wondered if that was her parting gift to me.

"It is *Captain Blood*," Mr. Braun said.

"But it's yours," I said, holding the book in both my hands.

"I will get another copy for myself," he said. "Open it."

I did. On the front page he had inscribed, "To a man of action and a true swordsman. We shall meet again."

I looked up at him and he looked away.

Siggy and I wrote to each other at first, but his letters stopped coming after a while so I stopped writing him. Mr. Braun went into the army to fight the Japs, and Baltimore became the Brauns' home. I sent Tomik letters, but he never replied so I stopped writing him, too.

In the end, Mr. Braun was right about the finding of a relative. The nuns and administrators at St. Agnes did find one, along with a place for me to live, though it took them five years to do it. The relative's name was Winston Arnolf Leftingsham and he was my father's cousin.

Mr. Braun was wrong about seeing me again.

PART II - PASSCHENDAELE

Ten

THE BELLS OF HELL, 1943

The dog kicker was the father I had. Abel Braun was the father I'd wanted. Winston Arnolf Leftingsham was the father who chose me.

I heard him before I saw him. His voice rasped like coarse sandpaper. Hesitating, then sliding forward, it pulled itself around the corners of St. Agnes's halls and shambled through Sister Bernadette's office door, accompanied by the slow, rhythmic tapping of shoes on the waxed floor.

"The bells of hell go ting-a-ling-a-ling
For you but not for me;
And the little devils how they sing-a-ling-a-ling
For you but not for me."

I sat in a wooden chair in front of Sister Bernadette's large bare desk. My feet touched the floor that had seemed too far away five years before. My peg-pants looked like knickers. My lip was swollen and I was missing a tooth. My tongue played with the empty space. The room was

a single lamp lit in the corner. The blackout cur-
...ade the room feel like a crypt.

Sister Bernadette was nowhere to be seen. She didn't
like to be in the same room with me. None of the Sisters
did.

"O Death where is thy sting-a-ling-a-ling,
O Grave, thy victor-ee?"

The footsteps landed—one dull, one sharp. *Tap-boom*,
pause, *tap-boom*. Then the voice became louder.

"The bells of hell go ting-a-ling-a-ling
For you but not for me."

I heard an intake of breath. It was Sister Bernadette.
She must have been waiting outside the door. The Sisters
did that at St. Agnes, standing outside of doorways, listening to us, watching over us, spying on us.

The singing stopped. There was a final *tap-boom*. The
sound of two heels clicking together followed in its wake.

"Winston Arnolf Leftingsham, at your service," the
voice rasped with a slight English accent.

There was silence, then Sister Bernadette's voice said
crisply, "There is no singing in the halls unless it's in the
service of the Lord."

"My apologies to the Lord, Sister."

Sister Bernadette snorted, then cleared her throat. "In
there," she said. "I'll be down the hall should you . . . need
anything."

"There is nothing I shall need."

"Very well," she replied, and I heard her footsteps re-
cede down the hall.

I was curious so I turned toward the door.

Winston Arnolf Leftingsham stepped awkwardly in the doorway, one leg bent, the other stiff. The light from the lamp shined onto his face.

The left side seemed to have melted down over his eye and off his chin. The cheek was sunken, covered mostly by a patch of white scar tissue. His hair was tan, sticking out of his scalp like sharp stalks of dead grass. It sat in random patches, surrounded by scarred and flaking skin. The right half of his face was untouched. He had no left arm and his empty sleeve was pinned flat to his side.

He focused his right eye on me and twisted his lips into a smile. He leaned on a cane that he held with his black-gloved hand. The gray suit he wore was too big and hung on him. The vest was threadbare and stained at its bottom edges. A tarnished brass pocket-watch chain dangled from its pocket. His left leg seemed longer than his right, tilting him to one side. A faded gray winter coat was draped across his shoulders.

"You are Wymann, son of Theodore," he said slowly, as a statement of fact.

I nodded.

He cocked his head and jutted the right side of his face forward, breathing heavily. His eye bulged outward. "You do not look like him."

"Who're you?" I asked.

"You sound like him, but you do not look like him."

I watched as he stepped forward and slowly lowered himself into the chair next to mine. His left leg wouldn't bend and stuck straight out in front of him. His pant leg pulled up and I saw both a shoe and an ankle made out of painted wood. He smelled of rotten fruit.

"Decaying from the inside out," he said. "Never get used to the smell." Then he laughed, a low, rattling sound that made my skin crawl. The laugh turned into a cough that doubled him over. He pulled out a wet, red-stained handkerchief and spit into its center. "Mustard gas, July '17, Passchendaele, Fourteenth Corps, Dover Brigade. Boche gun took off most of my left side. The gas took what remained—though it is still working on me. Doctors said I would not last until '18 but I am still here—not much good for anything, but still here."

"You were in Flanders, in the Great War?"

"Ee-pra Salient," he said, and coughed hard again.

"Did you kill a lot of Germans?"

He finished coughing, grasped the handle of his cane tightly, and locked eyes with me.

"Was it like in the movie," I said, "*All Quiet on the Western Front*? Were they like us or were they murderers?"

"We were all murderers," he whispered.

"Why are you here?" I asked.

Neither one of us moved. When he spoke again a smile crawled up the right side of his face. "Theodore was a right bastard. Met him a few times—heard of him before that. Was a bastard as a child—always kicking dogs and stoning squirrels. Thought he had grown out of it later on, but I was wrong. He was afraid of me—should have been, too. Are you afraid of me, Wymann? Do you like to kick dogs?"

I didn't move.

His cane, whistling in a large arc, cracked against the surface of Sister Bernadette's desk right next to my hand.

I made my fingers stay put. I didn't let my eyes leave

his. I counted in my head to three, then slowly clenched those fingers into a fist.

"You should be scared of me, Wymann. You will be my ward and you will do for me as I need done. I have been sent here by the family for this. They did not want me in London, not with the Blitz on." His voice sunk to a whisper. "No need there for such as I. Enough monsters in the air. Boche with wings, children screaming to their mothers in broken beds."

We stared at each other for a while, his chest rattling, the muscles of his right cheek twitching. I watched the cane out of the corner of my eye, waiting for the slightest motion to give his next move away. Then his face relaxed and he sat up.

"You are a fighter?"

I kept silent.

"Good," he said. He withdrew the cane from the desktop, scraping the wood with its metal tip, leaving a thick scar, then placed it solidly between his legs. He leaned forward and rested his chin on top of his hand, closing his eye.

I waited a minute, then when he didn't move, leaned forward to see what had happened to him.

His breathing grew heavier.

I leaned closer still.

His hand grasped the back of my neck and pulled my face to within inches of his. His one large eye loomed in front of me. The cane he'd released clattered to the floor.

"Are you afraid now, cousin?"

His breath washed over me and made me gag. I grabbed at his wrist and fingers with both hands and tried to pull them off my neck but they were as strong as steel cables.

"Are you afraid now, Wymann?" he repeated.

"No," I gasped.

He squeezed tighter and brought me to my knees.

"Here it is, Wymann. If I can catch you, I can hurt you. That is the first lesson of the trenches." He threw me back into the chair and rose unsteadily to his feet.

I came up slit-eyed and ready to fight.

He ignored me as he struggled with his balance while bending over to get his cane. I placed my foot against it and was about to kick it out of his reach when something made me stop. I had no reason to trust him and already enough reason to hate him. But he had said the *family* had sent him—my family. It made me hesitate. I slid the cane over to his outstretched hand. He picked it up without a word and, righting himself, rearranged the coat on his shoulders.

"Get your kit," he said. "I will wait out front for"—he pulled out his pocket watch, raised it close to his eye, then snapped it shut— "ten minutes. No longer."

Then he left, that awkward *tap-boom*, pause, *tap-boom* receding down the hallway, punctuating his song.

> *"The bells of hell go ting-a-ling-a-ling*
> *For you but not for me;*
> *And the little devils how they sing-a-ling-a-ling*
> *For you but not for me."*

Eleven

NEURASTHENIA

I met my cousin on the street. Sister Bernadette closed the front door behind me, her parting words echoing in my ears. "Mr. Leftingsham is your guardian by law of the state and by law of the Lord, Cedric. You are ours no longer. May the Lord be with you."

In a small sack that had been my pillowcase I carried my film notebook, my baseball cards, my three knights, Siggy's two letters, my father's drawing, and my dog-eared copy of *Captain Blood*. I had nothing else from my five years there except for the clothes on my back and a threadbare coat that was already two sizes too small.

It was February and cold.

Winston Arnolf Leftingsham leaned into the wind, using his list to his advantage, and headed uptown, not looking back to see if I followed. I gathered my coat tightly around me, pulled my cap down over my eyes, and walked in his wake.

By the time we reached Twenty-third Street, my fingers and toes were numb. The wind off the Hudson tore at my cheeks. The sun had already set and there were few people out. With the war going badly, a curfew at night, and blackout curtains everywhere, evenings on the streets were quiet and dark.

The few people we passed were bundled in thick coats and scarves. Some of them were soldiers. Some were missing limbs. I hadn't noticed the missing limbs before, but with Leftingsham's empty coat arm flapping in the wind in front of me, they seemed to be everywhere. Down dark alleys, shielded from the wind, I could see the glow of fires burning from metal garbage cans—men huddled around them, hands extended.

We crossed Sixth Avenue, going west into Chelsea. My markers for the neighborhood were two theatres, Barclays on Twenty-third near Seventh Avenue where they still did vaudeville, and an RKO on Twenty-third and Eighth. I'd escaped from St. Agnes once to see *The Mask of Zorro* at the RKO, and Maddie and I had seen *Fury* with Spencer Tracy at Barclays when I was back in Sunnyside.

We crossed Seventh Avenue. A large building appeared on the left rising up into the night sky. Fancy iron balconies pushed out from the brick face in upward rows until they disappeared above us. Light filtered through windows covered by drapes, marking the sky with soft yellow patches. A red sign above a heavy wooden-and-glass door stated simply THE HOTEL CHELSEA.

Leftingsham reached the door and rapped so hard with his cane that I thought the glass would break. A bellhop in a short red jacket and cap appeared—a thin red-haired kid, slightly older than me. He opened the door and shivered as the wind grabbed at him. Leftingsham elbowed his way in and I stepped into the small hall on his coattails.

"Have a hold there," the bellhop said, putting out his arm to stop me.

The cane descended lightly on the bellhop's arm. "He is with me."

The bellhop let me pass, flinching from the cane's touch.

The inside of the hotel was warm, with a fireplace surrounded by benches and worn chairs. Pictures covered the walls. One, a large painting of a round, fat, dark-haired man and woman, hung above the fireplace. The eyes of the man and woman seemed to follow me as I walked by. A staircase with an iron rail and dark wooden banister wound its way up from the back. A restaurant and barbershop stood beside it. There were two lifts, both small, opposite a ladies' lounge, and a front desk that smelled of oil. A dark-skinned woman at the open door to the ladies' lounge, her black hair pulled tightly back into a bun, her eyebrows dark and thick, made me stop and stare. Her lips parted. "Fuck, fuck, fuck," she said.

I didn't know who she was talking to, but I knew the word she said was dirty. If the nuns heard you say it at St. Agnes, Sister Bernadette would wash your mouth out with soap. But this woman with the thick eyebrows said it in a way that was different, forbidden even.

"Wymann," Leftingsham said over his shoulder. He was already climbing the staircase. I shook myself and followed him.

My cousin was winded by the time we reached his room on the third floor, and a vein stuck out on the normal side of his forehead. He fumbled for his keys and dropped them. I bent to pick them up and his cane rapped my knuckles.

"Leave them!"

I leaned back against the wall and watched as he carefully lowered himself on his good leg. His body shook as his fingers stretched out toward the keys.

Across the corridor and two doors down a woman in a white bathrobe took one step out into the hall and watched us. Her cigarette burned red as she inhaled. A man's voice called to her to come back inside. She waved him off with a flick of her other hand.

Sweat dripped down Leftingsham's face and fell to the floor. Finally his fingers touched the metal and he clutched the keys into his fist. Using his cane to keep from falling over, he rose from the floor and joined me with his back against the wall. We stayed there while he regained his breath. Then he pushed himself forward and opened the door. With a glance at the woman down the hall, I followed him in.

The room was small with its own sink, bath, and toilet. The walls were white. There was a wooden dresser with a mirror above it, a bed, and a cot. I assumed the cot was for me. Bedding was tucked in and sharply folded. A toothbrush, washcloth, and towel lay at the bottom of the cot. There was a glass door that opened out onto a small balcony. I walked over to it and looked out. Behind me I could hear Leftingsham struggle with his coat and clothes. Buckles clattered. Suspenders unsnapped. Drawers opened and banged shut. Something slid along the floor and then the springs to his bed creaked.

I turned around.

Leftingsham sat on his bed with his back against his pillows and the wall. He wore ancient button-front shorts and an undershirt. Two stumps—an arm and a leg—extended from his left side. His wooden leg leaned against the wall next to him. A black metal box, badly dented and scratched, sat on his lap. Ignoring me, he took out a cloth and placed it on his thigh next to the box. A syringe, a small bottle of clear liquid, and a belt followed.

I backed up a step, unsure what he was going to do with them.

"They are not for you," Leftingsham said, without looking up. "They are for me."

I stood and watched as he loaded the syringe, pulled the belt tight across the upper part of his thigh, and found a vein on the inside of his leg. The syringe turned pink, then he pushed the plunger in, waited, and took out the needle. Seconds passed. He undid the belt. The right side of his face slowly relaxed. His head eased back until it knocked against the wall. The syringe fell out of his fingers and rolled onto the bed. His eye closed.

"I've seen those before," I said. "The nuns use them for kids in the hospital, for pain."

"Morphine," he whispered.

I'd heard of morphine but I'd never seen it. "They use it on soldiers who've been hurt."

Leftingsham nodded.

"What do you want," I asked, "and why am I here?"

"Neurasthenia," he said.

"What's that?"

"Degeneracy of the mental and moral constitution, they said. *Le cafard*—the cockroach—the French called it. It put me in hospital three months in '15 after the first Eepra. They thought I was scrimshanking but changed their minds. They did not know what it was then. They had not seen it before. I sat in hospital. There were hundreds of us. Some clawed their mouths. Some could not hear. Some were blind. Some were dumb. Those that could watched the larks fly above us.

"I could not move. Then I could. I saw the sun. I saw the hospital. I ate my breakfast. 'What happened,' asked I. 'Shell burst on your trench,' said they. 'The others?' asked I. 'What others?' said they. I could not remember. They were there, then they were not. To this day I cannot remember. They sent me back. They sent me back two more times. I was five years in hospital after the gas attack. The war was long over, but not for me. Now, off with your coat."

I blinked, but didn't move. It was as though I was listening to another man, different from the one I'd met. The morphine had changed him, made him softer—perhaps more like the man he'd been before the war and the gas had done its work. I didn't understand half of what he said but it made me hurt to listen to him.

"Sit, Wymann," he said. So I did. "You are staying a while."

"Why should I?"

"I knew your mother."

I felt as if a hand had seized my throat.

"She was a young thing, pretty—in love with that dog kicker. Poor thing. A Jew."

"You're lying."

"I will forget that you said that."

"You're lying," I said, standing up.

"I will forget it twice but not a third time."

"How could you know her?" I asked. I could feel my face twitching from side to side and I couldn't stop it.

"They let me out of the asylum. They could not keep me forever. My friends could not bear to be near me. No woman would touch me. 'I am the Basilisk,' says I. I turned them all to stone. I found a boat to *the colonies* and met Abigail here."

Her name burst into my skull and I had to shake my head to clear the noise.

"Her brother went to trade school for textiles, across the street."

"Your brother?"

"*Her* brother, Abigail's brother."

"She had a brother?" I asked.

"I saw her waiting outside one day. No one talked to me. She talked to me. I will never forget that she did that."

"Where is her brother? My—my uncle. Is he alive? Why didn't St. Agnes find him?"

"Long dead."

"Why?"

"'Why?' asks he. He died of influenza. It was a simple thing. Thousands died of it but few talk of it. Abigail cried over him."

Her name again. "Was she—," I began, "what did she look like?"

"Never saw a picture?"

I shook my head. She'd never even been described to me. My hands trembled and I clasped them together.

Leftingsham looked at me, then looked away. "She called me *Lefty* because that was the part of me she said she would always miss not having known."

"What did she look like?"

"Pretty."

"Pretty," I repeated. He could have beaten me for six weeks solid and I would have followed him into hell for that one simple word.

"Sixteen. Young." He hesitated a moment and something moved across the right side of his face—a half smile perhaps. "Too young for me. I introduced her to my cousin—the dog kicker. She saw me with him one day and asked me who he was. I had no choice."

Suddenly I knew what I'd seen on the right side of his face. "You loved her," I said.

"I could not then, nor can I now, afford love," he said harshly, the other Leftingsham sneaking through. "Not since Passchendaele." He remained silent. His breathing eased into a steady rhythm until I thought he'd fallen asleep.

"I killed her," I said. "I was born, and I killed her."

"The Lord took her," he whispered. "She was not marked for long life—not like you and me." Laughter escaped his lips in small fits, then larger bursts, like exploding shellfire. He grasped his chest as if in pain, then sank back against the wall, his eye still closed.

"What do you want from me?" I asked.

"Honor, and memory. Both serve me still."

"You said you came because of your family in England."

"*Our* family."

"I don't have any family."

"You do. Oh, yes, you do."

I shook my head. "Why did Maddie never mention you? She always said I had no family. That all there was was here, in my father and her."

"She was wrong. You cannot leave your family. They follow you like bloodhounds."

"Why'd it take five years?"

He reached into his pocket and took out a creased letter—tossed it lightly toward me. I caught it and opened it. It was from St. Agnes's. The date was from the spring.

"I believe there were letters before this one, but I never saw them."

"Why not?"

"I came when I could."

I folded the letter again and extended it back toward him.

"Keep it," he said, without moving.

The paper felt warm in my hand. "What else do you know about her?"

"A little."

"What else?"

"That is enough for tonight."

"You can't just stop now. You have to tell me what you know."

"I do not have to do anything."

"But— "

"Turn off the light when you are ready for sleep."

"What if I leave?"

"The door is in front of you, Wymann."

"You'd just let me go?"

"I am a crippled old man." A lopsided smile creased his ruined lips.

"What about the first lesson of the trenches?" I said.

"You have a good memory."

"I'll take my chances out there." I placed my hand on the doorknob.

"What will you do then?" His voice stopped me again.

"Get a job. Maybe . . . join the army."

"They will not take you. You are too young. And you do not know a trade."

"I could pass." I knew I looked older than my fourteen years but I wasn't really sure I could pass for eighteen.

"Learn from me," he said.

"What do you mean?"

"Look at me. I am a walking lesson."

He was also a connection to my mother and my family. A family I had never known—one that had sent a man to me across an ocean.

✝

I awoke to the sound of Winston Arnolf Leftingsham screaming. I jumped out of bed and stared about me in the darkness. He sat where he'd fallen asleep, with his single eye glowing like a moon. The smell of rotting fruit was strong in the air.

"They are coming," he said, speaking in his morphine voice, human and clear.

I looked around.

"The shelling's stopped. Where's Roger? McCourt? Devlin? Winslow? I can't hear you. Speak louder. My ears are bleeding. Here they come. Here they come. Roger? McCourt? All dead. All dead. Where's my leg? My ears? They're bleeding. Of course they're bleeding."

His eye closed. He screamed again. "Get it off! Get it off!" His hand slapped at the empty spaces where his missing limbs should have been.

I crawled over to the door and sat down. Sometime before sunrise we both fell back into sleep.

I awoke by instinct. I moved my head and Leftingsham's wooden foot smacked into the door, missing my head by an inch.

"Well," he growled, "if you are here, you are here, so you bloody well better get up!"

Twelve

Short Sixes

I called him Lefty, but never out loud.

"Call me 'sir,' " he said, "and I will call you Cedric."

"I like Cid."

"All right, Cedric," he responded, and so it stayed, though when he was angry he called me Wymann.

"You must first get a job," he told me the next day. "I will give you one. You will be an orderly—an officer's servant. I need one. You need work. The fit is good."

"You want me to be your servant?"

"Are you deaf?"

"I can hear."

"Then do not question me."

"How much does it pay?"

"Room and board."

I agreed.

It wasn't hard work. Lefty wouldn't let me open a door for him or call a cab—though he usually couldn't afford one anyway. He only expected me to wash his clothes, press them, and lay them out in the morning. I made trips to the laundry, ironed in the room, shined shoes, made the beds to military standards, kept the room in order, and made tea when needed. I found these tasks easier than any I had ever had to do before—it was like a holiday. Since Lefty spent most of the day out, it left me a lot of time to explore my new home.

The Hotel Chelsea was full of a kind of life that was new to me. Down one end of our hall, a group of people called Communists met twice a month. Their rivals, the Trotskyites, met on the sixth floor on alternate weeks so they didn't run into each other. The Communists met in a man named Dalton Packer's room. I could hear them arguing even with their door closed. Packer was a poet and friends with Virgil Thomson, a music critic, who lived on the fifth floor. He and Thomson argued about music and politics in the lobby after concerts, and on their way up to their rooms afterward.

Packer was a thin, blond man in his thirties with pockmarks across his cheeks who walked around in trousers and a white undershirt, and who sometimes left his door open for a cross breeze. He had a typewriter in plain view from the door that I never heard him use. I don't know if he ever wrote a thing. I stopped by his door one day to see him staring out the window onto the street below, a piece of crumpled paper in his hand. When he saw me, he closed the door in my face, shouting, "What are you looking at?"

Mrs. Esslinger, who I'd seen across the hall that first night, had a habit of opening her door after midnight and yelling, "The mice are in the halls!" Her husband usually responded with, "Then kill the anarchists and come back to bed. I need a good fuck." It seemed everybody used the word *fuck*. It made me wonder what the difference was between a good one and a bad one—never having had one of either type myself. Her husband was a painter who used a studio on the roof. Mrs. Esslinger was a singer. Whenever I saw her she was rubbing the small of her back with both hands and eyeballing me as if she thought I was up to no good. It seemed to me she was up to less good than I was.

One night, while I was shining his shoes, I asked Lefty what he'd done before The Great War.

"I was an actor," he said. "Royal Shakespearean, class of 1910. I played Mercutio and was a reasonable Iago. There is enough of the villain in me for it, but I was too young in 1910 to give it its due. *Dangerous conceits are in their nature poisons, which at the first are scarce found to distaste, but with a little act upon the blood, burn like the mines of sulfur.*"

"What's that?" I asked.

"Othello."

"O-who?"

"You have a lot to learn."

"Did you like being an actor?"

"Not a lot, but I enjoyed the applause."

"You were like those guys at the movies?"

Lefty laughed. "No. I acted on stage."

"You did the live shows?"

"Yes, I did the live shows."

I couldn't believe Lefty had been an actor. I'd never thought about what I wanted to do with my life up to that moment. I'd never looked that far into the future. Then, struck by an image of Lefty on the stage, I knew what I wanted to do. "I want to be an actor, too," I said.

"What?"

"You said I had to learn a trade. Well, that's the trade I want to learn. I want to be an actor."

Lefty frowned. "Only fools act."

"Then what are you?"

"A fool," he said. We stared at each other for a while, neither of us moving. Then he added, "I will teach you at night."

That night, after Lefty went to sleep I took out my film notebook and wandered through its pages, imagining myself as Errol Flynn, Gary Cooper, Tyrone Power, or Cary Grant. Only this time, instead of seeing Zorro or Robin Hood, I saw myself with two faces, one the hero of the film projected on a silver screen, the other the actor who played him. At first it was a little strange, then, with some time, I got used to it.

Lefty sent me to the Central High School of Needle Trades on the south side of Twenty-fourth Street and Eighth Avenue—the same place he told me my uncle had gone. I didn't argue with him.

After my first day at school I returned to our room—for I quickly came to think of it as our room—my school bag filled with texts and my head bursting, only to find a stack of books on my cot. Lefty stood next to them.

"Shakespeare's war plays and tragedies," Lefty said.

"Where'd you get them?"

"What does it matter? They are for you."

"For me?" I looked down at the worn hardcovers:

Romeo and Juliet, Macbeth, Hamlet, Othello, Henry the IVth, Parts I and II, and *Henry the Vth*, then back to Lefty. "Seven books . . . for me?"

He didn't speak.

"What do I do with them?"

"Read them, you bloody idiot."

"What about the acting?" I asked.

"Read them," he said, "and we will talk about the acting later."

I'd shined Lefty's shoes to a luster that morning and I noticed they were already scuffed from his day's journey.

"Where do you go during the day?" I asked without thinking.

"That is not your business," he said and opened the door to leave.

"Does it matter which one I read first?" The door closed on me. Before the week was up I had read them all. I read them on my way to school and almost got hit by a bus crossing Eighth Avenue. I read them between classes and between chores. I read them into the night after Lefty had gone to sleep. *Romeo and Juliet* in particular grabbed me. I read it three times through, remembering the film I'd seen of it as a boy with Norma Shearer and Leslie Howard. I noticed all the plays had one key phrase written in their texts, set off by either italics or parentheses, that sparked my imagination: *They fight*. There were other pretty words within their covers—half of which I didn't understand—but none of them interested me nearly so much as those two simple words. I assumed the fights were with swords—though what kind of swords I didn't know—because all of

Shakespeare's plays took place in times when swords still ruled. But what happened in the fight itself? In *Captain Blood* Sabatini described the duels from beginning to end. Shakespeare told me nothing. Only, *They fight.*

I told Lefty when I had finished the plays.

"All?"

I nodded. "Now teach me about acting."

"Henry the Fifth. Act three, scene one. . . *or close up the wall with our English Dead.* Act four, scene three. Saint Crispin's Day speech."

"You want me to memorize the speeches?"

"Understand the words—all of the words. Then define them—write down what they mean."

"I want to know something else," I said.

"I liked you better, Wymann, when you were quiet."

"You've unleashed my tongue," I said.

"What did you say, Wymann?"

"I'm talking like this Shakespeare. What do you think? Have I got a future as a writer, too?"

Lefty stared at me.

"Okay. Here's the thing. When it says 'they fight,' what does it mean? It doesn't say how they fight or with what. It only says 'fight' and that someone is either wounded or dies. He leaves out the best part there, doesn't he? So what does it mean, 'they fight'?"

"It is a call to the Master of Fence."

"Howzat?"

"*Who* is that."

"Who-zat?"

"He is the man who stages, marks out the moves, then

teaches the actors the moves with the swords." His voice grew harsher as he became more and more irritated.

I continued, caught up in the moment. "He teaches you the moves? What do you mean, moves? It's a fight. A fight is a fight. If there's one thing I know a lot about, it's fights."

"Listen to me."

"So . . . the fights aren't real?"

"Listen to me." Lefty looked at me with his single eye and shook his head.

"No. I'm not an idiot," I said. "I know they're not *real* fights. But aren't they . . . fighting still?"

"Square eights. Round eights. Short sixes. Long elevens," he said, spitting the words into my face.

"What the—"

"Square eights. Round eights. Short sixes. Long elevens." His horrid breath was tinged with a sweet-sour smell. I realized he'd been drinking. All at once I knew I was in trouble. The Chelsea Hotel, the new school, the books and the reading, the information about my mother, they had all made me forget what the world was like—what Lefty could be like. Even his face had become familiar, ugly but familiar—in a strange way, comforting. Still, I couldn't stop myself from saying, "I don't get it."

"Square eights. Round eights. Short sixes. Long elevens," he said a third time, only his voice was even harsher.

"I still don't—"

He grabbed me by the back of my shirt and lifted me onto my toes. He pushed his single eye up close to my face, glaring at me like a drunken Cyclops. Inside my head I heard his voice repeat over and over, *First lesson of the trenches—if I can catch you, I can hurt you.* Then he let go of my shirt and turned away from me. His body swayed slightly as he found his balance. Then he turned back toward me and the right side of his face pulled his working lips up into a grin.

"Follow me," he said.

Thirteen
THEY FIGHT

Clouds covered the stars. The sky was black wool and pitch. My fingers and cheeks were numb by the time we passed Ninth Avenue, prickling from the cold. After Tenth Avenue we passed beneath the elevated train and went north, then turned off onto a side street. We were in the lower part of Hell's Kitchen. Lefty stopped midstreet in front of a rundown building's stairway. A small wooden sign swayed beneath the stair's lower arch, its paint chipping at the corners and worn by the sun. O'HANRAHAN'S it stated in script. Its rusted chain creaked.

"Where are we—," I started to ask but Lefty leaned down and placed a finger to the center of his lips, dividing his face in two.

" 'They fight.' You want to know what it means? Watch." Then he descended three steps, found the doorknob, and leaned into the heavy wood. As always, I followed.

We stood in a small space, another door directly in front of us. Faint wisps of cigarette, cigar, and pipe smoke pulled at my clothes and touched my skin. My ears hummed with the sound of many muffled voices. Lefty pushed the second door open, and the sounds and smells of a crowded tavern washed over us. The place was filled with men who'd been working on the docks and at construction sites, their faces lined with dirt, their caps set at cocky angles, their clothes covered with brick dust and caked mud. A tall man on a raised platform in one corner, stooping so as not to hit his head on the low ceiling beams, raised his bow and, with a downward slash, sawed his fiddle to life.

Lefty hesitated a moment, then waded through the crowd to the bar. A short, wide bouncer with burst blood vessels across his nose stood when we entered, then sat when he noticed Lefty's missing arm. Lefty ignored him.

People stopped talking as we passed. Those in front of us moved out of the way. They didn't look away, like so many of the finer dressed ladies and gentlemen did on the street—these people stared. Lefty was a walking carnival sideshow. I could hear the hawkers from the Clyde Beatty Circus near Broadway in front of the Forty-second Street palaces calling his name. *Come see the three-eyed man and the chicken-headed goat with the birthmark of the Christ child on its belly.*

Lefty hooked the head of his cane onto his cuffed sleeve. Leaning onto both the bar and his wooden leg, he kicked a stool out of his way. The circus barker's words scattered from my head.

"Have any good *English* beer?" Lefty asked in a thick English accent, loud enough for all around him to hear.

The bartender, a short round man with no hair, placed his hands on the bar top and said, "Think you're at the wrong place, Mac. Got mixed up perhaps in the cold? Came in the wrong door?"

With what seemed like a force of will, Lefty leaned forward and said each word slowly: "Some say the Irish are in league with the devil. They say they have Boche friends. They say they are Nazi sympathizers. I say they are just stupid bloody Micks."

"You aren't in England now, so have a care," the bartender said softly.

"Nor are you in papist Limerick."

Many things happened at once.

A large hand landed on Lefty's good right shoulder.

The music stopped, as did the rest of the noise in the bar.

All faces turned toward us.

The hand covering Lefty's shoulder was huge, thick-fingered, and calloused. I followed the muscled forearm upward with my eyes to where it disappeared into a rolled-up sleeve, and a neck that seemed so wide it spread from one shoulder to the other. The man stood over six feet tall, with cheeks and forehead made of slate and eyes already swimming with the effects of several pints.

"Now what would you want with us?" he asked.

"Think you can take a cripple and a boy, Eagon?" a slurry voice asked from the crowd.

The man called Eagon threw the words off with a toss of his head.

I felt, more than saw, space clear around us.

"Cedric," Lefty said, turning toward me and ignoring Eagon. He grabbed a full shot of whiskey that was near his hand and downed it in one gulp, slamming the glass onto the bar with a crack.

I cringed at the English sound of my name but nodded. Then I nodded a second time to make sure everyone knew I was with the crazy English bastard.

Lefty smiled at my gesture. "Short sixes," he said, the words slurred. "Three attacks—head, flank, belly—ripostés of the same. They are prearranged moves. They are preset and known in their entirety by the actors." He placed one finger against the side of his head as if it were a gun. "Memorized."

"I said"—Eagon squeezed Lefty's shoulder just enough to regain his attention—"what business have you here?"

"*Good king of cats,*" Lefty said, his voice suddenly clear, his diction crisp, his single eye fixed wholly on the man in front of him, "*nothing but one of your nine lives, that I mean to make bold withal, and, as you shall use me hereafter, dry-beat the rest of the eight. Will you pluck your sword out of his pilcher by the ears? Make haste, lest mine be about your ears ere it be out.*"

I recognized Mercutio's words to Tybalt from *Romeo and Juliet*, then watched as the words sunk into Eagon's brain. A furrow wrinkled across his brow, then disappeared. His eyes widened, then closed to slits.

Lefty turned slightly toward me. His lips moved in a whisper: "*They fight.*" And then louder to all, "*I am for you!*"

His arm moved up, outward, and down, breaking Eagon's hold on him. Then his cane windmilled to his outside and smacked Eagon down the forehead, shattering his nose and tearing skin as blood sprayed across the bar and onto the bartender. Lefty's arm swept the cane, like a rapier, back to his left, then forward quickly, where it cracked into Eagon's hip. Never stopping its movement, the cane whirled over Lefty's head in a flashing arc and descended, as if clearing a tabletop on his other side, aiming toward Eagon's belly. Before the cane connected the third time, Eagon's right fist smashed into Lefty's jaw, sending him sprawling to the floor. Lefty's leg unbuckled when he hit the ground and came out of his pant leg with a clatter. Eagon hesitated a moment and the whole room seemed to gasp.

"Now you done it, Eagon," his slurry-voiced friend said from the crowd. "You're goin' to hell for sure."

That's when I hit the big man in the side. I couldn't help myself. Lefty was all I had. I aimed for Eagon's kidney and caught it hard, but it was like hitting wet cement and my hand went numb. Out of the corner of my eye I could see Eagon draw back his fist, ready to send me into the hell of Mad Maddie's dreams, but I got my second punch off before he got off his first, slamming my other fist into his balls. As he doubled over, I threw my knee into his side and heard ribs crack, then hammered blows to his back until his knees touched the floor.

I thought he was finished and couldn't believe my luck—I hadn't even been hit. I should have kept at him but I felt the room's eyes on me and let my gaze drift up, a cocky, stupid-assed grin on my face. I don't know what he hit me with—an elbow, a fist, or a chair—but the next thing

I knew my jaw snapped back and I bit into my tongue. Then I was watching the ceiling and flying as fireworks popped inside my head. I landed on my back, cracked my head into the floor, and bit down on my tongue a second time.

My eyes closed, then opened. It could have been a second or an hour. Eagon stood over me. Blood dripped from the torn skin of his nose onto my cheek and one of his hands grasped his side as if he needed to hold in his ribs.

I tried to speak but my mouth was filled with blood and all I could do was gurgle. I heard a voice shout, "Look out, Eagon!" Then I caught sight of Lefty's thigh as it hit the back of Eagon's head—only it wasn't a flesh and blood thigh, but wood that cracked against the large man's skull. Eagon's eyes rolled up into his head and he fell forward, knocking the wind out of me. Gasping for air, I passed out again.

I ended up facedown on the sidewalk staring at Lefty's foot as he sat beside me on the tenement steps, buckling on his leg. I heard the door behind us close on laughter and a sizzling fiddle. My cheek against the cool cement, I spit out a mouthful of blood. My tongue felt like a sausage. Everything hurt.

It took us half an hour to get back to The Chelsea, leaning on each other as we went. In our room I fell onto my bed and closed my eyes. A wet cloth landed on my face and woke me up.

"Wash," Lefty said.

In slow motion, I washed my cuts and scratches.

"You will live," Lefty said. He sat on the chair near the window and night table. Our washbowl, now filled with my

113

blood and a red cloth, sat beside his extended elbow. Blood dripped from his split lip down his chin. It was then I realized that he'd been hurt also. His good side was marred purple and swollen.

"You'll live, too," I tried to say, but the words didn't get past my swollen tongue.

"Get my box," he said.

I stood for a moment, swaying, not sure what he meant.

"Morphine," he said. "Get it. Give it here."

I bent down under the bed and drew it out, placed it on the table next to him. He slid his trousers down to the floor and injected.

I lowered myself carefully to my cot and watched.

"Do you remember the fight?" he asked, his trousers still bunched up around his ankles.

I nodded.

"Could you do it again?"

"Whad ou mee?" I asked.

"The moves, boy. The moves. Attack to head. Attack to flank. Attack to belly?"

I nodded again.

"That is a fight—"

"I know what a fight is," I interrupted. "I've had some experience—enough so that I didn't need more tonight." Only none of my words came out the way I wanted them to. They slurred together and stuck in the wrong places. I shrugged and gave up trying to respond.

"Stage fights have to be repeated every night—seven nights a week—exactly the same way each time. Nothing different. But every night it must be as if it has never oc-curred before. That is what it means by *They fight*."

"Thir," I said, drawing out the word slowly.

His head rolled back, the morphine working, and his good eye, now partially closed from swelling, centered on my face.

I chose my words carefully, pushing them out around my aching tongue. "'ext ime ou coul jus fucking teh me."

"Leftingshams are like Wymanns. My father was a Leftingsham, my mother a Wymann. They both liked to fight. It is in the blood."

I closed my eyes and time passed. "Who are Rosher, McCour, ad Devin?" I asked.

"Nobody," his disembodied voice replied.

"'ou dream—"

"Cover your ears."

"Were hey freds?"

He snored in response.

I would ask Lefty about those men again, but each time I asked he refused to talk—at least he refused while he was awake. He dreamed every night, so I learned more anyway, probably more than he wished. Lefty's war was not the war they showed on the movie screen. There weren't heroes like Flynn or Wayne or Cooper. There were only screams, the shouting of names, and the words, "Get it off, get it off." I didn't want that war to be the war I'd read about in history books—to be the war I read about every day in *The Times*. I wanted the other war, the one where the flag waved at the end and the soldiers always marched on proud and free. Death, when it came, was glorious.

I went to school the next morning. When I returned to the room, Lefty was gone as usual, off on his mysterious travels. On my cot were two books. One was my copy of *Captain Blood*. The other was a new copy of a book titled *On Fencing*, by Aldo Nadi. There was a note in Lefty's elegant script set carefully on its cover.

Shakespeare's fights are not with fists. To fight his fights, you must learn to fence. Nadi is a master and his words will be your bible. As an enthusiast of Sabatini you should understand this.

✛

Beneath the note stood Aldo Nadi. He was poised en garde. I could still see him leaping forward against his opponent that night in The Savoy Plaza Hotel, so fast I could barely follow his blade.

I placed the book next to my Shakespeare and attended to my chores, for there were clothes with bloodstains on them to clean. A smile split my tender mouth in two as I worked. My scalp tingled and my heart ached. I couldn't stop smiling.

I didn't miss a day of class, injuries or no. At St. Agnes we'd had school every day but I'd enjoyed little of it. The School of Needle Trades was different. Most of the students wanted to learn and came into class prepared with their homework. The teachers did not use a ruler across the knuckles or the back of the head like Sister Bernadette had. I wasn't interested in making friends. I didn't need any. And even if I had been interested, most of the kids were in groups already. Still, roaming the halls, imagining my uncle walking the same halls, books under his arm, filled me with joy.

One month later I was thrown out of school when an upperclassman knocked my books out of my arms in the hall. He didn't know me. He didn't apologize. He stepped on my texts as he walked by. I beat him senseless. At St. Agnes, that was the kind of thing you learned your first day there. If anybody tried to hurt you or take your things away, they had to pay for it. If they didn't, you would be the one who paid for it every day from then on. The principal told me to find another school to learn in.

Lefty said nothing to me when I told him I'd been kicked out.

"I'm sorry," I said finally.

"For what? He will not cause you trouble again and there are other schools."

Within a week I was taking classes in another school farther downtown.

I read Nadi's book from cover to cover and waited for Lefty to bring up the subject of fencing again. It took two months, but I was patient, and when he finally did speak of it, his next lesson made the wait all the more worthwhile.

Fourteen
EN GARDE

On May 13, 1943, I received a letter from Siggy.

February 8, 1943

Dear Cid:

My father was killed by the Japs. It happened about a month ago—they're not sure of the exact date. The funeral will be on the 30th of March. I hope you can come—that the sisters will let you out. My mother says they will if you ask in a letter, so I am asking. She would like to see you. She has spoken of you often and asks me why you haven't written.

I had not heard from Siggy in years. A knot tightened in my stomach.

He was killed in the Pacific on Truk. His commanding officer said he was brave, but he could say nothing else. They would not let us see him when his body came to the airfield. My mother cried a lot.

Moonlight lit Siggy's words from the open window next to my cot. It was just past midnight and the city was in curfew. Lefty snored.

At the bottom of the paper lay Siggy's signature. He'd added a curved flair to his name. I crumpled the letter into a ball and tried to throw it out the window, but I couldn't. I flattened it out and placed it on my bed. There was no mention of all the time that had passed, of Mr. Braun's promise to return for me. I placed the letter under my cot, on top of my books, and went to sleep.

One week later I skipped school and waited under the awning of a tailor's shop across the street for Lefty to leave. I followed him to the West Side Highway and out onto the piers where he spent the morning feeding the pigeons and watching the boats load.

At lunch he returned to the hotel and climbed to the roof, where apartments stood alone like small houses in the clouds. He stepped past them to the edge of the black tar and the retaining wall. I watched him stand there for a half hour before I approached him.

"Are you going to Baltimore?" he asked without turning around.

"Baltimore?"

"The letter was on your bed. Never leave letters on your bed."

"It was under the bed."

"The wind moved it."

"How long did you know I was behind you?"

"I heard you on the stairs. Your feet clip-clop like those of a horse."

"I'm not going to Baltimore," I said.

"Your friend has lost his father. You need to go."

"No, I don't."

"Liar."

"He *was* my friend. He isn't any longer."

"What has passed has passed. Is that right, Cedric?"

"Something like that."

"He needs friends."

"You do fine without 'em and so do I."

A slight breeze ruffled the pinned sleeve of his jacket.

"Why do you come up here every day?" I asked.

"I do not."

"Yes, you do. Your shoes always have dust and tar on them. I clean them. I noticed."

"You are a smart boy, Cedric."

"Why do you come up here then?" I knew I was pushing him, but I was annoyed he'd read my letter and angry that he was telling me what to do.

"I took your mother up here," he said and turned to face me.

"My mother?"

"She said she wanted to see the city. A friend of hers rented a place here after the war. When she found out that I stayed here, she told me she liked the view and would like to see it again."

"What was she like?"

"I do not remember."

"Yes, you do. You must. You remember everything. You've got whole passages of Shakespeare stored up inside your head so I know you got a picture of her, too."

He turned away. "I remember nothing," he repeated.

I waited.

"She asked me questions, like you," he said. "She asked me about the war. She wore red lipstick and black stockings. She wanted to sing. She sang to me up here. I still hear her sometimes."

Many days of sorrow, many nights of woe,
And a ball and chain, everywhere I go.

"It was her favorite," he said. " 'Ma Rainey,' said she. 'She is a colored woman. She sang the blues.' Your mother liked the blues. She said Jews and coloreds had much in common—only Jews could not sing Nigra."

"Why did she marry my father?"

"She had no one else. Her parents were dead. Her brother was dead. The dog kicker loved her."

"I don't believe that."

Lefty shrugged. " . . . *and a ball and chain, everywhere I go,*" he sang, then hawked up some phlegm and spit. "Go to Baltimore."

"Why didn't you tell her you loved her?"

"One day, up here, she touched my cheek with her hand. 'If you ask me to dinner I will go with you,' said she. I took her hand away and told her I was broken—that I could have no children, even if she could be near me. 'You are young,' said I. 'You should have children.' 'My mother,' said she, 'told me that my hips are too narrow—that I can never have children.' She was wrong. Go to Baltimore."

"No," I said. "Besides, it's too late. He's been buried already."

"Then go to school and stop following me."

I asked him to tell me more about my mother, but he refused. He was that way. He could go days without speaking. But so could I. Lefty had talked about my mother twice and I knew, given the right time and place, he'd do so again. As for Siggy Braun and a trip to Baltimore, I could be just as stubborn and just as stupid.

In June flowers bloomed in bursts of red, yellow, orange, and white on the balconies to either side of us. Lefty called them zinnias.

"They grow quickly from their seed," he said.

Their perfume greeted me each morning.

The school year ended and I passed my class exams. Lefty chose speeches for me from each of the plays and I committed them to memory. The words I didn't know I either found in a dictionary or discovered in an annotated version of Shakespeare's works that I found in the public library. I learned that *anon* meant soon or presently. That *cock-a-hoop* meant to pick a quarrel or play the bully. That a *luce* was a pike and a *mountebank* a quack. To me the words sang. I found them to be like a secret code, each phrase needing to be deciphered.

At night, before Lefty came home, I practiced my lines, back straight and head held high, the way teachers in school taught us to make speeches. Then Lefty came home early one night and saw me. "Each word must be spoken as if you have just thought of it at that moment," he said. "You have to speak the character's thoughts. You must have a strong fantasy life to be an actor."

"What do you mean?" I asked, sitting down on my cot.

"You have to pretend to be someone else."

"How do you do that?"

"You never played pretend before, as a child?"

"You mean like playing war?" I remembered the war for Sunnyside Gardens with Siggy and Tomik. "I've done that, but it was a long time ago."

"Is that all you played at St. Agnes?"

"I didn't play at St. Agnes."

"All children play."

I stared at Lefty. Others at St. Agnes had played those games—the younger ones—but I never did. Playing meant you had to make friends. It wasn't any good to make friends, because they only left. Siggy and Tomik had taught me that.

"No games? No hide and seek?"

I kept silent. Lefty tapped his cane on the floor and looked down for a moment. "Did you ever daydream?" he asked.

"Sometimes. But if the sisters caught you staring off and your floors weren't clean or the pews not oiled, they'd box your ears."

Lefty looked up.

"Wait," I said. "I've seen movies."

"They took you to see them?"

"No. We weren't allowed to see them." I rubbed the back of my hand without thinking. It was where Sister Bernadette had hit me with a ruler when I'd asked her if I could leave for an afternoon to see Flynn's *The Adventures of Robin Hood*.

"Then how did you see photoplays?"

"I escaped."

"How often did you 'escape'?"

I shrugged.

"Did they find you and bring you back?"

I shook my head. "They didn't search for me. I went back on my own."

"What?" he asked, cocking his head to one side.

"Listen," I said. "I think I can pretend. I can be someone else. Just teach me how to do it."

Lefty sat down on his cot, shaking his head slowly.

"You think I can't do it but I can. I know I can."

He lay his cane to the side and took off his coat, unhooked his leg.

"Do you want your box?" I asked.

"No."

I waited.

He looked at me. "Think of something . . . grand. Then when you have that in your mind pretend you are a prince. Can you do that?"

"What do you mean, grand?"

Lefty stared at me a while. "In acting if you think a sad thought it can help you to act sad. A happy thought can help you to act happy. Do you understand?"

I nodded.

"Now, imagine you are the King of England."

"Which king?"

"Do you want to learn how to act?"

I nodded again.

"Then be the King of England. The one alive today."

I closed my eyes a second, stood up as tall as I could and looked at Lefty with half-closed eyes.

"Why are your eyes half closed?" he asked.

"I'm the King of England. I'm pretending not to care about anything that's beneath me—which is just about everybody."

"Good. You recall *Romeo and Juliet*?"

I nodded.

"Act three, scene one. Tybalt looks for and finds Romeo. '*Romeo*,' says he, '*the love I bear thee can afford no better term than this: thou art a villain*.' Romeo attempts to remain calm but Tybalt continues. '*Boy*,' says he, '*this shall not excuse the injuries that thou hast done me. Therefore turn and draw*.'"

"I remember it," I said. "It's right before they fight and Mercutio is killed—then Romeo kills Tybalt."

"That is correct. Now say Tybalt's first line."

I raised my chin and spoke the line with an English accent. "*The love I bear thee can afford no better term than this: thou art a villain*."

"Now imagine you are angry."

"At Romeo?"

"That would be good, but you can choose anyone in the play or in your life."

I thought of Sister Bernadette. "Do I have to still pretend I'm the Kind of England?"

"No. You are Tybalt and I am Romeo. Say your lines and be angry. You want to kill me. Show me that you want to kill me. Say your line."

"*The love I bear—*," I began, gritting my teeth the way Maddie used to when she was angry.

"Why are you gritting your teeth?" Lefty stopped me and asked.

"I'm angry. People do that when they're angry."

Lefty sat for a long time, looking at me, then past me, out the window.

I waited.

"Tell me something," he began, as if he'd made a decision.

"What?" I asked.

"How much do you hate Sigfried Braun?"

"What do you mean?" The question took me off guard.

Lefty waved his hand to cut me off. "Just answer the question. How much do you hate him?"

"Enough."

"Enough for what?"

"What does this have to do with anything? If you're trying to get me to go to Baltimore I already told you—"

"Answer the question," Lefty stated.

"I hate him," I said.

"If you saw him now," Lefty said, "in front of you, what would you do to him?"

"I don't know."

"You hate him?"

I nodded.

"You would hurt him?"

I nodded again.

"What"—he raised his voice—"would you do to him?"

"I don't know."

"Tell me what he did and *I'll* tell *you* what you would do to him."

I shook my head. "That's enough."

"You want to learn to act?"

I nodded.

"Then tell me."

I said nothing.

"Tell me." The two words hit me. "Tell me," he said again. "Tell me!"

"He left me. Him and Tomik. They left me at St. Agnes. They left me and didn't come back. Mr. Braun said they'd come back but they never did."

"And you hate them for it. All of them?"

I nodded.

"Do you feel that anger in your belly?"

I nodded again.

"Pretend that I am Siggy and say the line to me. Make me fight you."

"No."

"You wanted to learn how to act! This is acting. It is an

ugly method but it may work for you where other methods do not." Lefty raised his voice. "Do you want to learn to act?"

"Yes!" I said.

"Then make me fight you."

"No!"

"Make me fight you!" he yelled into my face. "Say Tybalt's words."

I felt all the rage of five years waiting at St. Agnes boil up and out of my stomach. It singed the back of my throat and entered into my mouth. *"The love I bear thee can afford no better term than this: thou art a villain."*

"Tybalt," Lefty said, *"the reason that I have to love thee doth much excuse the appertaining rage to such a greeting. Villain, I am none. Therefore farewell. I see thou knowest me not."*

"Boy," I said, and for a moment Lefty was not Lefty, and he was not Romeo. He was Siggy. And I was not Tybalt but I was saying Tybalt's words. *"This shall not excuse the injuries that thou hast done me. Therefore turn and draw."* The sound of my words were the sound of death. I stood in front of Lefty, gasping for air, my hands shaking. My mouth hung open and air escaped the back of my throat.

Lefty slowly leaned forward and touched my arm. I pulled it away and looked at the place his fingers had been, Siggy's fingers.

"That is how much Tybalt hates the Montagues," Lefty said, his words soft, still extending his hand. I looked up and he was Lefty. His hand touched my arm again and took hold of it. It was firm but there was no threat in his grasp. I looked into his good eye. He nodded slightly and released my arm.

"*That* is acting," he said. "And you were right. You can act."

✛

On the last Saturday of June Lefty took me to see *Romeo and Juliet* at a theatre off MacDougal Street in the Village. Rapiers clanged and clashed in each of the fights as weapons were banged together and those of us in the first row, sitting on wobbly-legged chairs, ducked half a dozen times along with the actors. The actor playing Tybalt attacked Romeo so savagely that sparks flew from their blades. He battered Romeo to the floor and backed him up against a wall before he seemed to realize that he was supposed to be the loser of the fight. He opened his arms wide, his face flushed, while Romeo carefully thrust home.

The actors sweat and spit and thudded when they threw themselves onto the floor. They flinched when steel clanged together too close to their ears, truly afraid they would be hurt. It was the first live theatre that I had ever seen and I fell in love with it.

I couldn't stop talking about the play as we walked back to the hotel. Lefty listened quietly. After he went to bed, I stared at the ceiling, my heart thumping, until, unable to stand it any longer, I dragged the play out from under the bed and read it again, this time picturing how I would fight, if I were Tybalt, the king of cats.

And I did know how to fight with a sword, or I thought

Joseph Lunievicz

I did. I'd read Nadi's book and practiced the positions in the room when Lefty wasn't there. I knew the guards and the invitations: quarte, sixte, tierce, and octave. I knew the words of attack and defense: parry, thrust, lunge, riposté, remise, redoublement, flèche, bind, beat, and counter-beat. Nadi also wrote about a duel he had fought, a real sword fight. I'd read and reread this chapter—even asked Lefty about duels, if he'd ever fought one, but he hadn't. What I had were a book, pictures, and my imagination. What I didn't have was the experience of what it was like to fence for real, steel against steel.

The following morning Lefty woke me with a rapping of his cane against the cot near my head. He told me to get dressed and follow him.

It was Saturday. I usually had errands to run for him and breakfast to buy from the corner grocer's, but there was none of that today. We went to the roof, to the rear of our building, where an apartment was nearly hidden behind a larger home and between two chimneys. It was small and shabby, its door covered with black soot.

Lefty knocked.

A man shouted from behind the door in a language I didn't understand. I thought it might be Russian.

Lefty knocked again, harder this time.

The door flew open and a short squat man stood there, squinting into the sunlight. He pushed a patch of thin gray hair back over his head to cover a large bald spot, and belched. His thick nose was round and red, his skin white like paper. His eyes focused on Lefty and a smile creased his lips.

"*Zdràhfstvyjti,* he mumbled and gave Lefty's tall, thin frame a bear hug. He asked him something and Lefty replied in the same language without missing a beat.

They went back and forth for a moment. Then the man's smile disappeared and he rubbed his speckled forehead. He asked Lefty something.

"*Spasíba,*" Lefty said and nodded. "This is he," he added in English.

"*Da,*" the man said. He reached forward with his right hand and tried to shake Lefty's, but the cane got in the way. When he reached for Lefty's left arm, he found only empty space. Narrowing his eyes to slits he searched the empty space a few times, as if in disbelief that he hadn't encountered an arm. Giving up, he tossed back his head, laughed, and threw both arms out to his sides for another bear hug, but lost his balance and toppled over backward instead.

I reached down to help him up. He found my hand and threw up on it.

That was how I met Nikolai Varvarinski, one-time fencing master to the court of the Tsar.

Fifteen
THE GUARD OF TIERCE

"This man will teach you to fence," Lefty said, turning toward me as Nikolai Varvarinski struggled to stand.

"Sir?" I said, not quite believing what Lefty was telling me.

Lefty lowered himself to look me in the eye. The right side of his mouth twitched upward into a grin. "He will teach you."

"Fencing lessons?"

Lefty nodded.

"Has he ever been in a duel?" I couldn't stop myself from asking.

Lefty's grin disappeared. "Do not talk to him of dueling. He is mad—madder than most. You will do well not to encourage him in that line."

I stole a quick glance down at the man below me, who was still trying to get up. "You're sure he can fence?"

His eye seemed to glaze over and lose focus. "In the trenches," he rasped, "you must use what you can find."

I nodded, knowing not to ask more. This man in front of me would be my teacher, and that was that. The tool

Lefty found for me to use might not fit exactly with what I had pictured—which had been a combination of Errol Flynn and Aldo Nadi—but he would do the job. I felt the vomit hardening in the space between my fingers and wiped them against my pants.

"You want to learn how to make a fight look real on the stage," Lefty interrupted my thoughts, "then you must learn how to fence. Nadi's book is only what it is—a book. Varvarinski owes me a favor. He will teach you the art of the blade. Later, I will teach you what is used on the stage."

"Hey, sir?" I stopped him as he was turning away from me.

He looked back and lifted his head.

"Thank you."

He grunted. "Do not thank me yet. You have not seen him teach."

I saw Varvarinski reach toward me seeking help to stand, and I offered him my still partially wet hand. The grip wouldn't hold and he slipped off, back onto the floor. I looked at his unfocused eyes and watched his hands tread the air as though they were in water.

"Sir!" I said, back over my shoulder, but Lefty was no longer there. I heard the door to the stairs click shut. Then two hands grabbed my forearm and I had to concentrate on helping the Russian up or be pulled down onto the ground with him. Finally standing again, he clapped me on the back and belched into my face. I had to push down the reflex to throw up and shivered when it passed.

Varvarinski turned away from me and disappeared into the darkness of his apartment. I followed him in. Before he left the light of the doorway, I had a closer look at him. He was old, probably in his seventies—older than Lefty, at least. Then Varvarinski spoke, his words alien and incomprehensible.

In the dim light I saw something fly toward me and I ducked, raising my hands to protect myself. A wet towel, dark with stains, landed on them.

"*Tíkha!*" he ordered.

"I don't understand—"

"*Sadítis!*" he snapped and slid a chair across the floor. It banged hard into my knee.

"Hey, watch it, buddy!"

He ignored me. Blinds creaked open and more light came in from a window over what was a small space that served as living room, bedroom, and kitchen. Shiny lengths of steel, small cups, and wire mesh masks littered the floor and leaned up against the walls. I stared at it all, the towel clenched between my stiffening fingers. Varvarinski turned on the water at his sink. He pushed his head under it so the water hit the back of his head and neck, splattering the counter around him.

I reached down to touch a shallow silver hilt with a hole in its center.

"*Nyet!*" he shouted.

I kept my hand extended, forcing myself to withdraw it slowly, then stood.

"Arnolf say you are smart boy," he said, his accent heavy.

"You speak English?" I asked.

"How can boy be fencer if he ask such stupid question?"

I bit my lip.

He said something in Russian.

"What's that mean?"

"I am Russian."

"I figured that out a while ago."

"*Da*. That is good. You figure out something. American boys always try to figure out something. Now you listen. You let brain rest. Do not make it work hard. I am to be *uchítil*, teacher. You call me Nikolai, and if you are lucky I will not kill you in first lesson."

"Kill me?" I said, unable to stop the laugh from escaping my lips.

"Why do you laugh?" His question was soft, but cold.

It chilled me and made me stop. "I'm sorry," I said. "I didn't mean to laugh."

"You did, and you are not sorry. Now tell old man from Russia why you laugh at him."

I shrugged, not wanting to go on, knowing it would make things worse.

"What is wrong? Afraid to tell what is on mind?"

"No."

"Then tell me, *boy*. Tell me what make *boy* laugh?"

The second time he called me *boy* my mouth opened. "You don't look like much of a fighter."

"What do I look like to you?"

"An old drunk."

"Old . . . Russian drunk?"

I nodded.

He didn't speak for a while, then moved forward into a patch of light. Water beaded on his head. He wiped it away with a towel in hands that shook. "I am each of them. I am also teacher. You will learn or you will not. Does not matter to me which. Matters to Leftingsham. I have debt to pay, and Nikolai Varvarinski pay all debts."

"Mr. Varvarinski—," I started, but he interrupted me.

"You want something of me?"

"Mr. Leftingsham told me not to ask you about dueling. Why did he tell me that?"

"Because he is smart, unlike *boy* in front of me."

"The father of a—" I stopped myself, then continued, "Someone I knew fought duels with schlagers in Germany."

Nikolai spat onto the floor of his apartment. "That is not duel."

"Why not?"

"Did man die?"

"What do you mean?"

"Was man killed? Did man die?"

"No."

"Then there was not duel."

"But Aldo Nadi fought a duel and nobody was killed."

"Aldo Nadi"—Nikolai's lips lifted up into a sneer—"writes book."

"I have the book."

"Then it is on paper already." He swayed for a moment and grabbed the back of his chair to steady himself. I thought he was going to throw up again, but it seemed to pass. "Now . . . before we begin lesson I tell you what you learn. I teach épée, only épée. I not teach for *sarivnaváh-niye*, ah, um, com-pe-ti . . . ti . . . ."

"Competition."

"*Da*. Compe-tition. *Spacíba*. If you want competition, you go to Fencer's Club."

"I've read about that club."

"Good. You can read. At Fencer's Club, you learn sport. Épée still weapon of duel—still weapon of fight. I teach you to fight. I teach you to kill. Now take off shirt."

"What?"

"To take off shirt!" he said, raising his voice. He brushed past me and walked out into the morning light, shielding his eyes from the sun.

I followed him, unbuttoning my shirt as I went.

"Off!" he shouted and turned around to face me. He wore black knickers with gray socks and shoes. His shirt was a ragged turtleneck that had once been white. Its collar hung loosely about his neck, damp from vomit and splashed water. A fleshy gut pushed out against the shirt and over his pants. He looked even worse in the light. I had to stop myself from laughing again.

I took off my shirt and felt the sun touch my skin. It was warm even if there was still a spring breeze. Nikolai walked around me, inspecting me.

"What about your shirt?" I asked.

"My shirt not in question." He reached out for my chest and I blocked his hand automatically. But I missed as he switched direction and grabbed my bicep instead. "Fast," he said, "for old Russian drunk, huh?"

"Hey, watch it," I said, throwing off his hand, but only after he'd pinched my skin and left a welt.

"Quiet!" He stopped and examined the scars my father's strap had lined my back with. They had grown smaller, almost disappearing as I grew up and out of them, but I knew they were still there. Lefty had seen them and said nothing. I'd ignored him as I'd ignored the kids who'd stared at me at St. Agnes.

"Who make these?" Nikolai asked.

"Nobody," I said.

"Someone make these."

"Nobody did. Now what about a lesson, *teacher*?"

He stared at me for a moment, then said, "Good," and pinched my belly before I could stop him. "Skimmer," he added and nodded. "Good for épée. Blade miss when you are skimmer. I am fat!" he said, slapping his own belly. "You are skimmer! Aldo Nadi is skimmer."

"You mean thinner?"

"That is what I said." Then he took my shirt from my hands and threw it against the chimney. "We practice afternoon—three to four each day during week until summer end. Then three day each week—Monday, Wed— . . . middle day, and Friday, until New Year. Do not be late. We begin today. We begin now. We continue Monday. Understood?"

That night, before I went to sleep, Lefty asked me about the lesson. It was near midnight and both of us lay on our beds with the lights out. Lefty's eye had been closed and I'd thought he was asleep. I was glad he wasn't.

"Why did you tell me not to talk to him about dueling?" I asked.

"You must learn to fence, not duel."

"When you duel, you test your courage."

"Who told you that?"

"Someone I used to know. He had four schlager duels and two scars because of them." I ran my finger across my face where Mr. Braun had been cut. "Here and here," I said.

"Dueling is not a game to be played by children or students in university. It can get you killed, or worse."

"What could be worse than getting killed?" I asked, then realized what I had said. "Forget that. I'm sorry. I didn't mean—"

"I met Nikolai Varvarinski after the war. We were two cripples—"

"He's not a cripple—"

"He is as much a cripple as I."

"How'd you meet?"

"A pub in London. He was drunk. So was I. I heard him say words to a soldier in Russian—words about the soldier's mother and a goat. He did not think anyone in the room could understand him, but I learned Russian in prep school and spent a summer in the Ukraine, near the border, with my father."

"What did you do?"

"I called him a coward. He said he could not fight me because of my injuries. I took him to task with my cane, but he disarmed me."

"So you're . . . friends?" I asked hesitantly.

"Nikolai does not have friends. The Bolsheviks killed his wife and two daughters. I do not know how he came to London, only that he did. He was homeless. My family took him in. Then he killed two men and I threw him out."

"In duels?" I asked.

"Yes. One was a friend of mine."

"Then why is he teaching me?"

"Because he is here and he must repay his debt. It is a question of honor."

Sixteen

COLPIRE SENZA ESSERE COLPITO

Over the next two weeks Nikolai introduced me to the art of fencing. He drove me up and down the roof with footwork until my legs felt so heavy I couldn't lift them, shouting out, "Advance, retreat, passatta forward, passatta back, and lunge." He taught me all these things without me touching a weapon. After two weeks, my hand was itching to hold one.

"You are not ready," he said when I asked him why. "Legs are engine. Legs carry body. Legs carry point. Where legs go, point go first. Make legs strong is first goal. Make legs strong, you make point bite."

I willed myself to be patient.

Each afternoon when I finished school I ran up the stairs to the roof and rapped on Nikolai's door. He would come to the door with a towel wrapped around his head and his bloodshot eyes half closed, smelling of alcohol and sweat. Then he'd shout, "To take off shirt!" and we'd begin. He taught me in Italian, Spanish, French, English, and Russian, mixing them each day in a soup of fencing terminology. I asked him why.

"Before I become master," Nikolai said, "I go to Italy in 1908 and study in Rome. When I return to Russian court I can fence like no other. Russian nobles like devils to fight in duel. Want to be like French. Like devils to be French. Everything French. I call French fencing master coward and kill him in duel. His students come to me."

"How many men have you killed?"

"Quiet! I not finished. I bring them fencing book, *La Spada e la Sua Applicazione*. Book by Greco. I show them to speak with sword must speak Italian. 'First to be Italian!' I say. My students live—opponents die."

"But, how many men have you killed?"

"In war I lose count. It is what happen in war."

"How many in duels?"

"In first duel I place my point in other boy's chest"—he pointed to the center of his chest—"here. Into heart, I think. Blade go into body—go into body far. I let go of blade—stare at boy. He stare back at me but does not die. I think, why does boy not die? While I think, he put blade in my side and almost kill me." He lifted up his shirt and showed me a thick puckered scar above his hip.

"How many did you kill in duels?"

"Six or seven."

"You don't remember?"

"There are many things I not remember."

"What happened to your fencing school?"

He did not answer for a while, then his hand trembled a moment and he clenched it into a fist. "Enough talk. Now back to work!"

He didn't allow me to drink any water or to rest for

more than one minute—which he timed on an old silver pocket watch—until we were finished. He always saved the lunges for the last half hour. But I was determined not to fail and stayed on my wobbling legs until he said, "*Kónchit'!* First position! Lesson finished!"

Lefty and I began a nightly ritual. Before we went to sleep, he asked me how the lesson went and what I had learned. I told him.

Some days he would come up to the roof and watch the whole lesson, sitting on a stool in the shade, leaning against the wall. They exchanged greetings, then took their places, Lefty the sentinel and Nikolai the barking hound. Those nights, in the darkness before we slept, there were no questions for Lefty to ask. We'd pass into sleep without a word.

One night after Lefty had watched a lesson and before he was asleep, I asked him why Nikolai had killed his friend.

"His name was Higgins. He fought in Ypres in 1918. He blamed the Russians for the final German offensive—called them traitors to the Allies. Nikolai heard and took offense. At Ypres Higgins and his company ran. He was a poet with a gentle heart, but this stain he could not remove. 'I ran at Ypres,' said he. 'We all ran at Ypres,' said I. But it did not matter. Nothing matters when you believe you have lost what it is to be a man. I was his second. Nikolai drew blood four times, pricking hand, arm, wrist, and shoulder."

Each hit Lefty marked in the air where his arm would have been. "Higgins refused to apologize. Nikolai drove his blade through his lung."

"He should've stopped when he was hit."

"He could not."

"Have you ever fought a duel?"

"Never," Lefty said. "I killed at Passchendaele. That was enough."

"But the fight at the bar—," I started.

"There are fights and there are fights. Be smart enough to know the difference."

I nodded.

"Do you know why Nikolai is teaching you?" he asked after a while.

"Because he killed your friend while he was your guest."

Lefty's mouth moved into a half grin. His eye remained closed. "Nikolai does not know how to teach for sport. He only knows how to teach for the duel. For him the blades are always sharp, the points are always lethal. If you do not want your stage fights to look like two actors banging sticks together, you will need this perspective. If you do not truly fear for the character, then you do not care about the character. You must hate Tybalt for desiring to kill Mercutio and love Romeo for his burning to kill Tybalt. Sport fencing will teach you bad habits."

"I don't understand," I said. "Do you want Nikolai to teach me to duel or to fence?"

"To Nikolai they are the same."

"But what if I want to fence against others?" I hadn't really thought about what I was going to say until I'd said

144

it. I hadn't even held an épée in my hand yet. But I'd thought that when I did, I would eventually fence someone. Perhaps it was the influence of Aldo Nadi's book or the articles I had read about the sport in *The Times*. Or maybe it was just my competitive nature. "Listen to this," I said, leaning over my bed and pulling out my copy of Nadi's book. I squinted so I could see the words by the moonlight. "Paul Gallico says this in the foreword. 'A touch of imagination and instead of working on the strip of the Salle, masked and padded, the sword tip blunted, you're standing, naked to the waist in some glade, facing an opponent with a deadly weapon in hand. Only one of you will leave the scene.' That's pretending the way you have taught me. Nadi's duel in the first chapter was brilliant. I'm not saying I want to fight a duel, but I do want to fence."

Lefty was silent a long time. I placed the book back under my bed and threw myself solidly onto my cot, thrusting my hands behind my head. After a while I thought he had gone to sleep, so I took a deep breath and closed my eyes. Then from the darkness came his harsh voice. "When you are ready, I will take you to the Gotham Club."

My body ached every morning when I awoke and every night when I went to sleep. But after two weeks of daily footwork I could see myself changing shape. My legs became harder, the muscles in my thighs and calves visible in bunches. My breathing became less ragged during drills. My run up the stairs to the roof became easier.

Then, on the first Monday in July, Nikolai placed an épée in my hand.

It was an Italian grip with a crossbar and a large cup hilt. Fitting my fingers and hand around it, Nikolai drew a worn leather strap from his back pocket and tied the grip tightly against my palm and wrist. The blade was thick and stiff. The tip was blunt like the head of a nail. The metal of its hilt was battered with dents and scratches. It was perfect—part of my arm from the moment it was placed in my hand.

"With foil you aim point at chest, at pit under arm, at belly—nothing more," Nikolai said. "Rules of foil are many. Who may strike first? Who may strike second? When you learn foil, you learn art. With épée you target body, whole body with point—head, toe, arm, leg, cock. Not need to be pretty. Need only to touch with point." He placed a finger on my forehead, then on my chest. "Head. Heart. Lung. These will kill. Hit and not be hit. *Colpire senza essere colpito*. You remember this?" He pulled up his shirt and showed me the scar he'd received above his hip during his first duel. "It is not about who hit first. It is about who hit and not be hit *at all*."

"Aldo Nadi says in his book that he can tell more about someone in a few minutes of fencing than from hours of conversation. You think that's true?"

"En garde!" he said and stood in first position in front of me.

I didn't mind the weapon's battered condition. I created a history for each mark and scar. I saw it being used in duel after duel, piercing flesh and tasting blood. It was Captain Peter Blood's. It was the Black Pirate's and Don Diego Vega's from *The Mask of Zorro*, and it had once belonged to Flynn's Geoffrey Thorpe from *The Sea Hawk*.

Nikolai adjusted my grip, placing my two fingers through the loops created by the crossbar, the ricasso, and the inside of the hilt. I gripped it tightly.

Nikolai shook his head. "*Nyet*," he said, loosening my grip with his fingers. "Think of weapon like woman. Beautiful, but dangerous. You hold tight so it fit good. Too tight and she bite you. Too loose and she find other man to bite."

"It feels light," I said, hefting the weapon from side to side.

"It grow heavy soon. You see." Then, instead of bending my sword arm the way Nadi showed in his book, Nikolai had me keep it almost fully extended and pointed at his chest.

"But Aldo Nadi—" I started to say and Nikolai cut me off.

"You want Aldo Nadi to teach, or Nikolai Varvarinski?" Stalking off into his room he returned a moment later with a wire mesh mask in his hand. He placed it roughly over my head, adjusting the back so that the fit was snug. I looked out at the world from behind a curtain of steel. Reaching into an equipment bag, Nikolai took out a leather plastron and put it on over his shirt, then donned a mask of his own.

"Don't I get a jacket?" I asked.

"If you are hit one time you not want to be hit second time. Pain make blade move faster."

He was right about that.

Nikolai took pleasure in carrying home his thrust or lunge when I was slow in my defense. Every hit upon my body was followed by a shout of "You are dead!" After one day, my parries became faster.

Seventeen
REMISE

In July Lefty and I saw *Macbeth*.

The show played in front of forty fold-out seats occupied by ten audience members of which—as I gathered from overhearing people talk prior to the curtain going up—Lefty and I were the only ones not related to a member of the cast.

The curtain opened on Macbeth and Banquo behind a gauze screen. With a light on behind them, we could only see their dark outlines. There they made war against an army. Back to back they fought what seemed like swarms of soldiers entering from either side. Broadswords clashed and soldiers screamed in the throes of death. The stream of soldiers seemed endless, Macbeth's and Banquo's energy boundless. There was no music and at times the scene seemed to move in slow motion. The lights went out on their victorious figures—their silent forms replaced by the cackles of three witches.

"It was like watching a whole battle," I said to Lefty afterward.

He nodded.

"There must have been twenty or thirty men playing soldiers to keep that going for so long."

"There were six."

"That can't be," I said, incredulous.

"There were six," Lefty repeated. Our irregular footsteps sounded dully on the cooling summer pavement.

"But—"

"There were three on each side. When one was killed he crawled off or was helped off by another while the third fought. The illusion was successful."

"That's incredible," I said. "Absolutely incredible. It's so easy to believe it's real—"

"When you want to believe it is real," Lefty finished for me.

I nodded.

✝

After Macbeth, we saw a film together at my request. It starred Humphrey Bogart and was called *Sahara*.

Sahara affected Lefty in a strange way. The images of the Germans—in wave after wave assaulting the desert oasis, lips cracked from the heat and no water while Bogart and his allies held them off with their lone tank, a machine gun, and rifle fire—disturbed him deeply. Afterward, he wouldn't talk about the film at all. When we got home his hand was shaking and he couldn't use his key at our door. For the first and only time he allowed me to open it for him. I never asked him to see a war film again.

On September 3, Italy surrendered to the allies and I

had my first day of school in ninth grade. Two weeks later I got into a fight and broke the nose of an upperclassman who called my mother a Jew.

That night, when I told Lefty, he reminded me that my mother *was* a Jew.

"Why do people hate Jews?" I asked.

"Why do you hate Jews?" he replied.

"I don't hate Jews. I just don't want to be one of them."

"Why not? Your mother was a Jew. You are one by birth."

"If I wasn't one, I could have—"

"You could have what?"

"Nothing."

"You were going to say something. What was it?"

"Mr. Braun, Siggy's father—"

"The boy who wrote the letter?"

I nodded. "He said they couldn't take me with them to Baltimore because I was a Jew."

Lefty sat for a long while, not moving. Then he got out his box and started his nightly routine. I got undressed in silence and lay down on my cot.

"Maddie said all Jews were devils," I said finally, "that we had horns and were cursed."

"She *would* say that."

"Nothing good has ever come to me from being a Jew."

"Little good has ever come from any religion."

"You don't believe in God?"

"I stopped a long time ago."

"During the war?"

Lefty didn't answer.

"Then why do I have to believe in one?"

"You don't have to believe in anything."

"Then I don't."

"You believe in nothing?" Lefty lay back on his bed as the morphine began to take effect.

"I believe in myself."

"That is a good start."

"I believe in you when you're not too angry, and Nikolai when he's not too drunk."

This made Lefty laugh.

"What else is there to believe in?" I asked.

Lefty said nothing.

"Then I don't believe in God and I'm not a Jew."

"God can go to the devil."

"Good."

"But your failure to believe in God does not stop you from being a Jew. It just makes you more intelligent than the average sod who wets his pants when the priest calls. Your mother told me that you were a Jew by birth, whether you practiced the faith or not. It was important to hcr, so it should be important to you. You are still a Jew. Accept it and you accept the part of you that is your mother. It is that simple."

Lefty found me another school, this time farther up into midtown. In the halls my first day, I heard students whisper about me.

"He's the kid who busted some guy's teeth."

"I heard he carries a knife."

I pretended not to hear them. I did my schoolwork and the other kids left me alone. The teachers did, too.

My fencing lessons continued five days a week. Nikolai never cut back on my time and I didn't remind him that he'd said he would. He drilled me even harder through the fall until the moves came to me without thinking.

"When you find blade," Nikolai said one afternoon, "you return attack—you riposté. It arrive *un fulmine*."

"What does *un fulmine* mean?" I asked.

"Like thunder-lock. You parry at last moment. Make opponent attack, then strike him like thunder-lock."

"You mean thunderbolt?"

"That is what I said!"

He taught me to attack my opponent's blade with beats, to pressure and thrust against it with glissades, coulés, and froissements, and to attack into my opponent's attack with stop-thrusts. "To hit head. To hit heart. To hit lung," rang in my ears until I heard it in my sleep.

At the end of each lesson we would salute and he would disappear into his apartment. Moments later, while I was carefully putting on my shirt, he would reappear wearing another shirt, usually black, repack his equipment bag, throw it over his shoulder, and leave.

One night I asked Lefty where Nikolai went with his equipment.

"He sells his lessons to rich American children at a private school on the West Side," he said. "I would not ask him about it, though, if I were you."

I itched to fence someone. Nikolai would sometimes

spar with me but it was always controlled—aimed only at teaching me the movements from my lesson, never letting me make up my own moves or combinations.

"What about finding me someone to fence against?" I finally asked him.

"*Nyet*," he said.

"Why not?"

"Learn form first. When feet move and you not think about moving feet—when hand moves blade and you not think about moving hand—then you are ready. Not before."

"But Mr. Leftingsham told me he'd take me to the Gotham Club."

Nikolai stopped with his mouth half open in reply, then turned his lips down into a scowl. "What do you say?" he asked slowly.

"Mr. Leftingsham said he would take me to fence at the Gotham Club so I could compete there when I was ready."

"*Da*," he said, nodding. "You have time on head you can think of Gotham Club? We see about this." He turned away from me, then back, a shadow over his face. "Today you learn remise."

"Aldo Nadi says—"

"I am not Nadi," he shouted and threw his glove onto the ground. "You want to take lesson from Nadi you find Nadi!"

"I didn't mean—"

"*Kónchit'!* No more questions. You learn. I teach! Remise is attack, then attack."

"What do you mean?" We had been working on parry-riposté drills, Nikolai pushing me to parry later and later, and to riposté faster and faster.

Nikolai picked up his glove and épée. He cinched his leather wrist strap tight and secured the grip against his palm. "With foil you extend arm before attack. *Da?*"

I nodded and rolled my eyes, having heard his explanation of foil what seemed like a thousand times before.

"Good," he said, ignoring me. "You know difference between foil and épée?"

"Yes, yes," I said, nodding and mouthing the words with him.

"If you parry, I withdraw arm, extend again before I attack in redoublement," he said, showing me with his blade in quick, sharply etched movements.

"That sounds French," I said.

"Quiet!" he shouted and launched an attack at my chest so quickly I barely had time to parry. Only instead of relaxing his arm back into en garde he kept his arm extended and attacked again to my hip. I stumbled back just in time to parry his strike in seconde and retreated again, now off balance, parrying another attack to my shoulder in sixte, only the third time I was too slow and his point touched my upper arm. Nikolai didn't stop. His momentum threw him forward and pushed his point into my flesh. I tripped over my feet and fell to the ground. My arm felt as though it had been pierced.

"Remise!" he said, looking down at me, anger seething out of his lips.

"Remise," I repeated, my own anger building in return. I touched the bruised skin of my arm. There was some blood where the point had hit. It was sore and would be black and blue in the morning. "Remise," I said again, quietly. The world slowed down and my senses expanded. I heard the rasping sound of gravel shifting beneath Nikolai's front foot and the dull thudding of my heart. His breath was ragged. A high-pitched buzzing floated by one of my ears and passed around to the other.

It seemed impossible for such a large and out-of-shape man to move that fast. In drills he pushed me with his own attacks, but they were timed and rhythmic, beautiful in their own way and mesmerizing in their patterns, but never blinding in speed. I'd thought he was fast enough to touch me only if I made a mistake. Now, watching him walk awkwardly away from me, his shoulders slumping forward, his belly hanging again over his pants, my anger grew. "Why don't you try that again?" I said, the words seeming to elongate out in front of me as if in a dream.

Nikolai stopped in his tracks, then turned to face me. "You want to fight me?" His words were crisp, dangerous.

"Yes," I said.

He stepped toward me, out of distance but with his blade angled down toward the ground. It was an open invitation to attack—a dare. His arm swayed almost imperceptibly from side to side—his body forward and back. He was waiting for me to move so he could attack into my attack.

I eased into the en garde he'd taught me. A fraction of a second passed, then a full second. Then two.

Then Nikolai's body moved differently and I saw the attack coming. He would not wait for me after all. He thrust quickly to my belly and I stop-thrust to his wrist, attacking into his attack. He parried in sixte, pressuring my blade out and down with a riposté glissade thrust to my chest. I parried just in time and jumped back out of distance.

"You go to Gotham Club when I say you are ready. Not before," he shouted.

I feint-thrust to his arm over his guard and he stop-thrust to my wrist, but I expected it and counter-parried in sixte. I took his blade and pushed against it, thrusting to his chest in a glissade. Nikolai barely had time to parry, countering in quarte and retreating.

We stood looking at each other, breathing heavily, our bodies poised like two compressed springs.

"He is ready now," Lefty said from the stairway door.

"Stay out of business!" Nikolai shouted, never taking his eyes off me.

"You have done your job," Lefty said. "Now he will learn from others."

"He is done when I say, not before!"

Lefty stepped toward him with his awkward gait. "He is your student, Nikolai, not your enemy. Put the blade down. You too, Cedric."

"No one tells Nikolai Varvarinski to put down blade." His blade swung in line toward Lefty's throat.

"Lefty!" I shouted.

"Stay out of this, Cedric," Lefty said. "This is between Nikolai and myself."

"Listen to man, Cedric. We finish lesson later."

"Is your honor worth so little these days," Lefty said, "that you would attack a helpless cripple?"

Nikolai's face was flushed, burgundy patches marking his cheeks and neck. His blade hovered inches from Lefty's jugular. Blunt tip or not, the threat was real.

"What is honor, Leftingsham? Did it save leg or arm? Did it save daughter?"

I stepped forward and raised my blade.

"Cedric!" Lefty said, his voice barely above a whisper. I froze.

Nikolai spoke slowly. "You are not cripple, Leftingsham."

"I am what I am," Lefty said.

Nikolai lowered his blade. His face drained of color and his body collapsed. His shoulders fell forward and his chin sunk down to his chest.

"Next week we will go to the Gotham Fencer's Club," Lefty stated. "We shall take your student, Nikolai, together. And once there, you shall behave yourself."

Eighteen
GLISSADE

Hi-ho, hi-ho, it's off to Tokyo.
We'll bomb the Japs right off the maps,
hi-ho, hi-ho hi-ho hi-ho.

It was a schoolboy chant echoing through the halls that November that I couldn't get out of my head. I wondered if it worked the same way with Lefty and his "bells of hell go ting-a-ling a-ling."

It took not one but two weeks before I made it to the Gotham Fencer's Club. Lefty kept to himself the whole time. After the first week I was disappointed but busy enough not to feel as if he'd forgotten. He started me on Shakespeare's histories instead. "Read them," was all he said. *Henry V, Richards II* and *III*, and *King John* were the first four I tackled. It left us silent at night. I noticed that he was drinking more, too, so I kept out of his way and did not press him.

Nikolai also had been quiet. He spoke to me less and would not look me in the eyes, except when he had to during our lesson.

Then one afternoon I came home from school to find

Lefty in our room waiting for me. "We shall go to the Gotham Club," was all he said.

"Now?" I asked.

"You will need this," he said, awkwardly reaching down under his bed and sliding a large bag out from beneath it.

By its shape I knew it was a fencing bag. It was black, worn around the edges, and holed at the top, with an épée point sticking out of it.

"Épée, tennis shoes, jacket, glove, and mask are inside," Lefty said. "Nikolai said you have a wrist strap."

I nodded, my mouth hanging open.

"You will catch flies," he said.

I closed my mouth.

"You have a birthday?"

I nodded again. "It's in February."

"It has come early this year. Remember *the immortal passado, the punto reverso, the hay!*"

"Mercutio dies," I said recognizing the quote from *Romeo and Juliet.*

"Yes," Lefty said. "But then he had to, did he not?"

"What do you mean?" I asked.

"Shakespeare had to kill him. Mercutio was stealing the play from Romeo. That is a good lesson to learn. Never upstage the star. Shakespeare knew that."

"Thank you," I said.

"For telling you a simple fact?"

"For your gift."

Lefty grunted and stood.

"Will Nikolai be coming?"

Lefty hesitated a moment, then said, "Yes."

"Do you think he'll cause some kind of trouble?"

Lefty stared at me, his body swaying onto and off his wooden leg. "One day Nikolai Varvarinski will kill or be the cause of killing again."

"Then why does he have to come?" I asked, knowing full well the answer.

"Because he has to," Lefty said.

Nikolai met us at the corner of Twenty-third and Sixth, appearing out of the twilight shadows of the Mason's Building. He fell into step behind us, even more drunk than usual. He swayed as he walked, stumbling on uneven pavement, mumbling to himself. We walked up to Twenty-fourth Street, then east almost to Broadway, but stopped in front of a glass-and-mahogany door. Lefty pushed it open. I followed him in.

I knew there were only a few places to fence in New York City—The New York Athletic Club, The Fencer's Club, and the Gotham Club. The sign above the door said GOTHAM.

Ever since Lefty had mentioned the Gotham to me, I'd read everything I could about it and the other clubs in the city. Outside of tournaments, which were held in hotel banquet halls, you had to go to one of the fencing clubs if you wanted to fence. The few fencing masters not teaching at the clubs taught in a hotel suite or dining hall, as Aldo Nadi had. The poor ones like Nikolai taught where they could find space.

Inside, the Gotham Club smelled of cigars and sweat. The walls were paneled a dark brown and the room was lit by a crystal chandelier. The main salle was more than fifty feet square—the walls run round with racks of foils, épées, sabers, antique smallswords, and rapiers.

A man stopped us as we entered, taking our hats and jackets. He was a large man, wearing a wool sports coat over his sweater and tie. He asked us if we were members, eyeing Nikolai, who used the doorway to hold himself up.

Lefty said something about visiting, and that he would like to pay the floor fee for me to bout in open competition. I heard it all in the background while my eyes drank in the sights before me.

On the salle there were three strips. On one, an instructor was giving a lesson to someone close to my age. The boy's back was to me, and he was engaged in a parry-riposté drill with foil. To the right were two pairs of young men fencing foil, each with an older man acting as a judge and presiding over their match. All the fencers stopped as we entered, anonymous behind their wire masks.

Lefty came up behind me. "The locker room is below us." He pointed with his cane toward the stairs at the end of the hall.

I nodded.

Then he and Nikolai took chairs in the corner and sat down. I watched Nikolai close his eyes and pass out. So, true to his word, he behaved.

There were others in the room, men in dark suits—probably fathers or uncles—but I had no time for them. This evening I was going to enter Paul Gallico's glade to fight an opponent with naked steel. I would be Geoffrey Thorpe, Major Vickers, and Zorro—my blade alive in my hand—and nothing could stop me.

I found my way downstairs and to the locker room. It was damp, the tile floor crusted over with mold in the corners and near the shower stalls. The smell of body odor and cigar smoke was everywhere. I placed my gear on a scored wooden bench and changed. Two other boys had just finished dressing and walked past me as I sat down. I nodded, and they carefully nodded back. They were wearing white fencing knickers and jackets.

The new tennis shoes fit snugly on my feet. I'd never worn tennis shoes before and their lightness thrilled me. They were white the way only new canvas can be, gleaming against my old street trousers and worn jacket. I tested their rubber on the floor. They squeaked on the tile and gripped the floor as if they had glue on their soles. With these shoes on I felt invincible. I packed my bag with my street clothes, slung it back over my shoulder, and ran up the stairs two at a time. Before I reached the top, I heard the two boys talking, then saw their backs as they stood at the top of the stairs.

"Who are those two clowns?" one asked the other, his tone educated and moneyed.

"Someone should tell them that the freak—," the other started to say, then turned and stopped talking as soon as they heard me behind them.

I knew they were talking about Nikolai and Lefty. In my rush to fence, I'd forgotten who I'd come with. I'd become used to Lefty, his appearance, his smell, the rasping sound of his voice. And Nikolai had long since stopped being anything but a fencing master to me.

I stopped midstep and saw then and there that I should

not have come. It was not Nikolai who would be trouble, nor Lefty—only me. I had forgotten my place in the world. The two boys in front of me wore clothes that, if they weren't new, were close to it. Their foils and masks shone with the brilliance of a servant's soft polishing touch. I looked at my loose pants and belt, my worn jacket, gray with years of use, my battered mask and weapon.

The echoing words of the two boys settled inside of me. I digested them and felt my stomach rumble.

"Excuse me," I said and pushed past them, knocking one off balance.

"Watch where you're going," he said.

I walked toward Lefty and Nikolai. The fencers still stood talking in the middle of the room; the master and student were still engaged in their lesson. I saw a group of five older men whom I'd barely noticed earlier—spectators in finely cut suits, smoking cigars in the far corner by the stairs that led up to the next floor. Two of them had brandy glasses in their hands. They pointed at the snoring Nikolai and statue-like Lefty and shook their heads.

Two young fencers stood in front of me. One pointed at Lefty and said, "Tom, since when do they let riffraff like that in this club? If that were a child, it would have been better to have killed it at birth." He spoke just loud enough to be heard.

I dropped my bag to the floor and ran the last few steps, pushing that boy from behind. The flats of my hands hit his shoulders, forcing him to stumble forward. He turned around quickly, expecting a friend who was playing a joke.

"Shut up!" I shouted.

His face shifted from surprise to anger and then to indignance. "What the hell do you think—," he began, but I stopped him from saying another word by hitting him in the mouth.

The other boy took a step toward me.

I turned on him with my bloody fist still raised. "This isn't your fight," I said, "but I can make it yours."

He stopped where he stood and stared at me. His friend moaned on the floor, turning over onto his hands and knees. Blood ran out of his mouth in a thick stream.

I saw Lefty stand up out of the corner of my eye.

"You'll pay for that," the boy shouted from the floor. "Just like the Japs and their sneak attack." He spit blood out of his mouth to clear it. "You'll pay."

The five men and the other students gathered around us, the men quickly grabbing for my arms. I threw them off.

"You're a coward," the boy said, and spit blood onto my new tennis shoes.

I leapt for his throat.

Arms wrapped around me again and pulled me away. The man who had greeted us at the door stood in front of me. He was much taller and broader than I'd realized.

"You are not welcome here," he said slowly, his voice menacing. "This is a club for gentlemen and you are not—"

Then Lefty's cane cracked him on the side of the head and he crumpled to his knees as the cane splintered in two. The men in suits stepped back and gave us room, the students following their lead.

"It seems we are not welcome here," Lefty said, sliding my bag over to me.

"No," I said, "we're not." I picked up the bag and slung it over my shoulder.

"Who are you?" demanded the boy I'd punched.

"Cedric Wymann," I said, "and that's one riffraff's name you won't forget for a while."

"Remember that, Tom," he said to the boy next to him.

The man who had been giving lessons came forward with his weapon partially raised. He stepped in front of the others as more foils were raised, their tips pointed toward us. "Now is time for you to go," he said, his Slavic accent thick. Lefty and I backed our way toward the door where Nikolai leaned, barely holding himself erect.

Then Nikolai pushed out from between us and stood with an antique smallsword in his hand, swaying from side to side.

"Nikolai," the teacher said softly.

"Joska," Nikolai replied, slurring the word.

"They call me Joseph here."

"Then they are wrong."

"You are drunk. Take your friends and go. There is nothing to prove tonight."

"There is always something to be proved," Nikolai said and launched into an attack, thrusting at the man's chest. Even drunk, Nikolai was quick. His opponent retreated and parried, matching Nikolai move for move. Then Nikolai stumbled to the floor. The men and boys around him stepped forward, but the teacher raised his hand to stop them.

"Let them go," he said.

I helped Nikolai to his feet and the three of us left.

✛

We stumbled back to the Hotel Chelsea in silence. Nikolai passed out on the floor of our room.

"Leave him there," Lefty said. "He will wake up in the morning." Then he took out a bottle of whiskey, poured two glasses, and gave one to me.

We both drank. The liquid burned a path down my throat.

"*The bells of hell go 'ting a-ling a-ling*," Lefty sang.

"*For you but not for me*," I added.

Lefty nodded, poured another, and offered it to me.

"Sure," I said.

Sometime later that night we both fell asleep. I awoke once to throw up. Staring into the small sink, my feet straddling Nikolai's snoring body, it came to me. The friend of the boy I'd hit at the club—the boy named Tom—had not struck me or even attempted to hit me. If it had been *my* friend, I would not have hesitated. But no, he'd stopped when he saw me, as if he'd recognized me. Then, closing my eyes as my head spun in circles from the alcohol, I knew why. Opening my eyes, I was sure of it.

The boy whose friend I'd punched in the mouth was Tomik Kopecky.

Nineteen

DECEIVE

Neither Nikolai nor Lefty said anything about the events at the Gotham Club.

Nikolai barked and drilled me again over the next few days. "Ceedric!" rang across the rooftop salle while his puffy eyes bore into mine. "Ceedric, how are you to be great fencer if you cannot move faster? The shoes with rubber spoil the feet. Waste of time in real duel. In real duel, you have bare feet or strong shoes. . . ."

Late at night Lefty's familiar rasp came to me while my eyes were closing. "What did you learn at your lesson today?"

The memory of Tomik ate at me. On Monday I went from school to the Gotham Club and waited until a few minutes before three to see if Tomik would show. Then I ran back to The Chelsea, where Nikolai waited for me. I did the same thing each day that week.

On Friday, he finally showed. A long-nosed Chrysler Crown limousine pulled down the block from Sixth Avenue. It passed where I was hidden next to the overhang of a newspaper stand and stopped in front of 19 West Twenty-fourth. A tall man in a long coat and driver's cap, unmistakably Tomik's father, stepped out of the driver's side and opened the two passenger-side doors. A large man in a suit with broad shoulders and a green fedora stepped out, his back to me. He pushed the brim of his hat up onto the back of his head, scanned the sidewalk, then motioned inside the car. The boy I'd punched came out, ignoring Mr. Kopecky and followed by Tomik. There was something about the boy's face, now that I saw him in the daylight, that seemed familiar.

Tomik was older, his curly brown hair fuller and longer, but he was still Tomik. He stood taller, his shoulders and chest wider, and his face had been etched with sharper angles. It made me wonder what I would look like to him.

Tomik looked across at where I stood. I was about to step out from the shadows when the large man in the suit turned to look in my direction, too. I recognized him instantly. Even after six years I hadn't forgotten the face of Rick Scarpetto. I stayed in the shadows. Tomik's friend called his name from the door to the club and he turned away.

Scarps turned toward Mr. Kopecky. "Tell Mr. Farthings everything's okay over here." Mr. Kopecky nodded as Scarps followed the other boy into the club and pushed some money into Tomik's hand before he could follow. Tomik looked down at the money and then back up at his father. He nodded and followed his friends into the club, carrying both of their fencing bags.

Then I knew who the boy I'd punched was. It was the same boy I'd seen Tomik and Scarps with the day I'd left Sunnyside, and his name was Edward Farthings.

✛

Christmas came cold, but without snow. Lefty's words about not visiting Siggy in Baltimore haunted me. "You will regret it," he'd said, and I found that I did. After seeing what had become of Tomik, I missed Siggy even more. Finally I wrote to him. I apologized for not coming to the funeral and for not writing sooner. I sent my condolences for his father's death and gave him my new address. I wrote nothing about Tomik.

Although Lefty had already bought himself a new cane, for Christmas I bought him another one I'd found at a pawnshop on Hudson, deep in the West Village. The wood was scarred and its carved ivory ball handle was worn smooth at the top. It seemed made for Lefty.

We had neither tree nor wreath, but when I placed the cane on Lefty's bed, wrapped in brown butcher's paper and tied with green grocer's twine, it felt like what Christmas was supposed to be. He seemed surprised when he entered the room that evening and saw it there. He unwrapped it and held it out before him like a jeweler examining a priceless gem. The ivory ball fit neatly into the palm of his hand.

"That top will give someone a nasty whack, too," I said, as he placed its tip solidly on the floor next to him.

He laughed, and though for most people his laugh wasn't a pleasant sound, to me it was music. I laughed with him and realized, for the first time since entering St. Agnes, that I was happy.

Lefty withdrew a small package from his coat pocket. It was wrapped in a stained red cloth, tied up at one end with the same green twine. He threw it to me and I caught it.

"Open it," he said, and sat on his bed.

I did. It was *The Chronicles of Captain Blood*, by Rafael Sabatini, a collection of short stories about Captain Peter Blood.

Nikolai came down from the roof near midnight, carrying a lit candle. "They turn off electric," he said and banged it on the table, splattering wax across it. He drank with Lefty by its light and I went to sleep listening to the sound of their emptied glasses knocking against the table's surface.

We ushered in 1944 quietly amidst rain and sleet. Then Nikolai left for two weeks. "There is business I have," he told me after my lesson on New Year's Day. "You practice footwork each day. Understand?"

I nodded.

The rainstorms of New Year's ushered in frigid temperatures and sheets of ice. On my way back from school one afternoon, I watched a Packard collide with a Chrysler at the corner of Eighth and Twenty-third. The Packard spun out on the ice and first hit a street pole, and then the parked Chrysler. The driver was thrown through his windshield and hung there on the broken glass, unconscious, the engine throwing up smoke around him. I watched from across the street, my hands stuffed in my pockets.

There was a folded note taped to my door waiting for me at the hotel. I pulled it off and unfolded it.

The note was written in pencil, the lettering refined but still recognizable.

"Come out and play," it read.

I stared at it a long time, remembering what it had meant to me when I'd first seen those words slipped under my front door in Sunnyside Gardens.

Inside my room, I crumpled the letter into a ball and threw it into the wastebasket. Then I took out my fencing bag, put on my sneakers, and changed into three layers of old loose pants and shirts. I grabbed my wool cap and gloves. Five minutes later I was on the roof, the door to the stairs closing behind me.

At first I saw no one, but it was cold and overcast, the shadows still winter-deep. Sweat trickled down my neck and I shivered from the chill. My breath frosted white as it left my mouth. I knew he was there somewhere. He had to be. Then a shadow in a thick wool coat, lapels pulled up over his face, head covered by a brown porkpie hat and hands cupped together in front of his mouth, moved from the space next to Nikolai's door.

A single white finger pushed the hat up enough to reveal the face.

"Cid."

The wind whirled around me, freezing the line of perspiration down my neck. I placed my bag slowly onto the roof's surface.

Tomik stopped a few feet in front of me and stuck out his pink hand. It shook from the cold.

I ignored it.

"Still the same old Cid," he said, withdrawing his hand slowly.

"Get out of my home," I said.

"The guy you punched at the Gotham Club—"

"Your friend," I said.

Tomik hesitated, as if examining the word, then continued, "He is . . . looking for you."

"I'm not hiding," I said.

"He's not looking for you alone."

I shrugged. "Then him and *Scarps* are not looking hard. It's been almost two months, and I live only a few blocks away from your club. *You* found me."

"You know about Scarps?"

"I saw you with him near the club."

Tomik waited a while before he spoke again. "I told him you lived in Brooklyn. He's been looking there."

"You're a real friend, Tomik."

"I knew you lived here. I knew about Nikolai Varvarinski, but I didn't tell Edward."

"Farthings?"

"He's the kid you clocked."

"I remember him from Sunnyside. Your father drives for him and you're his boy."

Tomik didn't reply.

"We said we were brothers."

"We were kids, Cid."

"We were *friends*, Tomik."

"It's not that simple."

"Yes, it is. You're either friends or you're not. I was your friend. Why did you come here?"

173

Tomik shrugged. "I don't know." He looked away. "It's been a long time. I guess . . . I owed you for that time with Scarps."

"You don't owe me anything."

"I did."

"Okay, then we're even."

He nodded and let his gaze slide back up to me. "I thought with a little time Edward would forget about what happened at the club—but he hasn't. Someone told him about Nikolai living here. Sooner or later he'll send someone."

"You? Scarps?"

"Not me." The lines of his face grew hard. "His father runs a munitions factory out in Newark. He's going to take down the Trylon and Perisphere from the World's Fair— turn the scrap into shell casings. Edward's got money and he doesn't like to lose at anything. His father's worse."

"So what?"

"He has different people to do different kinds of work for him."

"What kinds of work?"

"Watch your back, Cid. Edward doesn't fool around with his enemies."

"He called me a coward," I said, stressing the last word. "You tell him I'm here and I'll fight him anytime he wants."

"You hit him from behind."

"He deserved it and you know it. I heard what he said about my cousin and Nikolai."

"The man with the . . . face—"

"What about his face?" I asked, daring him to say something.

"Nothing," Tomik said. "Nothing."

"Nobody insults my cousin, and nobody insults my teacher. And you laughed along with him. What happened to you, Tomik?"

Tomik shrugged. "What happened to you?"

"I spent five years at St. Agnes."

Tomik didn't speak for a while. Then he said, "You talk a lot more now."

"I found things to talk about."

Tomik smiled.

"Mr. Braun was killed on Truk."

Tomik seemed to stop breathing. He shook his head slightly as if to clear it. "What?"

"He's dead, last spring. Siggy wrote me—which is more than I could say for you."

"You never wrote me either."

"I didn't know where you lived. I went by your house and you were gone. You disappeared."

Tomik pushed his hands into his pockets and was silent for a while. "You stayed in touch with Siggy?"

I nodded, lying, trying to make him feel worse.

"Is he still in Baltimore?"

I nodded again.

"I can't believe it . . . Mr. Braun." His voice softened. "He was the best. What happened to him? Did Siggy say?"

"What do you care?"

"I cared enough to come here." An edge crept into his voice. "Maybe I won't care next time."

"You think there'll be a next time?"

"Look, Cid," he said. "I came here—"

"Why *did* you come here?" I asked, raising my voice. "To give me a lesson? I get my lessons from someone else these days. Sometimes I hand out my own. I don't charge for them."

Tomik took a step around me and toward the door.

I thumped his shoulder hard with the flat of my hand and he stopped. "That's it?" I asked. "You show up after all this time, and then you leave?"

"You don't seem to want me to stay."

"Maybe I do and maybe I don't."

"Well . . . which is it?"

I didn't know. I was furious with him, but I was also glad to see him. I squeezed my hands into fists. I wanted to hit Tomik but I couldn't. With a big shrug I breathed in, opened my fists, and let my fingers rest at my sides.

Tomik looked at me, considering. "Do you get your lessons up here?"

"Five days a week," I said.

"What about the weather?"

"Duels are fought in all kinds of weather. Nikolai fought one in a rainstorm once. He says you've got to be prepared for all possibilities."

"Duels? Is that what Varvarinski calls fencing?"

"What does your teacher call it?"

Tomik shrugged. "Fencing."

"That's why I'll beat you if we fight."

"I'm not looking to fight you, Cid."

"Then come back sometime and we'll . . . fence."

176

"Maybe I will."

"If you don't, I won't lose any sleep."

Tomik smiled. Then the smile melted into a look of concern. "Watch behind you, Cid."

"You think your friend can do worse to me than others have?"

"This isn't Sunnyside."

"You don't know anything about what Sunnyside was like for me."

"Maybe I don't," he said and walked past me to the stairway door. When he got there he hesitated and turned back toward me. "I'll see you when I see you."

"Not if I see you first."

He nodded and left, the door closing behind him.

I stood in the cold for a long time, not moving.

Then another moving shadow caught my eye. The sun had fully set and the overcast sky showed no stars, creating a darkness so thick that at first I thought it was the fire escape that had moved. Then I realized it was a person—Lefty with his lurching step. He stopped just outside of the lighted area where my lessons normally occurred.

"You have enemies," he said.

"How much did you hear?"

"Enough."

"I'll take care of it myself."

"Was that boy a friend from Queens?"

I nodded as I realized he was a friend and might still be.

He stood for a moment thinking and swaying in the cold. I waited for him to speak.

"I had a friend from childhood. His name was Winslow Higginbottom. We called him Winny. We went to school together—acted together. Before the war began I fell in love with a young woman named Edith. I had her affections first. Winny came and took her from me. She said it was not his fault, but simply fate. 'It was in the stars,' said she. I could not forgive him. I had already joined the army. He joined two years later. We met in Passchendaele. Same battalion. Same trench when the shells began to fall. I had not talked to him in two years, but there he was. The shell that took my arm and leg also took him. Roger, McCourt, Devlin, and Winny. They told me in hospital that the four were untouched, each body without one scratch. None of them had been hit by the shell—only me. 'Concussion stopped their hearts,' said they."

"What happened to Edith?" I asked.

"She did not want half a man."

"There's no girl between Tomik and me," I said.

"There does not have to be."

Twenty
Riposté

A few days later, Lefty came to the rooftop salle wrapped in his coat, his breath frosting in the winter air. He watched me practice my footwork, sitting in the shadows. When I was finished, he stood up.

"Do you remember O'Hanrahan's and a giant named Eagon?"

I couldn't place them for a moment, then nodded as I recalled the place that Lefty had given me my first lesson in stage fighting. "Eagon's the man who hit us?"

Lefty nodded. "It is time you learned how to stage a fight with the sword."

"Now?" I asked standing up, tired from my practice but eager to learn.

"Would you choose another time?"

I shook my head quickly.

"Come here." He motioned me toward him. Then he shifted his weight onto his wooden leg, let his cane rest against his leg, and pulled a knife out from behind his back. "Hold your hand out."

I did.

He placed the knife flat in my palm.

"It is sharp," he said.

I could see that it was and nodded.

"It is real. It can kill you if held by a hand that intends to kill. Even by mistake, it can kill." In one swift motion, Lefty picked the knife up out of my hand and placed the point in my palm. It pierced my skin just by its weight. Lefty looked at me and I looked back at him, grimacing for a moment. Then he removed the blade and it disappeared behind his back. His weight shifted back to his good leg as he took hold of his cane again.

I looked down at the spot of blood on my palm.

"That is real blood," Lefty said. "Imagine if it had gone through your hand. Remember this and the swordplay will be real for your audience. Even with blunt tips and dull edges, you must pretend they are razor sharp. And do not fool yourself, stage weapons have been known to kill foolish actors who forgot there was steel in their hands. Given enough force, they can puncture skin and break bones."

"I know that," I said.

"Do you?" he replied. "The rapier, sword and buckler, rapier and dagger, longsword, and broadsword were Shakespeare's weapons," Lefty said. "In those times all gentlemen carried swords. You were born with one in your hand and taught how to use it by the time you were eight or nine. If your family had money, a real fencing master was your teacher. If you had a name but little money, then you hired a bully-boy veteran of the wars to do the job.

"'Excuse me sir, I like not the cut of your shirt,' says your enemy, walking up to you on the street. 'Tis more the pity for I like it fine,' says you. 'Shall we walk into the garden behind the church this afternoon at, say, four?' You did not want to fight a duel before lunch. It simply was not proper. But at four you would meet with your seconds and settle the issue by placing your blade between his ribs.

"Those times are long gone," he said softly. "Still . . . in here"—he tapped his head—"they have got to be alive." He stepped into the dark and returned into the light clasping two long pieces of wood in his hand. "Take one," he said.

The wood was the length of a sword.

"Pretend these are real. Think of the spot of blood in your palm. Carry them point down unless you intend to fight with them. Even in practice. Do as you would do with Nikolai. Then they will be real to you and to all who see you."

Lefty lifted his sword, pointing it at my chest. "Extend to my fingers—what would be my hilt."

I lifted my blade and extended my arm until it was in line with his, my "point" almost touching his fingers. I had to step back to be able to do it, but finally found the correct distance.

"Distance is important. If I cannot hit you, you cannot be hurt. We will create an illusion to the contrary. Now retreat." He stepped forward, swinging his blade toward my head in a slow but even circle. I raised my blade up and caught his.

"Head attack, head protect," Lefty said, then stepped forward again and cut at my right hip. "Remember a rapier has an edge. It is a cutting weapon first, a thrusting weapon second."

181

I backed up and pushed my blade out to the right in an exaggerated seconde.

"Flank attack, flank protect," he added and whirled the accelerating blade around his head to cut across my belly, pulling through my prime with a jarring crack of wood on wood. "Head, flank, belly. As you should recall, it is the first part of 'short sixes.' We shall call them 'threesies.'" He turned his back to me and returned to his starting position. "Now let us do these moves again, only faster." He raised his weapon to point at my chest. "Check your distance," he said, and I raised my blade to meet his.

An amazing thing happened to me while Lefty and I practiced back and forth across the rooftop—the same rooftop that Nikolai and I used to fence across. The world around us became hazy and out of focus. The area between us turned from color to shades of flickering gray, as if we were in a movie, projected up onto a giant screen. My heart thudded in my chest and my breathing deepened. The swords connected with a rhythm that soaked into my bones. When I fenced épée with Nikolai, every lesson was life and death. With Lefty, the choreographed movements lay in the space between fantasy and reality. Sometimes it was difficult to tell which was which.

Tomik was right. I should have watched my back.

Nikolai returned from his business in a foul mood, giving me lessons staggering drunk for two weeks, stinking the whole time. I asked Lefty what had happened to him on his trip.

"I know nothing of his ventures," Lefty said, "and care even less."

Then a letter came from Siggy.

It was good to hear from you, Cid. I wish you could have come to the funeral because then we would have had a friend with us instead of only my father's family. I'm hoping we'll be coming back to New York City soon. I'm not sure I can stand it here much longer. My father's family has not been very friendly. I know they're my family, too, but I don't think of them that way. My mother says they're angry with us for sending my father to the war. It's funny because my mother didn't want him to go and I did. So in a way, maybe I did send him. I'm glad you've got a relative to stay with and that you're out of St. Agnes. I can only imagine what it was like to live there. I'm sorry we didn't take you with us to Baltimore. I don't care what my father said. It's like that first time you met Scarps and I ran. My father told me it was a good thing to run and get help. Do you remember? But the thing is, you got beat up and I ran. I should have stayed, and we should have taken you with us. I'm going to tell my father's family that we're Jewish—that my name's Braun, not Brown. I'm tired of pretending to be something I'm not. Maybe we'll be back in New York faster that way. Thanks again for the letter. It meant a lot.

✛

Reading the letter again on my way home from school
and thinking, for the first time, about what it must have
been like for Siggy to move to Baltimore, I let my guard
down. I stepped onto my floor from the stairs and two rain-
coat-draped men in fedoras detached themselves from the
wall on either side of the door to our room. The hall light
near our door was out, the bulb's glittering pieces littering
the floor like frost. The two men stood in shadow as we
looked at each other for a moment. Smoke wreathed the air,
making their features seem even hazier. Two small red dots
near what should have been their mouths glowed bright orange and yellow. I saw a glint of brass around the knuckles
of a fist.

"Wiiiiman," one of them said.

I didn't run. I lunged toward them instead—attacked
into their attack the way Nikolai had taught me. Only they
outweighed me four to one and nobody was using an épée.
Still, I surprised them. Lunging between them, I threw a
punch at kidney level. I heard a hard grunt and felt my fist
connect through cloth into something hard. Then they hit
me. I saw the outline of one face—it was Scarps and he
was smiling. Then they hit me again. They hit me until I
couldn't move and the simple act of breathing hurt, until
blood flowed in a river out of my nose and mouth.

"'Dis one's for Billy," Scarps said as he kicked the
sharp point of his black leather wingtip into my eye. "And
deese are cause I missed you so much." His other wingtip
cracked in my chest three times, breaking one, then two of

my ribs. Lying on the floor in front of our door, my one good eye staring at the carpet, I heard them speak.

"You know dis guy?"

"Yeah," Scarps said.

"We didn't kill 'em, did we?"

"Nah."

"He's still breathin'?"

"Uh-huh."

"Good. Let's get outta here."

I heard footsteps. The floorboards creaked and their voices dissolved into nothing.

I woke up in a hospital bed. Something tapped lightly inside my head, like a coin against glass. Only one eye would open. My vision cleared.

Lefty and Nikolai stood facing a large window next to my bed, close enough to the glass to fog it with their breath. Lefty tapped the head of his cane—the cane I'd given him—against the window at a steady pace as if marking time. Nikolai stood, head bowed, shoulders slumped forward, hands on the windowsill.

I thought, *I have only one eye now. I'm just like Lefty.* Then I closed my eye and slept.

The next time I awoke, I heard them talking. Their voices entered my dreams and then I realized I wasn't dreaming. I kept my eye closed.

"He will try to kill boy," Nikolai said.

"Yes," Lefty replied.

"Boy should be kilt for what he done to Cedric."

"Yes."

"Cedric has hard head. Always thinking. Has too much time on hand."

"It is a bad thing to have, time."

"*Nikharóshij.*"

"*Khváhtit!*" Lefty said.

"He will never get to boy," Nikolai replied softly.

"No, he will not."

"He will try."

"He will."

"Will be hurt again."

There was silence, then Lefty spoke. "We shall have to see that he does not."

"*Da,*" Nikolai said. "*Da.*"

I had one final vision. It occurred at night. I opened my single eye and saw Tomik Kopecky sitting in the chair at the foot of my bed. In my mind I saw him as an old man, his face lined with worry, the skin around his eyes puffy and red. He saw that my good eye was open and he smiled, the lines melting away as if in a dream.

I closed my eye and fell back into sleep.

"Cid," he called after me, his voice a fading echo. It followed me into the darkness.

Twenty-One
The Disarm

I would make Rick Scarpetto and Edward Farthings pay for what they'd done to me. I would be patient and choose my time and place, but I would pay them back. I knew Lefty and Nikolai would try to stop me, so I would have to disarm them first.

When I got out of the hospital, my right eyelid drooped slightly, a result of the damage to the nerves in my eye socket. If I was tired, it made people think I had a lazy eye. The little finger of my right hand was broken in two places and never completely healed—it only looked normal when curled around the grip of a sword. There was a large bump in the middle of my nose and two others on my chest where bones had been broken and healed. My face was still a little black and blue, and I needed help walking, but otherwise I was fine.

I returned to our apartment to find Siggy Braun and his mother waiting for me. Lefty had not given me any warning.

Mrs. Braun sat on my cot with her hands in her lap.

Siggy waited by the window. When I entered, they both turned toward me.

Lefty ushered me into the room. I stared at Siggy and his mother, not knowing what to say, then looked at Lefty, who turned away with a smile on one half of his face. Behind him, in the darkened hall, stood Nikolai—his mouth slightly open, his eyes wide, as if in fear.

"Niko—," I began but Siggy interrupted me.

"Cid?"

I turned back to face him again, then glanced toward Nikolai, but the door had shut behind me.

"You look . . . terrible, Cid," Siggy said, as Mrs. Braun stood up. Taking my arm, she helped me to sit in her place.

"You look like your father," I said to Siggy without thinking.

"People tell me that. I like it, mostly. But you know, we have no choice in what we look like."

Siggy did look like his father. He still wore his wire-frame glasses, but his hair was short like his father's had been and he'd grown taller and wider across the shoulders. His face had the same angles as Mr. Braun's had had—only becoming the face of the friend I remembered when he smiled—and there was a belly where there had only been skin and bones before.

"Your mother's food finally caught up to you."

"Yeah," he said, patting his belly. "Right here." He paused for a moment, then continued. "Lefty told us someone did a real number on you, Cid. Who did it?"

I wondered what Lefty had told them. "It's a long story."

In the silence that followed, Siggy shifted from one foot to the other and Mrs. Braun looked out the window.

"What happened to your cousin?" he finally asked.

"Siggy," his mother said, reprimanding him with her voice.

"Sorry, Mother."

"Mrs. Braun," I said and tried to stand.

She shook her head slowly, looking back at me and smiling. "Stay seated," she said, and sat down next to me. She had changed as much as Siggy, but not in the same ways. Her hair had turned gray and her back was curved. There were deep lines etched into her forehead, and around her cheeks and eyes. Her smile flickered and faded, turning into a frown. I still thought she was beautiful.

"My cousin was in the Great War," I said.

"We've moved back, Cid," Siggy interrupted. "We're back for good. We've got a cousin, lives down on the Lower East Side, and she and her husband are giving us a room in their flat until we can get ourselves on our feet." Siggy grabbed his stomach. "I'll probably lose some of this, too. But you know my mother cooks and sews better than anyone so she should be able to get work easy, and I'm gonna get work, too. We can come see each other, if you want."

I took a breath in. My chest still hurt where the ribs had been broken. "Sure," I said. "That would be good."

It was quiet again.

"Let's leave Cid alone," Mrs. Braun said. "It's his first day back from the hospital and he needs his rest. We shouldn't have come today, only"—she turned toward me—"we didn't know until we got here."

"But—," Siggy said.

"You don't have to catch up all at once," Mrs. Braun interrupted, "and it looks like Cid has been through a lot."

"Okay, okay," Siggy said, turning toward his mother. "But we're back here for good and I hated Baltimore and"—he turned back toward me—"it's good to see you, Cid. Even if you're not sure if it's good to see us."

"It *is* good to see you, Siggy." In my heart I could tell that it was.

"Then . . . we'll see you soon, as soon as we get all settled and stuff, right?"

Only it wasn't soon. It was a few months before I saw Siggy again.

I left Scarpetto and Farthings in the back of my mind, but I didn't forget either. I focused instead on recovering, studying, and fencing. I learned to be silent again. I don't think Lefty and Nikolai knew what to make of me. So I believed I'd accomplished the first part of my plan—disarming them. Then I attempted my second.

"I thought," I began late one night staring into the darkness of our room, "I might join the Amateur Fencers' League of America."

"It has been three months and you have not said the boy's name," Lefty replied from his bed.

"Whose name?" I asked slowly.

"What I know of you, Cedric Wymann, I could place in a shell casing. But I know this. I know that you think of him every day. I know this because that is what I would do, were I in your place, and you and I are alike in that respect. Yet it has been three months and you have not spoken his name. What do you plan?"

"Nothing."

"You plan something. You do. The question is . . . what?"

"I want to compete," I said. "I wanted to know if you could front me the money so I could join the League for a year and compete at the city competitions. It costs twenty dollars."

Lefty grunted. "Leave Farthings where he is."

"Will you give me the money?"

Lefty was silent for a long time. "You will see Farthings at these competitions."

It was a statement, not a question, but I answered anyway. "Yes."

He nodded. "Have you spoken to Nikolai?"

"Yes," I said, lying. "And he said it would be good for me."

"Lying bastard, that is what you are. Nikolai has told me nothing. We watch you together, so do not think to trick us. That is too ordinary for you, Cedric, and you are capable of so much more. But . . . if you want to compete that badly, I will give you the money for it. Only, tell me, what will you do when you meet Farthings at competition?"

"Beat him, of course." *Beat him to a bloody pulp.* A picture flickered in black and white in my head, as if upon a movie screen.

Lefty laughed. "You are not subtle."

"I'll play by the rules."

"Make sure that you do. And Cedric . . ."

"Yes?"

"Why haven't you gone to see Sigfried Braun?"

I tried to answer Lefty, but I'd been asking myself the same question and didn't know the answer.

✛

The next day I got home by three, just in time for my lesson with Nikolai. I threw open the door to the roof and stopped in my tracks. Standing in the shade against the wall of Nikolai's apartment were Nikolai and Tomik Kopecky. They stopped talking when they saw me arrive, and Tomik smiled. He wore deck sneakers, loose pants, and a loose shirt, as if he were waiting for a lesson. His fencing bag leaned against the wall behind him, and the point of an épée stuck out of its top.

"I change lesson today," Nikolai said, turning toward me. "You fight Mr. Kopecky. I watch." With that, he sat down with his back against the wall and let his chin sink onto his chest.

"Hello, Cid," Tomik said. "You said to come back sometime and fence—"

"It's been three months."

"Thought I'd take you up on it, now that you're all healed." Tomik stepped forward and put out his hand.

I stared at it for a moment not sure whether I'd take it. "I saw you at the hospital."

Tomik nodded and kept his hand out, waiting.

Finally I extended my hand and we shook.

"I'm sorry about what he did to you. I tried to warn you, but you're stubborn, Cid."

"Yeah, well, did you come to fence or talk?"

"I came to poke holes in you," he replied.

I placed my bag down beside his and took out my equipment. We stretched a few minutes, then faced each other. Nikolai started to snore.

I noticed Tomik used a French-gripped épée. I would be attacking his blade and he would be avoiding mine. So I began the calculations a fencer engaged in when he observed his opponent during warm-up. I did it automatically—Nikolai had trained me well. We saluted each other, put our masks on, and stepped into en garde positions.

"How many touches shall we play to?" Tomik asked, advancing to within range.

"Let's not keep score," I said. "Let's just fence." As the last word left my mouth, I beat his blade hard in four and straight lunged to his forearm, scoring my first touch against a real opponent.

"Nikolai says most touches are scored with direct attacks. Compound attacks sell lessons. Direct attacks kill opponents."

"That won't happen again," Tomik said. He tried to beat my blade and begin an attack of his own. I saw it coming and dropped my blade down and around his, striking with a stop-thrust at his forearm, in the same place I'd touched him only a moment before. Tomik acknowledged the second touch by raising his left arm and retreating out of distance. "I liked it better when I beat you at everything."

"That was a long time ago," I said, and feinted with a thrust to his forearm again. He stop-thrust to my wrist and I parried in quarte, pressed his blade down, and lunged with a glissade under his arm, touching him just above the hip.

We fenced for twenty minutes that way. Tomik scored a few touches but I outscored him by far.

After touching Tomik three times in a row, he pulled off his mask and saluted me. I took mine off and saluted in return. Breathing hard and sweating, we drank water from a catch-basin near the gutter and splashed it over our heads.

"How long have you been fencing?" Tomik asked.

"One year."

"That's all?"

"I take a lesson five days a week and do footwork on my own on Saturdays. Nikolai lets me take Sundays off."

Tomik's mouth opened wide, then closed, as if he couldn't find the right words.

"How often do you fence?" I asked.

"Twice a week at the club when I can. Sometimes it's just once."

"Farthings pays for your lessons?"

"He got me into the club, Cid."

"Anybody can fence there. That's what Lefty told me. All you need is the floor fee."

"Lefty?"

"That's my cousin. His name's Leftingsham."

Tomik nodded. "Well, anybody can fence there, but only members can take lessons."

"Is that a reason to be friends with him?"

"You and Siggy left, Cid."

"We didn't have a choice."

"Neither did I. My father worked for Farthings and when he'd put in enough time, we got to live in his house. My sisters are finishing school because my father has work. My mother stopped doing extra work as a seamstress years ago. We left Sunnyside to live in a better place, not because the bank was foreclosing like everybody else. And I never heard from you. Edward can be a bastard and he's spoiled rotten, but his father's been good to us. If you can't understand that, then you can't understand anything."

"What about Scarps?"

"I've known him longer than I have you, Cid. A lot longer."

"Why are you *friends* with him?"

"His father works for Mr. Farthings, too. He chose me and Scarps. Times are hard. Neither one of us could say no."

"Scarps is one of the two who beat me up."

Tomik nodded and looked away. He knew.

We fenced another twenty minutes, rested, then fought for another twenty. Finally exhausted, we sat down against Nikolai's wall, the light fading from the evening sky above us. Nikolai had left sometime during our last session, his bag slung over his shoulder, a flick of his hand signifying goodbye. We had barely noticed.

"Hey," Tomik said, "the Bums sure came close against the Yankees a few years ago, didn't they?"

"Bonham took 'em out on three pitches in the seventh. It was embarrassing. Five games and it was over. Nobody will ever beat the Yankees."

"At least it wasn't a sweep."

"The '41 Dodgers. They got close."

"Wait 'til next year," we both said together.

"Only next year's already here," Tomik added and we both laughed.

"Want to fence again next week?" I asked. "Same time, same place?"

"Sure."

I reached over to shake his hand and, smiling, Tomik grabbed it.

Twenty-Two

BISH-BASH-BOSH

"I need servants!" a man yelled from behind the closed door of the office in front of us.

Lefty and I were in the damp basement of a brownstone in the Village off West Fourth Street next to the Black Cat nightclub. We sat on a wooden bench in a small hall, off toward what claimed to be a fifty-seat theatre in the back. A curling piece of paper with blue ink scribbled on it was taped to the frosted glass office door, stating, "Auditions." Behind that, stenciled onto the glass in letters that were already peeling off, were the faint words "Ridolfo Players." Shadows moved across the glass door as if someone were pacing back and forth behind it.

Lefty had told me what to expect. "Your Works Progress Administration is gone, as are their settlement project theatres. But new playhouses are rising up from their ashes. The Ridolfo Players is one of them."

"You think I'm ready to audition?" I'd asked.

"No. But they are looking for a fencing teacher."

"Where are my fucking servants?" the voice yelled again.

I stood up for a second.

"Sit down," Lefty said.

My palms were sweaty and my mouth was dry.

"How much does it pay?" I asked.

"It does not. This job you take for the experience."

Then a short young woman—a girl really—with black-rimmed glasses and brown hair cut in a short bob opened the door. A clipboard shielded her chest. "What did you say?" she asked.

"Nothing," I said and cleared my throat. Then my mind went blank.

She chewed gum loudly, cracking it like a machine gun, but stopped when Lefty stood up and looked into her face. She swallowed. "You're the fencing instructor?"

"No," Lefty said and walked into the office. "He is."

The girl looked at me and offered a half smile.

"Come," Lefty said over his shoulder.

I got up and walked past the girl. She cracked her gum as I passed, then followed me in.

The office was filled with manuscripts and props, some swords and bucklers—rusted and bent out of shape—and a red velvet hat covered with dust, sprouting a green peacock's feather. The window was closed and steam whistled out of a radiator beneath it.

"This the kid?" The man sitting by the desk didn't look up. The space behind the desk where he should have sat was filled with metal music stands and large cardboard posters. The theatre manager was balding, with wisps of gray hair on either side of his head and a couple of days' growth of stubble on his cheeks and chin. He wore a white shirt with a high, ruffled Elizabethan collar that was frayed at the edges, and stained yellow across its front. His legs were encased in worn green tights, and his shoes had large square buckles on their faces. He tapped a pencil against a clear space on the corner of his desk. "Betty," he asked, "what the hell is that smell?"

"Percy," Lefty said, still standing as there was no place for us to sit.

"Who are—"

"*I am not yet of Percy's mind, the Hotspur of the north, he that kills me some six or seven dozen of Scots at a breakfast, washes his hands, and says to his wife 'Fie upon this quiet life! I want work.'*"

The man Lefty had called Percy stood up slowly. "Fucking God . . . Winston? Is that you?"

"In the flesh, at least what remains of it. Did you expect someone different?" Lefty turned toward me without waiting for a response. "Cedric Wymann, this is Percival Clangor—an old school chum. Percy, this is my cousin, Cedric Wymann. He can teach your actors to fence. I would do it myself but my present circumstances . . . prohibit it."

Percival Clangor stood, still staring at Lefty.

The discourtesy made me angry. "*Captain* Leftingsham told me you needed a fencing teacher—"

"Here's how things fall out, kid," he interrupted, still not taking his eyes off Lefty's face. "Winston . . . sit."

"I will stand."

Percy sat back down. "What's your training, kid?" He waved his hand in the air and the pencil flew out of it, clattering against the wall.

"My teacher is Nikolai Varvarinski," I said, "and Mr. Leftingsham."

"What about this Varvarinski as a teacher?"

Lefty cut in. "You can't afford him."

"But I can afford the kid?"

"Anyone can afford Cedric. But only you are being offered his services. Consider yourself lucky."

The girl leaned back against the other side of the desk. The gum cracked in her mouth and stuck to the outside of her lip. She pulled it back in with her teeth.

"How old are you? Eighteen?"

I started to answer him and he cut me off with a wave of his hand. "Don't answer that. If you tell me you're eighteen, then you're just doing time until you're drafted. And if you're younger, I'd rather not know." He leaned forward, suddenly serious, his eyes boring into me. "I want my fights to look like a dance." He lowered his voice. "A dangerous dance, but a dance. I don't want my actors doing the bish-bash-bosh or the tic-tack-tic. And I don't want them just *going at it*. I lost a Hamlet a while back when an overzealous Laertes took out his eye. I want my fights to be worked out beforehand—to be choreographed, and our choreographer, well . . . let's just say he'll need help. And the rest of the cast is inexperienced with swordplay. We have three months before we start work on our next play, and I want them schooled in Shakespeare's hey, la, and punto reverso. Do you understand?"

I nodded slowly.

"You ever teach fencing before?"

I nodded again. Lefty had schooled me on this response. *Always tell them you have got the experience. You can learn what you need to learn after you have the job.*

"You don't by any chance act, also?"

I was about to answer when Lefty cut in. "No, he doesn't."

"Can he mark a fight?" Percy looked at Lefty instead of me.

Lefty nodded.

"It's a young cast. I've got them engaged in scene work. We rehearse Monday and Friday evenings." Percy turned toward me. "You can have them for an hour after each session."

I nodded.

"Remind me your name?"

"Cid. Cid Wymann."

"Well, Cid. Let's see what you can teach my kids. If I like it, we'll look at your choreography." Percy stood up. "The war's taken all the good actors. This cast is all I could get my hands on." He nodded to the girl—who smiled back at him. "Take the violence seriously and make sure no one gets hurt too badly. Our rehearsals start at six. You may start your work at seven-thirty. Don't be late."

"Betty . . . make sure Mr. Wymann finds his way out. Winston and I have . . . we have some things to discuss."

"Sure," the girl said, lowering the clipboard from her chest and leading me out.

"And Betty," Percy Clangor called out after us, "take that God damned sign down."

Betty tore the *auditions* sign off the door as she closed it. "Don't mind him," she said. "He's not a bad sort. Just moody."

"Will I be teaching *you*?" She wore a perfume that was familiar but which I couldn't place. While we walked her shoulder bumped into mine. The charge of electricity that went down my side made me forget about the perfume.

"Who will be teaching who, I wonder?" She darted her eyes at me, a smile at the corner of her lips.

I tripped on the edge of the carpet and she covered her mouth with her hand as she laughed.

"Carpet," I said, blushing. Girls and me didn't usually go along. In school, most of them left me alone and the few I'd tried to speak to had giggled and walked away. I swallowed hard. "What, what jobs have you had?"

She took her hand away from her mouth. "You mean roles?"

"Sure."

She sighed. "If you must know, Percy has me play boys—servants usually." She stopped and looked at me, then down at her flat figure. "There aren't enough real boys around and I've the look of a boy. That's what *Mr. Director* says, if you were asking."

"Me? Asking?" I shook my head. "I wasn't asking."

"You do think I look like a boy, don't you?"

I started to shrug, then, watching her eyes widen, thought better of it and scratched my shoulder instead. "No. I, well, I think you look like a, well—" I tried to think quickly. Girl? Dame? Broad? What was the right word? Then I found what I needed: "A woman." I wanted to tell her she was beautiful, though not in a Betty Grable pin-up way, but I couldn't think of how to put it, so *woman* had to do.

She smiled—smoothed her skirt with her free hand, and for a moment I relaxed. Then she took my arm again. "You're not so bad yourself, Mr. Wymann."

All the way home I couldn't stop smiling. I had no idea how I was going to teach fencing and the thought of it made my knees weak. But Lefty thought I could so I knew I had to believe it, too.

I ran the last few blocks to the hotel. I wanted to tell someone, only I couldn't think of who to tell. Nikolai wouldn't care and Tomik would not be by to fence for another couple of days. Then I thought of Siggy and, as I arrived at the front door, I realized he was the perfect person to tell. I ran up to my room and grabbed the scrap of paper I'd written his address on, then headed crosstown toward the Lower East Side and the Amalgamated Dwellings at 504 Grand Street.

Twenty-Three
Passatta Forward

I retraced the steps I'd taken with Lefty over a year ago, when he'd taken me from St. Agnes. I even stopped in front of the old orphanage and stared at its front door, remembering Sister Bernadette's words, *You are ours no longer*. I pictured the bed and room I'd slept in for five years. The building was boarded up now, the front door padlocked. The sight of the lock made my smile grow bigger.

I knew about Orchard and Division Streets. While at St. Agnes, I'd explored the pushcart market a few times, stealing pickles and bread from vendors and losing myself easily in the crowds. And I'd seen the ladies' clothing shops along Division, with their salesmen and -women waiting on doorsteps, trying to pull you in to their store and buy from them. *You, young man, you look like you could use a suit today to make your mother proud. Do we have a sale for you!* By the time I reached Grand, I'd heard young men shout "Jew-boy" twice before I realized they were shouting at me. The third time I turned around to see who was taunting me, only to find a sea of blank faces. I made a left onto

Grand and crossed Bowery, heading into a part of Manhattan I'd never been in before—what people called the Jewish Quarter.

It was crowded even at three in the afternoon. Old women sat on worn stairways, kerchiefs gathered around their heads. Men wearing long black beards and black skullcaps walked in and out of small buildings overshadowed by neighboring tenements. Inside were groups of men praying in a sing-song language I'd never heard before. People hung out of windows they shared with clotheslines and hanging laundry, while women with string shopping bags crowded into small food stores.

The Amalgamated Dwellings were on Grand between Columbia and Sheriff. I followed a girl and her baby brother through the front door and walked up to the sixth floor. When I found 623 I knocked on the door. An irritated woman's voice replied, "What is it?"

"I'm looking for Siggy Braun," I said through the closed door.

"He ain't here."

"How about his mother?"

"She ain't here neither."

"Well, who is there?"

"Sol Goldboig and his mother, dat's me."

I stared at the place where the door met the floor. Some light leaked out from inside. I heard a door to my left creak open. The prunelike face of an old woman poked out of the apartment door down the hall. She looked at me, squinting, hunched over, a shawl covering her head and shoulders. I wiped sweat from my eyes, then turned back to the door in front of me.

"Do they live here?" I asked the closed door.

"Who?" the voice behind the door answered.

"The Brauns. Do they live here?"

It was quiet a moment. Then I heard footsteps approaching from behind the door. The old woman down the hall disappeared and her door creaked closed just as the door in front of me cracked open. A white staring eyeball seemed to press itself toward me. It rotated in its socket a couple of times and finally stopped.

"I'm looking for Siggy Braun," I said, "and his mother."

Her hand wiped at her mouth. "She's at da bakery and he's at Orchard with da pushcart."

I couldn't believe it. I must have walked right by him. I leaned in. "What kind of pushcart?"

"Pickles." The door shut in my face.

I found Siggy on the corner of Orchard and Grand, selling pickles to customers standing in line while an older man sat beside the pushcart filled with barrels of pickles and covered in signs that advertised Cohen's New Pickles, Half-Sour Pickles, and Sour Pickles. The smell overwhelmed me: brine and garlic mixed with the odor of knishes, mustard, and the garbage thrown into the street. Siggy was listening to the man sitting next to him while reaching into the barrels for pickles and handling customers' change.

"Me, I made money in da Depression," the older man

was saying. "If I was in a desert I'd make money, because I'm willing to woik."

Siggy nodded.

"I don't eat many pickles because it cuts into da profits, but I eat some, 'cause you got to know what you're selling."

Siggy nodded again.

"Siggy," I said.

He had a harried look and a drawn face, and he'd lost weight since I'd seen him, shedding a good part of his belly and the cushion that had padded his face. Then he smiled. "Cid!"

"Siggy," I said again, returning his smile.

"I got customers, okay?"

I nodded and sat down at the curb to watch him work.

"He your friend?" the man next to Siggy asked.

"From my old neighborhood in Queens."

The man looked over at me and, squinting, told Siggy to give me a pickle while I waited for the line to work its way down.

"Abby Cohen," the man said reaching out his hand to me but not standing up.

I stood up and shook his hand, then took a pickle from Siggy. "Cid Wymann."

"You're a Jew?"

I hesitated a moment.

"You're not sure?"

"His mother was a Jew," Siggy said, "so he's a Jew."

I stared at them both.

"Looks like he don't realize it," Mr. Cohen said.

"What's there to realize?" an old gray-haired man with a stooped back asked from the line.

"Is he nonpracticing?" a younger man asked from behind him.

"What's nonpracticing?" the old man answered. "You haven't been to shul in years."

"And you, Marty," Mr. Cohen interrupted, "only go on the high holy days."

"I have to woik."

"Then God will forgive you."

Finally the line disappeared and Siggy was allowed to take a break. We sat on the stoop together, each eating a half-sour pickle.

"I've got a lesson soon so I can't stay long," I said.

"Oh," Siggy said, nodding. "What kind of lesson?"

"Fencing."

"You're learning to fence?"

"Épée."

Siggy's face fell for a moment, then he smiled again. "That's great, really great. I'm glad you came. I've been meaning to come by your place myself, it's just that we've been busy and haven't had much time. Mr. Cohen needed help and my mother is working at a bakery. We don't see each other much except late at night. She starts early before I go to school and I don't get home until late."

"Education is important," Mr. Cohen interrupted. "Perhaps it will toin you into a socialist. We could use another good socialist."

"Mr. Cohen needs help unloading the barrels," Siggy continued, "down into his basement. He needs . . . some muscle."

"I've got rats," Mr. Cohen added, examining his fingernails. "But dey only eat a few. I have to throw them out—da pickles you know—can't sell 'em with dose bite marks. Still, da basement. It keeps da pickles cool."

Siggy shrugged. "The room at the Amalgamated costs a lot. But we got it through our *landsmanschaft*. It's a small one, but our cousin helped us get some money from them to get started. The Goldbergs are nice, but they're short on money, too. The third bedroom's still nailed shut."

"What do you mean, nailed shut?"

"Well, the Goldergs got the apartment, but they couldn't afford the whole thing. So the Amalgamated keeps the doors nailed shut until they can afford the extra room. Then they take the nails out. It's the way they do things."

I nodded and we were both quiet for a while. "Tomik's here," I finally said.

Siggy stared at me for a while without moving. "Kopecky?"

I nodded.

"Where is he?"

"I found him at the Gotham Fencer's Club."

"My father said you would learn how to fence. He said you would do it because you were a swordsman at heart."

"Didn't he teach you?"

"Some foil. But we didn't have the money." Siggy shrugged. "And then . . . well, I'll get around to it, I think—when I have the time."

"I can teach you for nothing—I mean, that is, if you want to learn. My teacher is Nikolai Varvarinski."

"Who's that?"

"He's a crazy Russian, but a good teacher. He'll teach me and, you know, I can teach you."

"Do you know how to teach?"

"Well, that's the thing. I just got this job teaching a bunch of actors to fence on stage."

"They pay you to do that?"

"Well . . . not exactly."

Mr. Cohen, who was listening the whole time, laughed.

"But," I added, "it'll get me the experience I need to get paid next time."

"How'd you find your teacher?"

"Lefty knew him."

"What about Tomik?"

"It's a long story, but we fence a couple times each week on the roof of my hotel. Together, we could teach you."

"He's a teacher, too?"

"No, but the three of us could fence together, and that's a great way to learn."

"I never fenced épée."

"That doesn't matter, if you want to learn. You want to learn?"

Siggy hesitated, then nodded. "I could come on Saturday, after temple."

"I'll tell Tomik."

"Tell whoever you want," Mr. Cohen said. "It's time to sell pickles."

+

I told Tomik two days later, and he looked away from me when I mentioned Siggy's name.

"He's coming here on Saturday," I said.

"That's great." When he looked back at me, he smiled, only I'd never seen a smile that looked so sad.

Twenty Four
FOOTWORK

Friday, I was five minutes late and arrived at my first fencing class sweating and breathing heavily.

I entered the theatre door carefully, but the space was so small my entrance was hard not to notice. Mr. Clangor was in the middle of talking about something he called the method and someone named Stanislavski as I took a seat in the back row. He saw me and nodded without missing a beat. There were six young men and two women with their backs to me, trying to pay attention to what Clangor was saying, some failing miserably with nodding heads. One of the women, I could tell even from behind, was Betty.

A young man sitting in front of me, tall and thin with a hooked nose, sunken eyes, and pale white skin, turned around to face me and extended his hand. I took it and we shook.

"Harry Boles," he whispered, leaning toward me. "Percy is onto his Group Theatre days again—ends every rehearsal with it—Stanislavski the God, by Percival Clangor."

I nodded, having no idea what he was talking about.

"Glad you could make it, Mr. Wymann," Clangor said, startling me.

I nodded.

"Rehearsal and lessons start on time. Make sure that you respect your colleagues by following your timepiece more closely in the future. Mr. Wymann," he said, now looking around at his young players, "will be joining us after rehearsal to teach you the art of fencing in Shakespeare's time. He comes highly recommended by an old friend. And if schedules work out when we begin our season, he may help Mr. Everhart"—he pointed to a tall young man with light blond hair and a rounded chin sitting in front of him—"choreograph our duels."

Everhart sat up straight and sputtered. "I don't need any help!"

"Robert," Clangor said carefully, "we've already discussed your need for assistance in *marking* the duels."

"Mr. Clangor," Harry Boles interrupted, a note of concern in his voice, "you said Robert was not going to be in charge of the fights this time."

"It was only an accident, Harry," Everhart whispered loudly over his shoulder. "I told you that."

That's when I noticed that Robert Everhart sat with a ring of empty chairs around him.

"Mr. Clangor," Harry said, "I'm not going to—"

Clangor cut Harry off. "Would you rather have me audition others to take your place, Mr. Boles?"

Harry Boles swallowed, his large Adam's apple bobbing. Slowly he shook his head.

"Mr. Wymann," Clangor raised his voice again, "Mr.

Everhart is our choreographer but right now has other tasks to occupy himself, though he may well be of some help in getting you started. He will be available to you if you need him."

I looked at Everhart and he looked back at me. His right eye twitched as he nodded.

"Why don't we just go at it a bit and see what happens?" Everhart said, swishing his blade from side to side. "Show these others what it is *we'll* be doing?"

They were questions spoken in a manner that did not desire an answer. I had arrived with a lesson planned for the class, made up with Lefty's help, but the intrusion of Robert Everhart had thrown me. Inside my head Nikolai said, *Before duel check to see if blade is good. Measure blades. Must be same length. Find balance. Never swish. When you swish you make noise and show world you are idiot.*

Everhart and I stood on the large stage, surrounded by the Ridolfo Players.

"I thought," Harry Boles stepped forward, hands raised defensively, "Mr. Wymann was—"

"Are you afraid, Harry? Is that what all this pissing is about?"

"Robert," I said, finding my voice and carefully hefting the three-foot-long, inch-wide, five-pound replica of an Elizabethan rapier in my hand. "I don't think it's a good idea to just *go at it.* That's not how Mr. Clangor wants them taught." A few voices from the circle of young actors murmured their agreement. Everhart's blade swished again, this time in Harry Boles's direction, and Harry stepped back quickly out of range.

Everhart turned back toward me. "The name's Mr. Everhart," he snapped, and dropped into an en garde position. His eyes sparkled and his mouth hung open.

"Shit," I whispered to myself, knowing that he was both crazy and about to attack.

Then he lunged at me.

It was fast enough but easily anticipated as his whole body tensed before he set his blade in motion. My reflexes took over. I sidestepped my back foot to the right in a demi-volte, parried his blade with the flat of my palm, and easily placed my blade's point on his chest. I pushed him back a step with the point.

"I think that's enough for now," I said.

I saw Betty watching to my left, her bottom lip held tightly between her teeth.

I looked down at my left hand as Robert's face blossomed in rage and his breathing grew heavier. I saw there was a thin line of blood seeping from a cut across my palm where I'd parried his blade. The blade was worn and a burr must have caught my skin. It stung. While I looked at my hand, Robert slapped my blade away and swung his sword up and down in an arc toward the center of my head. Instinctively I stepped back and brought my blade up to parry. Our blades clashed together, my arm shaking from the force of the blow. Rust shot into my eyes and, blinking through tears, I saw Robert draw back and cut at my neck in a beheading move. I took a step back and stopped him with a parry in quarte. The sound of steel clashing rang throughout the room. He yelled loudly and stamped his foot forward as he swung his blade around to attack my neck from the other side. I ducked and dropped to one knee amidst gasps from those around us. I heard the heavy blade slice the air where my head used to be. I grabbed my hilt with both hands and swung the flat of my blade, like a baseball bat, into his stomach. He folded over my steel as air rushed out of his mouth in a loud groan. Struggling for breath, he dropped to the floor next to me.

"What's going on here?" I heard Clangor ask from behind me. My eyes were closed, the rust particles pricking at my eyeballs.

"The . . . bastard . . . tried . . . to kill . . . me," Everhart gasped.

"If he'd tried to kill you, you'd be dead," said a voice from the crowd.

"What happened?" Clangor repeated.

"The blades need to be cleaned," I said, between gritted teeth.

"Lay your head back," Betty whispered.

I felt her place her hand against the back of my head and I let her guide me.

"Try to open your eyes," she said. I did, and water ran over them, flushing the particles out. A cloth was placed into my hand and guided onto my face. Another hand tried to take away my weapon but I held on, pushing the hand away. I blinked my eyes through the water and tears until the pain subsided.

"Mr. Everhart," Clangor said, drawing himself up to his full height. "I can guess what happened here and I'll have none of it. You promised to accept help and to work with the group."

"You just try to put this on without me," Everhart said, using his rapier to help himself stand. "Who's going to play Romeo? Boles?" He pointed the blade at Harry, then shifted it to a short, heavyset young man with black hair and a large belly. "Pekarsky? He'll break the ladder when he climbs up the balcony."

He pointed his blade in my direction. I stood and beat it down to the floor. A short shout of surprise escaped Everhart's lips as his blade fell from his hand, clattered once, and lay still.

"You're going to let him do that, Percy?" Everhart shrieked, his empty hand shaking.

Percival Clangor was silent for a moment, as if weighing something.

"Percy!"

"You're done here, Robert."

"You can't—"

"I already have."

Everhart glared at me, then the rest of the cast, and stomped off the stage.

"Close the door behind you, Robert," Clangor whispered, then turned toward me. "Do continue, Mr. Wymann. I will be doing paperwork in the office if you have need of me. The class is yours." Clangor turned on his heels and followed Everhart out.

The theatre was quiet.

"I think I pissed myself," said the young man named Pekarsky.

There was nervous laughter, then quiet again.

I looked around at them, suddenly afraid. All day I'd told myself I could do it—I could teach a class of actors how to fence. But, standing in front of them, I was filled with doubt. Could I really teach? *No*, I thought, my whole plan for the lesson disappearing from my head. A bead of sweat rolled down my cheek and made me shiver. What was the plan? Someone coughed and the sound gave me something to hold on to. "Okay," I said, clearing my throat, "who's fenced before?"

"I have," Harry said, "on the stage, I mean."

Pekarsky nodded. "Me too, a little. I fenced Everhart after he took Mark's eye out last fall—though I don't know if you can call it fencing, more like blind panic and prayer."

"How about you?" I asked, looking at the other three young men.

They shook their heads.

"What are your names?"

"Ernie Stockwell," said the smallest and probably the youngest. He might even have been younger than me. A smile flickered across his lips, then disappeared. His eyes were big and blue. "I'm, I'm, I'm, I'm—"

"He's new," Harry said, and Stockwell nodded.

"And you?" I looked at the boy next to him, horse-faced with crooked teeth, near my height, and broad of shoulder.

"I worked with a settlement house theatre down by the Educational Alliance."

"His name's Kovacs," said the last boy, a round-faced, pug-nosed boy with a wicked smile. "I'm Dean and we came in together."

"We haven't fenced either," Betty spoke up, pushing her way forward. "And this is Di." A girl with long brown hair nodded from behind her. I'd almost forgotten the girls.

"Good, good," I said, stalling for time.

"You've done this before, haven't you?" Dean asked dryly. "We can tell you can fence." Around me heads nodded. "But can you teach it for the stage? We're not *fencers*. We're actors."

Inside my head I could see Lefty and Nikolai together, one teaching me about life and death, the other teaching me about the land of pretend. "Let's find out," I said. "Put all the weapons back into the bag."

"There's *only* two," Dean said.

"Then put *those two* away."

"As you wish, *my lord*," he said and bowed. Kovacs laughed, only stopping when I looked at him.

The lesson plan came back to me. I opened my mouth to begin as I'd practiced with Lefty, then closed it. Something was not right. I could feel it. Then I realized what it was. Smiling I opened my mouth and shouted in my thickest Russian accent, "To take off shirt!" My voice echoed throughout the theatre.

"What?" Betty asked.

"Except for the women," I amended, realizing my mistake.

"Why?" Harry asked.

"If you miss a parry once with your shirt off, you won't miss a parry a second time."

"We're going to just . . . go at it?" Pekarsky asked, his hand shaking slightly. "I thought we were done with that?"

I shook my head. "No one is going to get hurt. We'll mark every move. Anybody does anything dangerous, they answer to me. While you have the swords in your hands, you have to pretend they're real. At all times, you must pretend they are real. Then you won't forget in front of the audience." I took off my shirt and threw it against the far wall. Another addition to the plan. I heard the sharp intake of breath and knew they were looking at the scars on my back and sides.

"We'll answer to you?" Dean asked, stepping forward to pick up Everhart's blade. He stepped lightly for his build and I knew he would be one to watch out for.

"Yes," I said, turning back to face him.

"I've got no problem with that," Pekarsky said quickly. The others nodded in agreement.

"Mark move to move?" Harry asked.

"Move to move."

Harry nodded and started to unbutton his shirt. The others followed. Dean, after putting his and my blade away, was the last to become shirtless.

"If your shirts come off," Betty said, "then mine does, too."

"Fair play," Dean said, clapping.

"Betty!" Di yelled. "What are you doing?"

"Learning to fence," she replied and started to unbutton her shirt.

"But—"

"Di," Betty said, never taking her eyes off mine, "you can stay or you can go, but I'm learning to fence."

"I'll stay," Di said, "but my shirt stays, too."

Betty smiled at me and took off her shirt, throwing it to the side with a flourish. Her bra had frayed straps and stains under her arms. Her breasts were small, the too-large bra smothering them. She stood with her hands on her hips, challenging me, it seemed, to comment on them.

"To take off shirt!" Harry Boles shouted, imitating my accent, and the others responded in kind, their words a ragged cheer. "Now show us how you did that move to Everhart."

"First, the basics."

"What about the swords?" Pekarsky asked.

"After we work on your legs and footwork, we'll pick up the swords. Your legs drive your point forward. Your arm and hand aim the cut and thrust. The edge wounds, the point kills."

Pekarsky swallowed hard. "You're serious?"

"You want to learn how to fence?"

Harry Boles slapped Pekarsky on the back and smiled. "Yes! Right, Pecks?"

Pekarsky nodded.

I started them on footwork the same way Nikolai had started me—mercilessly, until their legs shook and the sweat dripped off their bodies and pooled on the floor. I barked out commands to advance, retreat, pass back, extend, and lunge, but I couldn't stop myself from watching Betty. Her throat and chest patched red from the exertion and her hair fell into her eyes. My stomach tightened at the sight of her.

For forty minutes I worked hands-on with all the other

actors as their muscles ached in protest, stopping them in their tracks, repositioning them in their en garde and lunge positions, even making suggestions to Di—but I didn't touch Betty.

"You move them into correct position," Betty finally yelled, "but you don't move me! What do I have, the plague?"

"No, no," I said quickly and came over to her. Harry Boles laughed and I shot him a glance to shut him up. Then I called out some footwork and held the group in a groan-inducing lunge. I placed my hand carefully on Betty's shaking calf and pulled it forward to its correct position. I pressed her sweating shoulder back and turned her left palm up, the movement broadening her chest. I pulled the tips of her fingers forward until her right arm was straight and the curve of her bare underarm opened to me. I hesitated there, gazing at her form.

"Good," I said, my voice cracking. I cleared my throat. "Before we go, there's one more thing I'll show you." I turned away from them and faced the seats. The house lights were warm on my face and I closed my eyes. My head swam and I tried to steady myself. Behind me I heard the others breathing heavily, shifting from foot to foot. *They're waiting for me*, I thought.

"Is he all right?" I heard someone whisper.

"Give him a second," Betty said.

I opened my eyes. The room moved from color to flickering black and white, the way it did when I worked with Lefty on choreography. *They're waiting for me*, I thought.

"You all right?" Betty asked, almost at my shoulder.

I didn't move. I tried to, but my legs and arms wouldn't budge.

"Tell me one thing," she said, low enough so the others couldn't hear, "and I'll wait an eternity. Because you're already ten times better than Everhart. But . . . you know what you're doing, Cid, don't you? You're not full of . . . shit, are you?"

My body unlocked and I turned to face her, then called Harry forward. "Threesies are a triple intention attack. One way, three cuts, one after the other—head, flank, and belly. We'll mark them first like this." I leaned toward Harry and spoke softly. "Can you parry head, flank, and belly?"

"Show me first," he said.

I showed him the parries, calling them out slowly one by one, while the others sat down to rest and watch. We did them twice more, as if in slow motion.

"I know these," Harry said.

"Can you do them fast?"

Harry swallowed. "Yes."

I placed us in fencing measure: just out of distance, but not so far that you could tell. We stared at each other from en garde, bodies tense. I nodded slightly, and when he nodded in reply, I launched into the three cuts as if my body had been propelled by lightning. Harry caught all three, just barely, and his backward momentum kept him moving a few steps after I'd stopped. The clanging of the blades echoed in the hall.

"You good, Harry?"

He nodded again, grinning this time. "Good, Cid."

I turned to the others. "Next week I'll work your legs until they ache again. Then I'll put a sword in your hands." I glanced at Betty. Her lips pressed upward into a grin.

Twenty-Five
THE DOUBLÉ

It was about an hour before dark, and Tomik and I were fencing on the rooftop when Siggy came up the stairs. Tomik's back was to him, but I saw Siggy out of the corner of my eye and the distraction almost made me give away a touch. Then I parried Tomik's lunge at the last second and riposté, striking him in the chest after a quick deceive. He threw off his mask and yelled, "Shit! I had you that time! I had you!"

I took off my mask and pointed at Siggy.

He turned around and stepped back as if struck. "Siggy?"

"Tomik?"

They stood for a moment, staring at each other. Then Tomik asked, "What's that smell?"

"Pickles," Siggy said. "I can't get it off me. Mr. Cohen gives me soap—says it gets rid of the smell, but it doesn't. Even though he says it does—it doesn't."

Siggy took a step toward Tomik. "I told my mother I was going to see you today and she asked me to send her regards to your family. How are they?"

"I'm sorry about your father," Tomik said. "I still can't believe it."

Siggy nodded. He seemed about to say more, then looked at me instead. "You going to teach me to fence?"

I nodded.

Tomik took off his mask and held it out to Siggy along with his blade. "Here, use mine. I need a rest after *my* lesson."

Siggy hesitated a second, then took them.

Nikolai was long gone and the rooftop was our own. We fenced until the sky darkened and the stars came out, sharing our weapons and masks with each other. I fenced with Siggy first, then Tomik, then we rotated against each other until our legs gave out. Siggy learned quickly, remembering the basic footwork, attacks, and parries that his father had taught him. The épée was heavier than the foil, but he bore up well under the added weight and surprised me with his aggressiveness when we fenced. He even scored against Tomik, who swore Siggy only got the touch because he was taking it easy on him while Siggy was still learning.

Exhausted, sweating, we sat with our backs against the wall of Nikolai's apartment and stared up at the stars.

"Do you want to come around again?" I asked.

"Maybe next Saturday," Siggy said.

"Not till Saturday?" Tomik asked.

"He works every day until late," I said.

Siggy nodded.

"Selling pickles?"

Siggy shrugged.

"Come back next Saturday," I said, "if you can."

"I will." Siggy hesitated a moment, then turned toward me. "My mom wants you to come for dinner some night."

"That would be good," I said.

Siggy turned toward Tomik. "You too, Tomik—if you can make it."

"When?" Tomik asked.

"I'll tell you next Saturday."

"Good."

"Tomik, how are your sisters? Are any of them married off yet?" Siggy asked, laughing as if it was an old joke.

"Just one."

"Which one?" I asked, suddenly embarrassed that I hadn't thought to ask Tomik about his family before.

"Bela." Tomik looked down at his hands.

"Who'd she marry?" Siggy asked. "How'd she meet the guy?"

"She married Rick Scarpetto," Tomik said.

"Who?" Siggy and I asked together, both sitting forward.

"Scarps."

"I don't understand," Siggy said.

"I better go," Tomik said, getting up.

"Cid, what's going on?" Siggy asked.

"I don't know. Tomik, why didn't you tell me this before?"

"What would you have said?" Tomik asked, anger in his voice. "I told you it was complicated."

"Scarps from our neighborhood?" Siggy added.

"Does he live with your family?" I asked, ignoring Siggy.

Tomik nodded. "Almost a year now."

"Does he know that you come here to fence?"

Tomik shook his head slowly.

"What's going to happen when he does?"

"He won't."

"But what if he does?"

"That's my problem." Tomik looked past me. He opened his mouth, then closed it. "Do you still want to fence during the week?" he asked.

"Yes," I said, and a smile flickered across his face.

He turned back toward Siggy. "I've got to get home. It's good to see you again, Siggy." He turned away, closing the roof door behind him.

"Cid, what's going on?" Siggy asked again as soon as the door shut.

"Scarps is one of the two guys who beat me up. He's one of Edward Farthings's boys and Tomik's dad works for Mr. Farthings. I didn't know about Tomik's sister, but now it all makes sense."

"Rick Scarpetto? How can that be?"

I watched the information work its way across Siggy's face. He leaned back against the wall and exhaled loudly. "I hate that things change," he said. I couldn't tell if he was speaking to me or himself. "I hate it. Why couldn't they stay the same—the way they were in Sunnyside?"

That night, with the lights out, Lefty's voice drifted over to me.

"Your friend came to see you this evening?"

"Yes."

"Good."

"Tomik was there, too. They haven't seen each other since we were kids. We were all friends then."

I heard him take in a morphine breath, then let it out, slow and soft. "Did you have many friends?" he asked.

"No," I said.

"Neither did I. It is the Wymann blood. We either kill them or run them off. These two, Tomik and Siggy, should be kept."

"Siggy invited me to his place for dinner. Will you come with me?"

Lefty was silent for a long time. "No," he said, finally.

"Why not?"

"I said no."

"You can change your mind later."

"I won't."

Neither one of us spoke for a while.

"You were right about going to Baltimore," I said.

"Yes," Lefty said softly. "I was."

That night Lefty woke me with a scream that made me jump out of bed. I saw him in the moonlight, sitting in his bed, his single eye staring at the ceiling as if waiting for it to fall upon him. Tears poured down his cheek as his chest lifted and fell rapidly, the sheet grasped tightly in his hand. My heart felt as if it would jump out of my chest. I rubbed hard at the skin above it, then walked over to Lefty's bed.

"They're coming," he whispered.

"It's only a dream," I said. "You're dreaming again."

"They always come. Every night they come out of the sky, screaming. Boche murderers. Sky devils. Screaming . . ."

"They're not coming tonight."

"How do you know? Do you have intelligence? Have you spoken to the recon patrols?"

I helped him to lie back down. His eye remained open, but I knew he was asleep, somewhere in the Flanders fields.

"Yeah," I said, "the patrols said no attack tonight. Everyone can take it easy and rest." His face twitched toward mine and he grabbed my shoulder with his good hand, pulling me close as he lifted himself off the bed again, searching my face from one side to the other. "They say the Boche are using gas. It strips the flesh off the bone. If—if there's gas, wake me. Don't let me sleep. Don't let me sleep."

His mouth opened and I smelled the rot. I eased his fingers off my shoulder and lay his head back onto his pillow. "I'll keep an eye out for the gas. I'll wake you if it comes."

"Good man," he said. His mouth closed and the muscles around his good eye relaxed. "I'll sleep, then. Yes, I'll sleep."

Twenty-Six
FENCING MEASURE

When I arrived on Tuesday, the weapons were all laid out and polished, with not a speck of rust on any of them.

Pekarsky, Ernie, Betty, Di, and Harry were sitting around them, staring at their reflections in the steel. They stood up as soon as I arrived.

Dean and Kovacs followed me in. "Nice work, people," Dean said. Kovacs laughed.

"They look great," I said. "Thanks for cleaning 'em."

"Yeah, thanks," Dean added.

"We left yours," Harry told them uncovering the two remaining, rusty weapons. "The steel wool and oil are in the weapons bag."

"You're a bastard, Harry," Dean said.

"Everybody pays their way, Dean." Harry smiled broadly. "Even you."

"Pick up your weapons," I said.

"What are the parts called?" Betty asked, looking closely at her sword.

"Who cares?" Kovacs said.

"I do," Betty replied.

"If you were a seventeenth-century noble in Europe, you would care," I agreed, and Betty hid a smile. "You'd know your weapon from hilt to point." I watched as Ernie turned with his blade resting on his shoulder like a rifle, almost hitting Pekarsky in the eye. "Keep your point down, Ernie. If you believe the weapon is real, the audience will believe it's real. Besides, even with a dull edge and blunt point, it can draw blood or break bones." I motioned to the rest. "Gather round." I held my blade point down in front of me, the crossbar at eye level. I could see Betty through the wire of the cage hilt and forgot what I was going to say. Again she smiled and I shook my head, then pointed to the guard, remembering.

"Bell guard, *coccia*. Crossbar, *gavigliano*. Arches, *archetti*. Grip, *manico*. Pommel, *pomo*. The *forte* is the bottom third of the blade," I said, tracing its edge with my finger, "and is what you use to parry. The *foible* is the top third and is supposed to be razor sharp—it's what you attack with. What you kill with." I saw Ernie swallow and wince. "Now pair up."

I was going to take Harry as my partner, but when I turned around to find him, Betty was standing there instead.

"I want to work with you today," she said, one hand on her hip.

I saw Dean and Harry paired up together, Pekarsky and Kovacs, Ernie and Di—good pairings all. I nodded to Betty.

"Line up with us," I said to the others. "I'm going to teach you all two sets my cousin Winston Arnolf Leftingsham taught me. They're the same one's Harry and I did last week." I said it loudly, projecting across the stage as

Lefty had taught me. "He was in the Royal Shakespeare Academy, and in London they call these threesies and four-sies."

The others laughed, repeating the terms as though they were a joke.

"Betty and I will do it first and then you'll all follow our lead. First," I said, "make eye contact." Betty's gaze became steely-eyed and I swallowed hard.

"What's next?" she prompted.

"Make sure your partner is ready. Don't begin until you know they are."

Betty nodded and I nodded back.

"Get your fencing measure." I extended my blade and she extended hers. Our tips touched our hilts. We were out of distance to hit, but close enough for it to look real. "Now let's do a head cut and a head cut riposté." I showed her how to do a windmill cut or *moulinet*, moving her blade with a rolling of her wrist. Our blades crossed and I felt electricity run up my arm. I swear I saw it travel up her arm, too. Our eyes locked, and my lips and fingers tingled as we went back and forth, cutting and parrying until I broke off. "Now," I said to the others, "we'll all do it together." We fenced for another thirty minutes, practicing head cuts, belly cuts, and flank cuts, then finished the class with foot-work, weapons in hand.

On Friday a heavyset woman with dyed black hair showed up. Her name was Gertrude Blythe, and she wore baggy pants and a man's shirt. She smoked constantly, too, and spoke out of the corner of her mouth, around her cigarette. "I'm the stage manager," she barked when I asked her if she was going to join the class. "But I'll watch, just to see what the hell you're doing."

When I called for everyone to take off their shirts, she laughed so hard that her face turned blue.

Siggy never made it back that next Saturday or the Saturday after that. Tomik and I fenced, but our hearts weren't in it. I wondered if it was that way with the brothers in *Beau Geste*, none of them quite whole without the others.

During these two weeks of class, I made sure to fence with each of the other players, avoiding Betty as much as I could. It's not as if I hadn't seen or overheard enough to know what to do with a girl. A picture of Sister Bernadette at St. Agnes's getting bent over a friar's pew by Father Sinclair stuck in my mind, the pale white of her ass speckled red from being rubbed by the coarse wool of his robe. I guessed I knew what went where. But I had no idea how to get there, or if *there* was where I wanted to get.

But why did I forget where I was when I looked at Betty? Parries and thrusts disappeared. My heart raced and a pounding took over my brain. I didn't know how to deal with it so I tried to ignore her. Fortunately for me, Betty Sirocco was the kind of girl who didn't allow herself to be ignored.

At the end of one class, I invited Harry to The Hotel Chelsea's rooftop salle.

"Where?" he asked. The others had gone and we were alone.

"It's where I get my lessons and there's plenty of room to fence. We don't have enough time here to get everything in, and I wanted you to know the moves so you could help me teach the others."

"Me?" He seemed surprised.

"Yeah, you."

"Why not Dean? He's better at this than me."

"He knows the moves, but he goes too fast with the others. When you work with other people, you go at their speed. Dean cares more about looking good than taking care not to hurt his partner. Besides, they all laugh at Dean's jokes, but they trust you. I trust you."

His jaw dropped a little and he stared at me.

"Do you want to help?"

His jaw finally starting working. "Sure," he said. "Thanks."

"What about me?" Betty asked, stepping into a small circle of light. She must have been in the shadows packing her bag and I'd missed her. Betty and Di were generally two of the last to leave at night, and they usually left together because they shared a room on the Upper West Side. I'd seen Di leave earlier, so I'd assumed Betty had left with her. Betty's bare shoulders were still glistening with sweat from the practice and she hadn't put her shirt on yet.

"What about you?" I asked.

Harry laughed and turned to leave. "When shall I meet you?" he asked over his shoulder.

"Monday at four?"

"I'll be there." The emergency lights were the only ones still on, and Betty and I were alone.

"Well, Wymann, what about me?" she asked again.

"What do you mean?"

"Why don't you invite me to help? I'm good with a sword, too, or couldn't you tell?"

"Sure, sure you are."

She stepped closer to me and I stepped back before I realized what I was doing.

"Have you even noticed?" she asked.

"Of course—"

"How could you?" She stepped closer and I stepped back again. "You haven't fenced with me since the second class. You don't look at me. You don't even glance my way. I thought we'd settled this issue. But it seems I was wrong." She stepped forward again and I backed into the front row. "Can't go back any further, can you?"

"Where's Di?"

"Do you want to see her, or me?"

"I, uh, you. It's just that you always leave with her . . ."

She stepped closer again. "You told me when we met that you thought I looked like a woman. Well"—she stepped closer until her chest almost touched mine— "do I, or don't I?"

The smell of her sweat was thick and sweet, her perfume a ghost of a presence behind it. My heartbeat hammered in my ears and I saw a vein on her neck pulse lightly.

I opened my mouth to reply but she covered it with hers.

When her lips released mine I tried to speak again but she stopped me.

"Just shut up," she whispered hoarsely. "You're not in charge here." She kissed me a second time, and when we came up for air she grabbed my shirt. "Don't forget me again. You got that?"

I nodded.

She released my shirt and smoothed it onto my chest, then pushed me away and waved as she left.

The smell of her perfume lingered with me, and finally I remembered where I'd smelled it before. It was the same perfume Mrs. Braun had used.

Twenty-Seven
THE HANGING GUARD

"I need to see *Robin Hood*," I told Tomik.

We were sitting with our backs to Nikolai's wall, soaked with sweat. Nikolai was unconscious next to us, drool running out of the corner of his mouth in a small stream.

Tomik looked across me toward Nikolai, then leaned back against the wall. "I've got time."

We both stared up at the sky.

"You think Siggy will come by today?" I asked.

Tomik shrugged.

"The show is at Proctors in half an hour. I might need to sit through it twice."

"Okay."

The door opened and Siggy walked tentatively onto the roof. Nikolai stirred, then settled in again and started to snore.

I raised my finger to my lips and Siggy, seeing Nikolai, nodded. Tomik and I got up and walked over to him.

"Who's that?" Siggy asked, keeping his voice low.

"Nikolai Varvarinski, my fencing teacher."

"The crazy Russian?"

"The one and only."

"I'm sorry," Siggy said, "I couldn't make it the last two weeks. I had to help my mother at the bakery. The owner's not a Jew and they need extra help sometimes on the Sabbath."

I nodded. "We're going to see *Robin Hood*," I said.

"Over at Proctors," Tomik added. "It's nearby."

"You want to come?" I asked.

"*Robin Hood*? With Errol Flynn?" Siggy asked, his eyes lighting up.

Tomik and I nodded together.

Siggy's eyes lost their sparkle and he lowered his gaze. "I don't think I can."

"If it's about the money, I can cover you," Tomik said.

"We both can," I added.

"I can't—"

"'Course you can," Tomik interrupted. "You've got to. Cid needs our help. Isn't that right, Cid?"

"That's right. I was just saying to Tomik that I needed both of you to help me."

"What do you need us for?"

"The choreography."

"The what?"

"The moves of the fights," I said. "I need two other sets of eyes to catch everything, 'cause it goes so fast on the screen. Then we'll re-create the fights back here so I can mark them and teach the others in my class."

"How'd you get that idea?" Siggy asked.

"Cid's got all kinds of ideas," Tomik said, smiling.

I shot him a look and turned back to Siggy. "Lefty told me last night. He said I should look in front of me, to the places I've already been. 'A fight is a non-verbal dialog with a dangerous weapon,' he said. Only I have to make up the dialog with the moves. And I thought, where are there sword fights that I can see? Where is there non-verbal dialog?"

"'Non-verbal dialog,'" Siggy said, as if the words were magic.

Tomik laughed and shook his head.

"And of course," I said, "it was right in front of me. *Robin Hood.*"

"*Robin Hood,*" echoed Siggy.

"Welcome to Sherwood," said Tomik, pretending to tip a cap off his head.

"I've got to figure out how to put groups of moves into a fight," I said, "and the best place to learn is from the professionals and who's more professional than Basil Rathbone and Errol Flynn?"

"No one else that I know of," Tomik said.

"Me neither," Siggy added. "But why us? Don't you want to do this with your students?"

"He can't," Tomik said. "He has to bring in work that's baked, not half-baked, right, Cid?"

I nodded. "That's right. And I thought, who better to ask help from than you and Tomik."

"Your friends," Tomik said.

I smiled. "My friends. So . . . we'll go to see *Robin Hood*?"

"But," Siggy persisted. "I don't know anything about fencing on stage and acting."

"Cid will teach us," Tomik said. "You sell pickles. He teaches people to fence on the stage."

I nodded. "It's what I do."

Siggy hesitated a moment, then nodded. The sound of Nikolai farting made us laugh as the stairway door closed behind us.

We sat through two performances, going to the bathroom during the break and wandering back in for the second show as the next crowd was let in. Afterward we went back to the Chelsea rooftop and together wrote down all the moves of the final fight. Then, with the sun beginning to set, turning the sky red, we acted out the moves. First I taught Tomik and Siggy the basics of sword fighting for the stage, but having fenced already, it wasn't too difficult for either of them to pick it up and fight it at a slow pace.

I took a turn at each of the parts, and then watched Siggy and Tomik do the fight, making final adjustments because we didn't have a table to land on, a staircase to fight up, or a candelabra to knock over. I'd never really thought of the individual moves of a screen fight before, and Siggy and Tomik told me it was the same for them. At that moment I realized that the individual moves were, in fact, not so important as the overall *look* of the fight. As Siggy and Tomik fought with épées, I closed my eyes and pictured them in my mind's eye. I pictured Flynn and Rathbone clashing swords while their shadows were thrown up against the castle's stonewall, then opened my eyes and saw Siggy and Tomik, then closed them again. There was an ebb and flow to the fight, a rhythm and pace, a changing momentum that came from the cuts and thrusts, the aggressive repeated attacks, and the rebuffs of the single attack and counterattack. I had them do the fight again and again, then took each of their places until we all knew each part and were all too worn out to do it anymore. By now the stars had come out and it was approaching curfew. We had not eaten and our stomachs suddenly ached.

"I've got to go," Siggy said, bent over double and breathing heavily. "My mom is going to kill me for missing dinner and getting home so late."

"It's almost curfew," Tomik added. "We're going to have to run if we want to get home before the lights go out."

"I don't think I can run," Siggy said.

"I don't think I can, either," Tomik said laughing.

"Hey," I said, stopping them both as an idea came into my head. "You guys want to come to my class and show them the fight? You know, help me teach it to them?"

Tomik looked at each of us and shrugged, then said, "Why not?"

"I can only do it on a Saturday," Siggy said.

"Let me see if I can change the class date," I said, wondering what Percival Clangor would say to a change in schedule. "It'll be a few weeks, when they're ready, 'cause they're not ready yet."

"That would be great," Siggy said and headed down the stairs, finding enough energy to push his legs forward. He stopped to shout back at us leaning on the rail, "See you next week."

Tomik hesitated a moment after Siggy left. "You know there's a tournament in July at The Hotel Pierre—the last Saturday of the month."

"I didn't know."

"Well, there is. Are you going to compete?"

"Are you?" I asked.

"Yes."

"Épée?"

Tomik nodded again.

"Will Farthings be there?"

Tomik stared at me a long time, then nodded, his smile finally disappearing.

"Then so will I."

Harry Boles came by and I taught him the lessons I was going to teach the rest of the troupe during the week. Harry liked to go over and over each move until he got a sequence right before he allowed me to move on. "Come on, Cid," he'd say. "You've been doing this forever, and compared to you, I don't know shit. I don't want to look like an idiot and give Dean any ammunition to hit me with—the bastard."

"You hold your own with him," I said.

"Oh sure, with the sword. But he's got the looks I don't have. I'll be lucky to get Tybalt come the season, while he'll stare down at me as Mercutio."

"You're taller than him," I said.

"Not on stage. Everyone looks at him. I've seen it."

"You'll get to kill him."

"But he'll still have all the good lines."

I clapped my hand on his shoulder. "But Harry, nobody likes him except Kovacs."

Harry nodded and smiled. "Well, there *is* that. Anyway, let's do it again, okay?" So we did.

In class, Betty and I didn't have a lot of private time. She didn't want the others, or Clangor, to know about us, and the curfew at her boarding house was strict, so there were no after-hours or before-hours together. The truth was, I didn't even know what *us* was. So I rotated partners each session and made sure I demonstrated moves with her and fixed her stance at least once every class. Whenever our blades touched and our eyes met, my breath caught in my throat. I wondered if there'd be another kiss or perhaps more, though thoughts of *more* only turned my mind in the direction of Sister Bernadette and Father Sinclair, and that made my insides flip.

June came. I asked Percival Clangor if I could change the Thursday class to Saturday and he said it was fine with him if the troupe agreed. They all agreed with a rousing cry of "To take off shirt!"

"What else do we have to do on a Saturday night?" Pekarsky asked.

"Play with yourself?" Dean said.

"At least he has something to play with," Harry said.

"Touché Harry," Betty said.

With the Allied soldiers taking Rome and the invasion of Normandy putting U.S. soldiers onto French soil, my world seemed so bright I could hardly stand it.

✛

Siggy finally invited Tomik and me to his place for dinner the following Saturday, the first Saturday of July, the day before Independence Day.

That night I waited up for Lefty to return so I could ask him again to come with me to Siggy's. He didn't return to our room and I fell asleep with my face propped up against the wall. He didn't return the next night either. He'd left no note, and on Monday, at my lesson, Nikolai said nothing about his absence. A fourth day passed and I began to worry. I had an uneasy feeling in my stomach. The memory of my father and his final disappearance came back to me and I couldn't shake it.

Nikolai would not look at me when I asked him where Lefty was. "Drunk!" was all he would say.

"He's done that before," I said finally. "But he always comes back at night. He needs his morphine or he can't . . ."

Nikolai walked away. Our lesson was over.

"What's happened, Nikolai?"

"You and I are friends now? Comrades? Use first name?" he said, turning back to face me. "I am teacher. Do not forget." His words were harsh but his tone was not.

"Nikolai Varvarinski, you are my teacher and . . . my friend. Tell me where Mr. Leftingsham is."

"Morphine did not come this month, so he go to morphine."

"I don't understand." Then I thought about it. Lefty's morphine habit had become a normal part of our lives in that amazing way that the strange can become the everyday. Watching him inject it had become as commonplace a part of my night as brushing my teeth. His shipment came every month. Sometimes I went to the post office for it, sometimes he went on his own. Every night the wooden box came out from under the bed; there were no skipped nights. For more than a year, the package had always arrived.

"There was no package?" I asked.

Nikolai nodded.

"Didn't he go to the hospital or, or to a doctor?"

"Not same here. Cannot get it here."

"But there's a war on. There's morphine in every hospital."

"Morphine short everywhere. Not legal to write, how you say, note? Pre-scrip-tion?"

"Prescription?"

"*Da.*"

"But he needs it for the pain."

"Here, to drink was against law. Morphine is drug of devil."

"Then where is he?"

"Where he can get what he need."

"Take me to him."

"*Nyet.*"

"Please," I said.

Nikolai's eyes were heavy, alcohol filled. They focused on me for a moment, then began to wander. He nodded and went back into his room. When he came out, he was tucking a Colt revolver into the waist of his pants.

Twenty-Eight
FOIBLE

Nikolai took me to Chinatown. We took the IRT to Lafayette Street and walked over to the small, five-city-block neighborhood that centered on the triangle of Mott, Pell, and Doyers Streets—the neighborhood the St. Agnes boys had called Chink City.

It was early evening, and the hazy orange sun was low in the sky. The tenement houses, brownstones, and small shops of Little Italy cast deep shadows across the still crowded streets. The eight-hundred-foot-tall Woolworth building loomed above us from the southwest like a monster, its copper-peaked spire glistening and shimmering against the setting sun.

Stepping into the street to avoid the growing sidewalk crowds, we approached Mott from Worth. A few moments later a horn-honking tour bus pushed us up and back onto the curb. We could overhear its operator shouting at his passengers like a circus barker: "Take it easy, folks, and keep to your seats until the bus stops. Now I want to warn you to stay close together. Ladies, hold hands and stay on the inside of the group. Gentlemen, take the outside next to the curb. We don't want to lose anyone to the Tongs on this trip!"

An old Chinese man crossing the street in front of the bus made it slam on its brakes, stopping only inches from him. The driver leaned on his horn and the old man finished crossing without a sideways glance.

The singsong sounds of the Chinese dialects surrounded us. Large Chinese signs rose into the air above our heads, a few with English translations beside them.

We passed what looked like a temple, then there were grocery stores with cabbage, bean sprouts, water chestnuts, smoked squid, and shark fins all neatly stacked on tables in front of them with signs marking each item. Varnished ducks and roast pork hung from awning hooks, above broad displays of green bowls, brown paper fans, black cotton slippers, kites shaped like butterflies and dragons, and snakes steeped in rice wine, their eyes swollen, glazed, and milky. Nikolai had to pull me along behind him as I stopped again and again to gaze at the oddities like some dumb tourist.

"Want to find Leftingsham, or look like tourist in yap wagon?" Nikolai shouted in my ear as an old woman in front of me, wearing what looked like worn satin pajamas, reached into a large bucket and pulled out a tangle of crabs.

I nodded toward Nikolai and kept my eyes on his back as he threaded a path through the crowd. Across the street, up toward Bayard, I saw a large wall covered with Chinese newspapers where dozens of men stood, reading. To my right, Pell was completely in shadow. The neon lights above us cast flickering images across our faces as street and store lights switched on like giant fireflies. Halfway down the street I looked up to see a sign stating in English, LADIES, DRESSES MADE TO ORDER IN CHINESE STYLES.

As we turned the corner of Pell and Doyers, Nikolai slowed down. Another tour guide shepherded a group of tourists—women wearing real seamed stockings, men with their gray trilbies cocked at a fashionable angle. They stopped just before the corner building. "This is the head-quarters of the Hip Sing Tong," the guide said. As in-structed, the women huddled close in the center of the group surrounded by their men. "This is called the Bloody Angle because in the early 1900s the On Leongs and the Hip Sings battled for control of the gambling, white slavery, and opium rackets down here."

"Gee whiz," a small boy said, and his mother shushed him.

"Of course"—the guide paused for effect and leaned forward—"now under the Chinese Consolidated Benevo-lent Society, the Tongs are no longer at war. But . . ." He leaned in even closer and pulled the corners of his eyelids up into a slant. His voice took on a thick Chinese accent. "Who know what will happen with inscrutable Chinee?"

The corner building was the old Chinese Theatre taken over by a Rescue Society Mission founded by an ex-con named Tom Noonan. I'd seen his name and the mission's picture in *The Sunday Times* a while back.

Nikolai ducked into a dark alley next to the Mission. He pulled me in after him.

"Stay close," he whispered, grasping my shoulder tightly.

We waited a moment while our eyes adjusted to the darkness. A small amount of light filtered down from the darkening sky, illuminating moisture that glistened on the walls. Nikolai released my shoulder and I rubbed it to get the circulation flowing again. The alley was only a couple of feet wide and Nikolai had to walk sideways in order not to touch the walls with his shoulders.

The darkness grew deeper and the back of Nikolai's head merged with the blackness around it. I felt a breeze on my cheek off to one side, then another, as if we had passed openings. Just when I thought Nikolai had gone on too far ahead, he stopped and I bumped into his back. He placed his large hand over my mouth and whispered in my ear, "We go down. Do not speak." His eyes glowed in front of mine.

I nodded and he took his hand from my mouth. Then his head disappeared and I stepped forward into open air. I stumbled down the first step, caught myself, and then followed more slowly down twelve more, placing my hand on Nikolai's back to steady myself.

For a long time, Nikolai stood in the dark without moving. Finally I heard knuckles rap on wood. A few seconds later, a small panel slid open at eye level, bathing us in yellow light.

I shaded my eyes with my hand. A voice whispered a two-syllable word in Chinese, and Nikolai responded. I heard bolts click softly and slide. The door eased open, its hinges silent.

A lantern hung from the ceiling above us. A large, heavyset Asian man wearing a white shirt and black slacks, perspiration beading on his forehead, stood aside so we could enter. The air was thick and smelled faintly sweet. The door closed shut behind us. The passageway turned left, then right. A second door stopped us, the peephole easily visible in the glow of a hanging oil lantern.

Two eyes stared out at us.

Nikolai said something, again.

The eyes scrutinized us from head to toe, then disappeared as the panel slid shut and the door opened.

Smoke filled my nostrils with a sweet, pungent odor. Beneath it, masked by incense, was the smell of dried sweat and unwashed skin.

A small room greeted us, low and dark, its far corners lost in smoky shadow. A large table stood on one side, a small one across from it beside a wall filled with what looked like small glass lanterns and pipes. In front of us was an arch that led into another room, lined with bunks to either side, the wood on each bunk covered with etchings and varnished a dark cherry. Each bunk was fitted with a woven mat and a lacquered leather pillow. A single oil lamp, surrounded by thin red paper patterned with Chinese characters, hung from the center of the room. There were maybe seven or eight people in the bunks, some lying back with their eyes closed, others lying on their sides with a large box on a wooden tray next to them, smoking long thin pipes. One or two glanced up at us, their eyes glassy and uninterested. Their pipe bowls glowed orange, then red, as they sucked in on their stems.

"Where is he?" I whispered to Nikolai.

He held his hand up to silence me.

An elderly gray-haired man appeared out of the haze and stood before us in what looked to me like gray silk pajamas and a black skullcap. He bowed and Nikolai did the same.

Then Nikolai started to speak in Chinese, but the old man interrupted him with perfect English.

"It is admirable that you wish to speak our tongue and I am honored by your attempt, but it is not necessary, Mr. Varvarinski. It is a pleasure to see you again. Tell me your, and your young friend's, desire this evening." His voice was so soft it was almost a whisper, yet I heard it well enough.

"We look for man named Leftingsham. One leg, one arm, half of face. Is he here?"

"You know our policies," the old man said. "I do not allow my patrons to be bothered. They pay for privacy and I provide it. We have Fountain of Happiness available today for your pleasure should you care, instead, to sample it."

I felt the presence of two men at my back before I saw them. I looked over my shoulder and recognized the large man from the first door we'd passed. The other was equal to his size and could have passed for his brother. I heard the click of Nikolai's revolver as he cocked it and I snapped my eyes to the front. Two more clicks popped to my rear. Nikolai held the gun at his hip, aimed at the old man's belly, and I knew from the way my ears stung that two guns were pointed at our backs. The saliva in my mouth dried up and my palms broke out in sweat. I thought that was funny, to be dry in one place and wet in another, but I had to stop myself from laughing. My head spun from the opium smoke and I knew that at any second I would probably be killed.

The heads of the customers disappeared into the haze of their bunks. For a moment, nobody moved.

Then I heard it. Faintly at first, then louder, someone was singing. The harsh throaty voice was unmistakable.

"The bells of hell go ting-a-ling-a-ling,
For you but not for me.
O Death where is thy sting-a-ling-a-ling,
O Grave, thy victor-ee?"

The song was cut off by a raw, painful cough.

"He will die here," Nikolai said, when the coughing fit ended and the next verse began.

"Each man chooses his own means of death," the old man said. "Some with eyes open. Some with eyes closed."

"Need more money?" Nikolai asked.

The old man shook his head slowly.

Nikolai released the hammer with his thumb and pushed the revolver back into his pants' waist. "Then we take him."

"If that is all . . ."

"All," Nikolai said, and stepped past him.

I followed him into the far recesses of the second room, toward the corner where I knew Lefty must lie.

The sight of him made me draw in my breath sharply. His good eye was sunken in and his skin stretched tautly across his face. Then his stench reached me, like invisible fingers thrust down my nose and throat. I gagged and forced myself not to cover my mouth.

"Grab him," Nikolai said and I leaned forward to help. Lefty was like a bag of bones, their joints and ends sticking through his pants and T-shirt. "I'll carry him," I said and cradled him in my arms. Nikolai grabbed Lefty's wooden leg from the bunk, along with the cane I had given him six months before.

The old Chinese man stopped me before I left the room and held out his hand. There was a small card in it with what looked like a single Chinese character painted on it in black.

"Take this, young gentleman," he said. "I am Sammy Hing. This is my parlor. Should you require my services, you need only present this card at the door."

My hands were full and I did not intend to take his card, but he placed it in my shirt pocket as I left. His touch was as light as a fluttering butterfly.

We flagged a checkered cab on the edge of Chinatown. Lefty sang all the way home.

Twenty-Nine
BLOOD GUTTER

"He need doctor," Nikolai said when I put Lefty in bed and covered him. It was warm out, but Lefty was shivering, unconscious, and breathing roughly.

"He'll need morphine when he wakes up," I said. "Do you know a doctor?"

He shook his head, then stopped. "Ask Kopecky."

"No," I said. I'd already thought of him. I knew he would help, but it would also jeopardize his family's position with the Farthings and put Tomik in trouble with Scarps.

"Leftingsham will die."

"There's a girl at the theatre I'll ask. She has to know someone."

"Girl?"

"Yeah," I said. "She'll know of a doctor."

"It will cost. Everything cost."

"Then we'll pay."

"How?"

"Leftingsham must have some money. He has to have

some. He pays for the room here and for food. It's got to be somewhere."

"Where?"

I hesitated a second, looking at Nikolai. I remembered his lights being off around Christmas, his figure at our door with a candle. I looked at his clothes, the holes at the elbows, the wearing at the knees, and thought how far Lefty's money would go in his hands. It shamed me to think of him this way, but Lefty had always warned me to be wary when dealing with Nikolai, and for a moment this made me doubt him. Perhaps he saw it in my eyes.

"Because you are boy, I will let it pass," he said, as if reading my mind.

"I'm sorry," I said.

"Standing on your shoes, I would think same."

"Stay with him?" I asked and he nodded.

I ran down to the theatre and was out of breath when I got there. It was late and the theatre lights were dim. I banged on the door until my hand hurt. Gertrude Blythe opened it and I almost fell in on top of her.

"Wymann," she said, as if that covered it all.

"Miss Blythe," I said, between gasps. "Is Betty around? I know we don't have class until tomorrow night, but I need to see her . . ."

Blythe took the cigarette out of her mouth that I'd bent in half and threw it onto the ground. "That's not all you want to do with her, am I correct?"

"What do you mean?"

She stepped aside and lit up another cigarette.

"She lives on the West Side in a boarding house on Ninety-eighth Street. How come you don't know that?"

"Miss Blythe—"

"The name's Gertrude. Friends call me Gertie." She took a drag on her cigarette and blew out the smoke. "You can call me Gertie."

"Gertie, then. I know where she lives. I was hoping she was here. Ninety-eighth Street's too far."

"For what?"

"I need a doctor."

"You look in fine shape."

"Not for me—for my cousin."

"What happened to him?"

So I told her, simply and quickly. When I was finished, she dropped her cigarette to the ground and stepped on it. "Follow me, kid." She led me back through the theatre to Clangor's office and picked up the phone hanging on the wall. It was an old two-handed trumpet and she had to lean into the speaker to talk.

"Butterfield five, three-six three-six," she said and waited. Then her eyes opened a little wider as if she had just heard someone speak and she turned away from me. "Janice? Gertie. Yeah, I miss you, too. Remember the doc who helped your sister out with that little trouble of hers? That's the one. Got his number? Thanks. You're the sugar in my . . . yeah. That's right. Next week would be good." She hung up and called a new number. Her body stiffened when she spoke this time, her voice harsher. She spoke for a while, relating what I'd told her, then gave my address.

"How do you know where I live?" I asked when she got off the phone.

"You never worked with a troupe before?"

I shook my head.

She laughed and lit up again, the cigarette appearing in her fingers as if by magic. "I'm the stage manager. It's my job to know everything about everybody, even fencing instructors. Now let's go."

"Wait. You're not coming."

"The hell I'm not."

"You've done plenty already. Thanks, but he's *my* cousin."

"Nothing doing, Cid. You ask for my help, you get my help. I get to see this Leftingsham of yours. Us stage managers are the curious type."

I looked at the clock on the wall. I had been gone an hour already. We stared at each other a moment, then I nodded. "Just keep up."

Gertrude Blythe was breathing in great gulps of air by the time we made it back to the hotel. Shouting out "Fourth floor" over my shoulder, I took the stairs two at a time and heard her curse behind me.

"Isn't there a fucking elevator?"

I opened the door to our room and Nikolai turned from the window he'd been looking out of.

"Bring doctor?" he asked.

I nodded, catching my breath, and left the door open behind me.

Gertrude staggered in a few minutes later.

"Nikolai Varvarinski, Gertrude Blythe."

Nikolai's eyes widened.

"She's not the doctor," I said. "She's, well, she's the one who's bringing him."

They exchanged nods.

"This is my cousin," I said, pointing at Lefty. I had to give Gertie credit. When she looked down at Lefty, she didn't blink. She leaned in closer, as if to get a better look at him, then took a deep inhalation.

"You didn't say he'd been gassed."

"How do you know he was gassed?" I asked.

"My father was gassed at Belleau Wood. He lived for a year at home before he died. What type was it?"

"Mustard," Nikolai said. "Dirty thing. Kill from inside out."

"They used Phosgene on my father. I thought that was bad. This is worse."

"Everything dirty in war."

Gertie lit a cigarette in reply, and together we watched Lefty in silence while we waited for the doctor to arrive.

Yasha Chodakowski was the doctor's name. He'd come to New York from Poland just before the war started and practiced medicine without a New York license. During the day he worked as a nurse at a Roosevelt Hospital clinic.

"He's the only kind of doctor who can get you morphine today. No one else will do it for you," Gertie said. Nikolai nodded.

Doctor Chodakowski was a small man in his fifties who had a tired, sagging face and wire-rimmed glasses that he pushed up on his nose before he spoke. His Polish accent was still strong, but he was easy enough to understand. He'd seen the effects of mustard gas before, and after a quick check, shook his head. "Opium killed his pain. Smoke killed his lungs. Nothing to do," he said.

"What do you mean, nothing to do?" I said.

"He will die soon, that is all."

"How soon?"

"A day? A week? Maybe two? He has lived long with it already, so who can tell. All his time now is gift. Perhaps before it was curse, no?"

"There *has* to be something we can do."

"Make him comfortable. I will give him antibiotic and morphine. I have supply from friend at hospital."

"So he won't be in pain then?"

"What is pain to this man? Every day is pain. Every breath is pain. Morphine will help. Morphine helps for everything."

"But what can we do?"

"You heard the man, Cid," Gertie said. "Keep a pillow under his head."

"How much is cost?" Nikolai asked from the window.

Doctor Chodakowski stared at Gertie for a moment, lowered his eyes, then looked back at me. He pushed his glasses up onto the bridge of his nose. "I will get you morphine. A boy will bring it in package each Monday. Patient must take three times a day as he need. If he uses more, supply will run out quicker. I cannot get more. I will do this for one month, if he lives that long. But that is all I can do."

He packed his bag, shook our hands, gave us a phone number, and left.

"He owes me a favor," Gertie said as I opened my mouth to speak. "Leave it at that."

I didn't know what I was going to say. I had always known Lefty could die—that at some distant time in the future, he would die. But now, in front of me, while I watched—it was too much to accept.

Gertie bent down and kissed Lefty's ruined cheek. His skin twitched slightly where she touched him with her lips.

"He's going to die," I said, more to myself than to Nikolai.

"We all die," Nikolai said.

The words of Sammy Hing echoed inside my head as the night wore on and Lefty's breathing eased into a softer morphine rhythm. "Each man chooses his own means of death, some with eyes open, some with eyes closed."

Thirty
POMMEL

I didn't sleep. I sat and stared at Lefty throughout the night. The next day I didn't go to school. I didn't leave the room except to go to the bathroom.

I had no intention of ever going back to school. I had no friends there. The administration would not waste a truant officer's time on my trail. Besides, I'd learned more from Lefty and Nikolai than from all my schooling put together.

I told myself that when Lefty woke up I would take him to a real doctor. I prayed to God and apologized for not believing in him before. I swore to my mother's God and Maddie's God and every Greek, Roman, and pagan God I could think of that I would take better care of him, that I would make sure he took his medicine, that I would steal morphine if I had to, just so long as they let him live. But the slight rise and fall of his chest was my only response.

One day turned into two.

Nikolai brought me food that I didn't eat. He stood behind me and mumbled words in Russian that I didn't understand.

Finally Lefty opened his eye. I spoke to him. I told him what had happened. I told him how things would be different when he was better. But he didn't answer. He didn't even seem to hear. He let me wash him and roll him onto his side to change the sheets, but that was all. He looked at me, but didn't see me. He'd told me once about the thousand-yard stare that soldiers in the trenches got after the shelling had pounded them into the farthest reaches of their mind. Their bodies moved, but when you looked into their eyes, you saw nothing but the vacant stare of the beaten. I saw this stare now and realized that Lefty had given up. He was only waiting for his body to do what his mind had already done.

It didn't seem right. He should fight to live. I begged him to. I yelled at him. "Get off your ass and throw something!" I shouted. "Break something. Hit something. Don't give up!" When he didn't respond I cursed him.

"Why are you doing this?" I asked finally, softly.

His eye bore into mine.

"Why are you leaving me? Why are you doing this to me now?"

The skin beneath his eye twitched as if an insect had landed beneath it.

Harry and Tomik showed up on Wednesday evening. They'd met on the rooftop salle. I'd forgotten I'd told them both to meet me there. When I answered their knock at the door, they stood facing me, an awkward pair, Tomik with his leading man look, and Harry towering over him with his catcher's mitt of a face set in a heavy scowl.

"Varvarinski sent us down," Tomik said. "Your friend here," he pointed over his shoulder at Harry, "did not want to disturb you."

"If we're intruding," Harry said, "we can go. It's just that you had said to meet you here, and you weren't at class yesterday, and Miss Blythe told me you were here."

I shook my head trying to get rid of their voices. The air swam in front of me and my eyes were heavy. I tried to close the door on them, but Tomik stuck his foot out to stop it.

I heard Harry ask, "What's that smell?"

"Just ignore it," Tomik said.

"I don't think he wants visitors."

"Leave if you want," Tomik said, and pushed the door open. "Listen, Cid, what is it that Nikolai—," he began, but then stopped as he stepped into the room and saw Lefty.

"What in the name of Jesus . . . ," Harry said, the door framing him as he stepped in behind Tomik. "Who's that?"

"Cid's cousin," Tomik said, softly. He walked up to Lefty and placed his hand on Lefty's shoulder stump. Lefty stirred. Tomik turned to me. "What happened to him, Cid?"

I didn't say anything. I couldn't. Their images disappeared as quickly as they had come.

Betty came by with Gertrude.

I remember thinking that my room, in a few days' time, had already been host to more people than it had been in the whole last year.

Betty sat with me while Gertrude went to bring back

sandwiches from the Automat. A new one had gone up near Penn Station and she walked uptown to get them.

"Give you two some time alone," she said.

"Lefty's still here," I said.

I don't remember what Betty said. I didn't notice when she and Gertrude left, though I remember hearing their voices in the hall afterward. I remember at some point looking around and seeing that the sun had set again and left the room in darkness.

I heard Mrs. Esslinger shout in the hall. Her voice got closer to our door. There was a knock.

"Is Mr. Leftingsham sick?" her voice asked in a stage whisper.

"He's dying," I said.

"I'm so sorry," she said. "So very sorry."

There were no nightmares for Lefty now and perhaps that was a blessing. Or maybe he had them and just didn't shout them out. Maybe they were trapped inside of him. In a strange way, I missed them.

I slept at some point because I woke up in my bed. Nikolai must have placed me there.

Two days later, while I watched, Winston Arnolf Leftingsham died. His chest rose and fell, and then didn't rise again.

✛

I sat staring at him until morning. Then I went up to the roof and woke Nikolai. He was still drunk from the night before and staggered down the stairs after me. He closed

Lefty's eyelid. I called Dr. Chodakowski from the lobby phone and went back up to the room to wait for him to arrive.

Nikolai helped me wash his body. Under Lefty's bed was a black suitcase that held his clothes. I took out his captain's uniform and dressed him in it, pinning up his empty sleeve, and placing his wooden leg against the stump of his thigh so that he looked complete. Beneath the clothes, I found a large brown envelope, which held Lefty's will and a letter addressed to me covered with his crablike script, cross-outs, and inkblots.

Dear Cedric,

I am slipping. It has happened before and I have pulled myself out, but I will not do so this time. I spent four months in hospital before I came to New York. I would not tell you this, but I need you to know that my condition has nothing to do with you. You are not responsible for it and have never been.

I have been close to madness so many years now that I do not remember what it was like to be otherwise. Passchendaele did this. The Boche did this. My country did this. I did this. I should have died there. You asked me once where I went when you were at school. My foot travels on one plane, my head on another. My head is full of worms. You cannot see them, but they are there nonetheless, tunneling. I walk in the daylight to fill the tunnels that they make while I'm asleep. I end up on the roof of this hotel and stare down at the people passing below. I hear your mother's music from a long time ago and I talk myself out of stepping off the edge. My promise to her has kept me here. My meeting you has kept me here.

When I was an actor on stage I could forget who I was and become someone else. It was a useful skill for a young man—even more so for the remains of a man and that is what I am—pieces of what I once was. Do not make the mistake of forgetting who you are, Cedric. It is all you have.

When you have received this I will be dead.

It is a harsh but necessary solution.

Know that I have provided for you as I promised your mother I would. It might not be as she would have wanted, but it will have to do. Even your bright star cannot keep me here. I thought to come here and find nothing more than a boy. In many ways I found a son. In another time and place you could have been my son, a son I would have been proud of.

I failed you when I was sick. I am sorry for that. I knew who you were and where you were. I knew that you had been born. But I could not come to you then. In my dreams I asked your mother for forgiveness but she did not answer. Only the worms answered. I was in hospital a long time before I came here to see you—a long time.

I wish only for peace. Can you understand that? Have you heard enough of my dreams? The shells burst and I cringe with fear. Yes, I fear, Cedric. I fear *the nighttime and I fear the day. I fear the faces of dead comrades that greet me when my head sinks into the pillow. I fear their voices calling to me. I fear the pain of my burning lungs. I fear the stench of my rotting flesh. I fear the look of passersby on the street. I wish to be released from this cross. I wish the nails taken out of my palms and feet.*

Nikolai will legally be your guardian so you will not have to worry about a place to live. He is what was available in my trench so I have used him. He is as mad as I and yet he has survived longer. This is his strength. And I have no doubt, my young cousin, of your resiliency in the matter. The room is paid for through your eighteenth birthday. It was my last home and will be yours until you can find yourself another. There is a safe deposit box at 40 Wall Street, The Bank of the Manhattan Company, that contains records of importance for you, names and addresses of family in England. Perhaps you will make more use of them than I have.

I know you, Cedric Wymann. You are much like I was. One year is enough to see your light and shadow. One year is enough to see your strength and weakness. You are scarred as boys are sometimes scarred by their fathers, but you are not your father. It took me many years to realize this about myself, and you would do well to realize this now, before life disfigures you further. Your mother's bloodline runs thick in you. Our line is tainted—always has been. Let Abigail lead you to life as she did me. I wonder if I will see her on the other side? I wonder if, once there, I will be whole?

The letter was left unfinished, without signature. I sank down onto my bed and curled into a ball, cradling Lefty's letter against my belly. My hands shook, making the paper flutter against me like a moth's wings. I heard a roaring in my ears and closed my eyes.

Thirty-One
THRUSTING HOME

At daybreak on June 28, Grahams Funeral home packaged Lefty's body into a casket and took it to Pier 90 near West Fiftieth Street. Nikolai, already drunk, rode with me in the hearse. Stopped at a traffic light in midtown, I heard the paperboys on the corner hawking their dailies while we waited for the light to change.

"Seventh Corps surrounds Cherbourg!"

"Bradley assaults the hedgerows!"

I covered my ears with my hands.

There were two groups waiting for us. Tomik and Siggy waited together on one side, while Harry, Gertrude, and Betty waited on another. I couldn't remember if they'd all met before or not.

I looked at Siggy in surprise.

"Tomik told me," he said, looking up at me, then down at his feet. Tomik stood back from him, his porkpie hat low over his eyes.

Harry and Gertrude stayed back while Betty embraced me. I placed my hand on her back lightly. When she let me go, there were tears in her eyes. She wiped them away with closed fists.

A tired looking railroad steamer with patches on its funnel waited for us. The midtown Hudson piers were usually busy with many of the fancier Atlantic shipping lines working out of their wharfs, but for some reason they weren't busy that morning. The steamer seemed to be the only boat there. It was heading to England, and the captain had agreed to carry Lefty's remains along with his load of munitions. I touched Lefty's casket as the sailors, cursing quietly at its weight, lifted it from the back of the hearse and took it on board.

We all watched as the boat eased out of its berth and created a wake toward the Statue of Liberty and the open sea. Water slapped against the pier in short choppy waves. Nikolai finally broke the silence. "There go one dumb English bastard back to fucking motherland." Then he spit into the river.

I had a pain in the center of my chest. I rubbed at it, but it wouldn't go away.

"I go home," Nikolai said, still staring out to sea. "Do not forget your lesson today. Competition come in three weeks and you are not ready." His words hung in the air between us. Finally he turned and left, listing first to one side, then the other, as he walked downtown along the waterfront.

"I'm sorry about Lefty," Tomik said.

"Me, too," said Siggy.

Harry nodded, dropping his gaze uncomfortably.

Betty stared at me as if expecting something, only I didn't know what.

Gertrude turned toward me. I saw there were tears in her eyes. She ignored them and lit a cigarette. "Damned stupid war," she said, taking a long drag, then throwing the remains into the water. "Clangor couldn't make it. He said he doesn't like funerals. I told him he was an ass."

"He told me to send his condolences," Betty added, shooting her a look.

"You still going to compete?" Tomik asked.

Gertrude lit another cigarette.

I nodded slowly. I could still see the outline of the steamer on the horizon. Then it was gone. I turned toward Tomik. "Are you?" Now that he stood closer, I noticed a large purple bruise across his cheek. "What happened to you?"

"I walked into a door," he said. "I'll be at the competition."

I reached out and took off his hat. The side of his face was bruised and his eye was black. "What happened to you?" I repeated. "Was it Scarps? Did he find out?"

"Leave it alone, Cid."

"Was it Farthings then?"

Tomik shook his head.

The others gathered around us.

"If they didn't find out, then why'd they do it?"

Tomik would not look at me.

"I'll kill the bastard!"

"Edward didn't do it," Tomik said, looking back at me.

"Then it *was* Scarps?"

Tomik smiled. "It was my father."

"Your father? Why would he—"

"I asked for help from the Farthings family doctor. He helped my sister when she was ill last year. I thought he could help Lefty. My father found out." He shrugged. "You're not popular with my father these days, and neither am I."

"I didn't need the help. Dr. Chodakowski—"

"Everybody needs help, Cid," Tomik said. "Even you." His smile disappeared.

"Who is this Edward Farthings?" Harry asked.

"Someone I've yet to settle with."

"And Scarps?"

"Works for Farthings."

"I don't understand—"

"It's complicated," I interrupted.

Harry shrugged.

Suddenly the dock seemed full of longshoremen. The nearby warehouse doors opened, two boats pulled into piers, and crews began to off-load. A mosquito bit into my neck and I slapped at it. I rubbed at my chest again.

"You want to take a week off from class?" Gertrude asked. "I'll tell Clangor."

"I could teach 'em if you wanted," Tomik added. "Work with this guy here." He nodded toward Harry.

"I'll help, too," Siggy chimed in. "We said we would anyway."

"Cid doesn't need any help," Betty interrupted.

"Cid's *my* friend," Tomik said.

"*Mine* too," added Siggy.

Harry raised his hands in defense when Betty looked his way.

I half listened, unable to stop picturing Tomik's father's large hands striking Tomik's face. I wondered if Mr. Kopecky still had his shotgun.

"I don't know you well enough, *Mr.* Kopecky or *Mr.* Braun," Betty said looking at my two friends, "but Cid doesn't need any help teaching us. He's got a contract with my cousin and he'll complete it on his own, right, Cid?"

I looked at Betty. Her hands were on her hips, her jaw set.

I nodded slowly. "I'll teach on Saturday," I said. "I need . . . I need a few days to get Lefty's things settled. Then I'll be back." Betty smiled at Tomik and Siggy, jutting her chin toward them. "Tomik and Siggy will come with me on Saturday to show the class the choreography we worked out. It's the next step and they know it well. I was going to teach it to you, too, Harry, but . . ." I shrugged.

Betty's smile faded.

"It's okay," Harry said, looking at Tomik and Siggy. "I can work with these two."

"All I can say," Betty stated, "is you better be as good as Cid." She turned toward me. "You want us to walk back with you?"

I shook my head.

"We'll walk with him," Tomik said.

"No," I said. "I'm going to stay here a while, then head home."

"But Cid—," Betty began. Then Gertrude touched her shoulder.

"Let's get out of here, leave Cid alone. It's his cousin died, not ours."

Each shook my hand before leaving except Betty, who simply stormed off on her own.

I sat on the dock for an hour, then walked back to the hotel.

The ache in my chest grew worse. Before I reached the hotel, my hands were shaking and I was almost doubled over. Back in the room I sat on my bed, curled my legs up toward my chest, and lay my forehead on my knees. My stomach churned and I thought I would throw up but I didn't.

I looked down and saw Lefty's envelope in my hands. I didn't remember how it had gotten there. I upended it and when Lefty's letter didn't drop out right away, I shook the envelope up and down until it did. Only instead of one letter, there were two, Lefty's, and one I'd missed before. It was old, the stationery brown, stained, and creased, as if it had been folded and unfolded many times. A corner was torn away where it had stuck to the glue on the larger envelope. I checked to see if there were any others, but the big envelope was empty.

A piece of the second letter broke off when I unfolded it. It was a letter to Lefty from a woman named Abigail. It took me a few moments to realize that she was my mother.

The letter was in a simple script, workmanlike, without an extra curve or flourish—but feminine just the same.

✛

Joseph Lunievicz

February 22, 1929
Winston,

I am to give birth any day now. I need to speak to a friend and find myself with no one at hand. Maddie has banished the women I know from my life. My pregnancy has been difficult these last weeks and I have needed her to help me so I have not had the strength to fight her. Teddy does not know what to do for me and has never been one to listen to a woman's chatter. So I am writing to you because I know, if you were here before me, you would listen. You have been a friend and more than a friend. You would not think me a foolish woman led by her emotions. You would comfort me against this dark dream that I am loath to speak of. I fear I will not live to see my baby. There, it is said and written in black on white. It does not seem so bad, now that it has been said, and perhaps I have been a fool all along. But I have dreamed my death. I have seen it and I would have someone promise to care for my baby should I not live to see his birth. It will be a boy. I know this by the feel of him kicking against my belly. He will be all rough and tumble like my brother, and he will have enough of me in him to temper that which is his father. Will you make sure that he is cared for? Will you tell him of me? Perhaps we will laugh over this someday. Right now I would give much to be on the roof of The Hotel Chelsea with you, listening to Ma Rainey. Teddy thinks I'm daft listening to a black woman sing. But you, my friend, do not think that at all.

✛

Inside my head I heard her voice. *Son*. The word plunged into my belly and left a hole there. *Son*.

I read her words again. The ache in my heart became unbearable. When I closed my eyes I saw a woman lying on a birthing bed, blood-spattered sheets, pale dead skin, no face. I released the letter and it dropped to my lap. A breeze from my window tugged at it. My body shook.

✛

I opened my eyes and noticed that the shadows had changed from one part of the room to the other. In an apartment across Twenty-third Street I saw an old man sit on his windowsill, one foot on his fire escape and one in his apartment. He wore an undershirt and pants, with one suspender visible on his shoulder, the other hidden by his large belly. Eventually he slept, and I imagined I could hear his loud snores above the sounds of traffic below us.

Lefty's bed creaked as if he were sitting on it. I knew it was my imagination, but I turned to look anyway. When I finally looked away, I swore I could hear the knock of wood against wood, as if he was placing his wooden leg on the floor next to his headboard.

Betty knocked on my door that evening, after the sun had set. I didn't let her in. She knocked, then banged, but I didn't answer her.

"I know you're in there," she shouted, then lowered her voice. "I've only got a few minutes before I have to go. I've already been late once this week. One more time and Mrs. Armorie kicks me out."

I heard doors open down the hall and Mrs. Esslinger shouted at Betty, "What's the big idea? Keep it down out there."

Betty asked, "Do you know if Cid Wymann is in?"

"How the heck would I know?" Mrs. Esslinger said. "The captain's dead though, if it means anything to yah." Then I heard a door slam shut.

It was stupid, what I did. I should have let her in. Instead, I pushed the sound of her voice into the farthest part of my mind until it was barely a whisper.

Thirty-Two

SHARPS

Late that night I went down to the street—about an hour before curfew shut the city down. I went underground and took the Broadway line to Times Square. There I watched the Motogram on the face of *The New York Times* building switch off its fifteen thousand electric bulbs.

THE NEW YORK TIMES WISHES YOU GOOD NIGHT! rolled across its surface at the stroke of twelve. Then there was nothing. I walked east to Fifth Avenue, past the lions in front of the library, then uptown to the park.

Fifth Avenue was lit by curled lamps, two lights to a post. I remember Mr. Braun had called it "The Avenue," as if there were no other avenue in New York City. Approaching the park I passed St. Patrick's Cathedral, then the Plaza, the Sherry-Netherland, the Pierre, and the Savoy Plaza.

In front of the Sherry-Netherland, a man in top hat and tails stepped out of a black Studebaker. First the driver, then the doorman, held the door for him. He was tall and thin, and took off his hat and gloves by the entrance door.

"So Sam . . . ," he said to the doorman.

"Yes, Mr. Plant," the doorman said, still holding the hotel door open for him.

"I heard a joke today," Mr. Plant continued. His accent was tailored, patrician.

"What joke, Mr. Plant?"

"A man named Wentworth says to a waitress, 'I'll have a demitasse, please.' And a cabbie sitting next to him turns to the waitress and says, 'Gimme the same, and a coffee, too.'"

The doorman stood for a moment as if waiting for the punch line. Then, he smiled. "That's a good one, Mr. Plant. A demitasse. That's a good one."

Up to Sixty-fifth Street I walked, on to Millionaires' Row. Andrew Carnegie's mansion book-ended it at Ninety-first Street on the northern end of Central Park, and the hotels on Fifty-ninth Street held it up on the south. The Astors, the Vanderbilts, and the Whitneys lived in the palaces that lay in between, along with industrialists like Henry Phipps and F. W. Woolworth. Edward Farthings lived there, too.

Tomik had told me, "We're across the street from old Mrs. Astor's house on Sixty-fifth. She's a pip. Got a ballroom that can fit more than twelve hundred people for a soirée—at least that's what her maid tells my mom. That broad can throw a party for the bluebloods when she wants to. Hey, she's got a rug that's made of peacock feathers. Can you believe it? And I heard she's got some pictures of naked women painted onto her ceiling."

I stopped beneath a streetlight in front of the house on Sixty-fourth Street, though *house* is a strange word for a building that took up half a city block. The Astor house rose out of the night to my left, its head topped with a spiked fence like a thorny crown.

I stood there awhile.

"Hey, fella," a voice said. "You know the curfew's on. How about movin' on and gettin' home? Make my night an easy one, will yah?" It was a police officer and he was tapping his billy club lightly into the palm of his hand.

"The Farthings live here?" I asked.

"That's right, now come on. Move along before I have to get rough with yah. These folks over here don't like nobody ogling them at night."

"How do you know I don't live up here?"

"Don't need to take but one look."

I looked at my clothes. They were wrinkled, my shoes badly scuffed, my shirt stained brown and untucked. I felt a breeze run through a hole at one elbow. At some point in the day I'd changed for my lesson, but I'd never gone up to the roof for it. I realized only then that Nikolai had not come down to get me.

"Ain't you got a home to go to?" the cop asked.

I looked back at the stolid building. There was little of the flair of the surrounding buildings about it. It spoke of new wealth, an edging into society.

I heard a car pull up behind us. A door opened, then shut.

"Kopecky," the policeman said and I turned around, thinking it was Tomik. "I was just talkin' to the lad here about the curfew."

Mr. Kopecky came around the limo.

"Mr. Kopecky?" I said, surprised. He looked older. Up

close his face was deeply lined, and his hair was streaked with gray.

"You know this kid?" the policeman asked.

Mr. Kopecky's eyes opened wider and his skin flushed crimson. His hands closed into huge fists as he pushed past the cop.

I remembered Tomik's black-and-blue cheek.

"Hey—," the policeman said, losing his balance.

I put my hands out in front of me.

Mr. Kopecky slapped them aside and stopped inches from me. "Wymann!" he seethed. "You, Wymann."

"I'm taking care of it, Mack," the policeman said, trying to grab Mr. Kopecky's shoulder.

Mr. Kopecky threw off the policeman's hand. "You!" he said again, pointing a thick black-gloved finger at me. "Stay away from my family. You're going to get my son killed! Just like your father. You're just like your father!"

The policeman came up behind Mr. Kopecky and pulled at his arms. While the two of them struggled, I backed away, then ran.

"You're just like your father!" rang off the mansion walls and echoed down the avenue. I beat at the words as if they were gnats, but I could not get rid of them. I didn't stop running until I got home. I threw myself onto my bed, wrapped my pillow around my head, and covered my ears. "I am not my father," I repeated over and over until sleep finally took me.

✛

Looking into the mirror late the next morning, I saw my father staring back at me. I felt his blood sear through my veins, his anger, his bitterness. I reached under my bed and found the pictures he'd drawn that I'd saved, pictures I hadn't looked at since I'd entered St. Agnes. *The Spider, Master of Men* was still there, his colors only slightly faded, still grinning up at me, his cape flowing in an imaginary wind. *Blood is blood*, I thought. *I am who I am.* Hadn't Lefty told me in his letter not to forget who I was?

At three o'clock I went up to the roof for my lesson. Nikolai said nothing about my missing the lesson on the previous day. I was focused and sharp in a way I had never been before, scoring touches against Nikolai and bending my blade against his chest until it snapped. I looked at the jagged edge of the broken weapon and wondered if it could go through a canvas jacket.

"It can," Nikolai said, as if reading my thoughts. "Three places to strike, head, heart, and lungs. Mask and jacket are weak."

"There is a competition coming."

"*Da.*"

"I'm going to face Edward Farthings," I said.

"Then we must practice the killing," Nikolai said, and we went back to my lesson.

The days leading up to Saturday's class were long. I couldn't stay in my room and I couldn't leave it, yet staying was worse. My legs twitched. My chest ached. All through the daylight hours I walked, following Lefty's path and picturing him in front of me, the tap-boom pause of his step echoing between the factories and warehouses of the meatpacking district near the West Side Highway. I carried Aldo Nadi's book with me, even though I knew the words by heart. Most days I ended up on the roof. The gravel by the edge was missing in two places where Lefty must have stood time and again. I stood in his place and swayed with the summer breeze.

At night I took my lesson with Nikolai, then fenced with Tomik. We spoke little except with the movement of our blades. I didn't mention my meeting with his father. Neither did he.

When he left I retreated into the shadows of the flickering movie houses. I saw *Thirty Seconds Over Tokyo, Double Indemnity, Lifeboat*, and *Henry V*, with Olivier using Shakespeare's words to rally the Allies against Germany for their final push. I saw *Frenchman's Creek* because I'd read an article about it in *Photoplay* that mentioned Aldo Nadi's name. It said he'd worked on the choreography of the fights with Basil Rathbone and Joan Fontaine—fights between a man and a woman. But Nadi's name was not in the credits. The article had also said that Nadi had opened a salle in Los Angeles. I pictured the room I'd seen him in with Tomik and Siggy and Mr. Braun at the Savoy Plaza so many years before. In my mind the room was empty, its window open, an ashtray overflowing with crushed cigarettes placed neatly on a nightstand near the front door. In the darkness of the movie theatres, I slid down into my seat and disappeared.

✢

Saturday I was greeted by the troupe with a loud chorus of "To take off shirt!"

Siggy and Tomik were there, too, standing apart from the troupe but near Harry. Betty wouldn't look at me. I forced my lips into a smile.

That first class passed in a fog. I didn't say a word to Betty. She stiffened her jaw and quivered, then solidified and became like stone. I didn't know what to do. The pain in my chest wouldn't go away, and looking at her only made it worse. I didn't understand why.

Tomik and Siggy stuck close to me. They spoke for me, finished my sentences when I faltered, and demonstrated the moves that we'd written down when I had trouble getting them right. When class was over, the three of us walked back to the hotel together, Siggy and Tomik talking easily about the Dodgers the way we used to when we were kids. Siggy invited us both to his house for dinner the following Saturday, "and Nikolai, too," he added, "if he wants to come. My mother will like the company." Tomik and I agreed.

During my lessons with Nikolai that week, I saw the world in a kind of detail that was lacking everywhere else. We used épées with sharp tips. He didn't say anything to me about them. He simply brought them out and handed one to me. They were razor sharp. Each time we approached each other, the world turned black and white, its edges flickering like the world of a movie screen. It was as if the very particles of air around Nikolai and my blades were visible to me within this frame. In Nadi's book, he wrote of his first duel and the fear he had when he realized what it meant to need only one touch to win a fight. I felt no fear and the ache that was Lefty's passing disappeared while our blades clashed.

Only the first half hour of our lesson was with live steel, because even though my skill improved, I still finished each session with blood running down my chest or arm. Nikolai made me press an alcohol-soaked cloth onto each cut. They stung long into the night—a fresh reminder that I was still alive while others were dead.

Nikolai's harangues grew in intensity. "This weapon will kill you if make mistake," he shouted. "I will not kill you. Farthings will. You will not make mistake!" I pricked his skin with my point and made him bleed, too.

Nikolai made me put on a shirt for the second half of each lesson. "Do not let Kopecky see," he said; then, while I put a shirt on, he put the sharps away and took out our blunt-tipped weapons.

After each lesson Tomik came by and we either went to class or fenced until it was dark. He let pass without comment the fact that I now wore a shirt when we fenced. The members of the troupe said nothing either.

"We may fight against each other at the competition," Tomik said one night.

I nodded.

Tomik laughed and punched me in the shoulder. I winced. Nikolai had hit the exact same spot in our earlier lesson. "Just because you beat me here," Tomik said, "doesn't mean you'll beat me in competition. Competition is different."

Tomik had scored only one touch against me in the last three sessions and I knew he wouldn't touch me if we faced each other.

"If you are touched one time in competition," Nikolai said, as if reading my thoughts from the shadows, "you are dead."

Tomik rolled his eyes. "Hey"—he hesitated a moment, then continued—"what about Betty?"

"What do you mean?"

"If I had somebody like that looking at me the way she does at you—I don't know, Cid. I would talk to her . . . or something."

I stared at Tomik until he lowered his gaze. "All right. All right. Dinner at Siggy's on Saturday?"

I nodded.

Then Tomik pointed to my shoulder. "Did I do that?"

"What?" I asked.

"That."

There was a circle of blood the size of a quarter where he had punched me.

"No," I said.

"Cid, what's going on? Are you all right?"

"Nikolai was rough on me earlier," I said. "That's all."

Tomik nodded but I could tell he didn't believe me.

Thirty-Three
REFUSING THE BLADE

When I asked Nikolai about dinner at Siggy's he froze, his back to me, his weapon pointing down. Its sharp tip circled slowly a few times, then he nodded. "*Da.*" The word came out too soft for me to hear it, so he had to say it again.

For dinner at Siggy's, Nikolai came to my room relatively sober. I'd never seen him wear anything but his fencing clothes, so when I saw that he wore a clean white shirt and slacks, I stared at him with my mouth hanging open.

"Catching flies, Ceedric," he barked.

By the time we arrived at the Amalgamated building, Nikolai had beads of perspiration across his forehead and had stained his shirt badly. We knocked on the door I'd approached once before and this time it opened quickly. Siggy stood in the entrance, smiling, and welcomed us in.

"Glad you could make it, Mr. Varvarinski," he said and bowed deeply. "You, too, Cid," he added with a wink.

Inside Tomik was already sitting on an orange sofa,

next to the old woman with the wandering eye I'd met before. Tomik, too, was neatly dressed in shirt and tie, a glass of water in his hand. A box fan in the window pulled air in from the outside and dulled the sounds from the street below. Across from Tomik was a large wooden table, set with plain white dishes, tarnished silverware, and cloth napkins printed with small yellow flowers. Mrs. Braun came in from the kitchen with a hot plate of stew held between two thick wash towels. Wet hair stuck to her forehead; she blew air out of the corner of her mouth in an attempt to move a loose strand out of her eyes. It floated upward, then fell back down to the same place.

"Hello," she said. "Come in and take a seat. Siggy will get you something to drink. Perhaps Mr. Varvarinski would like something stronger than water?"

I'd taken two steps in before I realized that Nikolai hadn't followed me. I looked back and saw him standing in the doorway. His face looked shattered the way I'd seen him in the hall the day I'd come home from the hospital. I looked at Mrs. Braun and back at Nikolai.

"What's wrong?" I asked.

Nikolai swallowed and his feet moved him forward, his face pale. "Nothing," he said.

"Nikolai," I said, moving closer to him.

"It is gone," he said, pushing my hand away.

Siggy came over with a glass filled with clear liquid. "My mother thought you might like something stronger?" he said.

"*Da*," Nikolai said, smelling it. Nodding in approval,

he drank it down with one gulp, then handed the empty glass back to Siggy.

Siggy's eyes raised and he looked at me. I shrugged.

I watched as the alcohol rearranged Nikolai's features. He blinked a few times and motioned for me to leave him. I went over to Mrs. Braun to see if I could help with anything. She kissed my cheek and said no. "Sit and talk to Siggy and Tomik," she said, so I did just that, allowing the warmth of the room to envelop me.

Before we sat down to dinner, Mr. Goldberg came in from his room down the hall, followed by Mr. Cohen, Siggy's boss in the pickle business.

"He's here on *landsmanschaft* business," Siggy leaned over toward me and whispered.

"I apologize for being so rude," Mr. Goldberg said, addressing us all and introducing himself and Mr. Cohen.

"Ah, the Jew who is not sure he is a Jew," Mr. Cohen said when he saw me, reaching forward to shake my hand. "Have you decided yet?"

I shook my head, smiling.

"Have you become a socialist then?"

"What do you speak of?" Nikolai said from my other side.

I heard a warning in his voice that made me shiver.

"We need more good socialists in this woild."

Nikolai stepped forward. His jaw was set and his face flushed red.

"Nikolai," I said, facing him, "we're guests of my friend. Mr. Cohen meant nothing."

"What is it," Mr. Cohen asked, "that is bothering your friend?"

Nikolai pushed into me and I placed my hands on his chest, pushing him back.

"His name is Nikolai Varvarinski and he is a Russian who had to leave his country after the Great War."

I felt a hand on my back and turned to see Mr. Cohen standing close behind me. He looked into Nikolai's eyes, unafraid.

"We're all," Mr. Cohen spoke softly, "Russians and Poles in dis room—and Americans now—with da right to believe what we want to believe. Dat is how they do things here, Mr. Varvarinski. And they don't kill you for what you believe. Not yet anyway. I didn't mean any insult to your son."

"He is not son," Nikolai said. "He is student."

"Then you are da teacher he told me about. Is he a good student?"

Nikolai nodded.

"I thought he was. We should sit and eat together, no?"

Nikolai hesitated a moment, looking in the direction of Mrs. Braun, then nodded.

Mrs. Braun came up to Nikolai. "Mr. Varvarinski, would you mind helping me serve the stew?"

Nikolai backed into me, as if trying to get away from her, then stopped himself.

Mrs. Braun took his hand with a smile and led him into the kitchen. I breathed a sigh of relief and turned back to face Mr. Cohen, who had not moved.

"His wife and children were killed by the Bolsheviks," I said. "Please forgive him his temper."

Mr. Cohen nodded while he placed his hand on my

shoulder and squeezed it. I hoped that meant that he would not bring up the subject again. "It is that way with many of us," he said. "And before the Bolsheviks there were the pogroms. And before them, the Cossacks. What's a man to do? It is the way of the woild for a Jew."

Tomik was quiet that evening.

"What happened to the Tomik Kopecky I knew as a boy?" Mrs. Braun asked near the end of the meal.

Tomik smiled at Mrs. Braun but said nothing.

"This boy is carrying a heavy load on his shoulders," Mr. Cohen said. "Perhaps he should lighten it? That is what good company is for."

"Yeah, Tomik," Siggy added. "You're among friends."

"Mr. Cohen," Tomik began. "When would you go against the wishes of your father?"

"That is a heavy weight, indeed," Mr. Cohen said, his voice becoming softer and more serious. "For me the answer is simple. I wouldn't go against them. My father was usually right when we disagreed, and the few times he was not, it was of no consequence."

Tomik lowered his head, nodding, though his smile never left his lips.

"If my father was wrong," I said quietly, "I would go against his wishes. And if he used his fists to tell me he was right, I would use mine to tell him he was wrong."

"Then I can only say," Mr. Cohen replied to the silent room, "that we have very different fathers."

Tomik excused himself early from dinner. I asked him if he wanted some company for the walk home. He said no and left us to finish dessert in a respectful silence.

✛

Nikolai drank Mrs. Braun's vodka all evening long, and in the end, I had to half-carry him home. I dropped him at his door on the roof and turned to go but Nikolai stopped me. "*Sadítis*," he said, motioning with his fingers toward the inside of his apartment.

Nikolai had not invited me into his apartment since the first day I'd met him and he'd thrown up on me. I followed him in.

Nikolai sat on the one chair in his room and cleared a small table of debris with a swipe of his arm. Hilts and pommels clattered to the floor.

"*Sadítis!*" he said louder.

I found another chair buried beneath some foul-smelling blankets and pulled it up to the small table. Nikolai had two glasses in front of him and a bottle of vodka, the three objects appearing as if by magic.

Nikolai drank what was in his glass and pointed to mine.

I drank the clear liquid. It burned my throat and made my eyes tear.

Nikolai poured again.

Three more glasses and I could barely keep my head off the table. Nikolai sat upright still, the pale color of his skin the only marker that the alcohol was affecting him.

Then the world turned sideways and something thumped against the table. "What happened?" I asked.

"Your head is on table."

"What is it about Mrs. Braun?" I asked, shifting so I

293

could see out of both eyes, but unable to lift my head up. The world began to spin slowly to the left.

"Drink," Nikolai said in answer.

With his help, I lifted my head up slowly and found the drink in front of me. When I drank it, I toppled over backward, off the chair and onto the floor. A cup hilt's edge rubbed against my teeth.

"Sylvia would be older now," Nikolai said, then I heard the sound of his glass banging down onto the table. "But has look of her. It is trick. God is laughing. Always laughing at Nikolai."

"Who . . . who is Sylvia?" I asked, the words circling my head.

"Wife."

I don't know what else he said because I passed out.

Thirty-Four
BINDING THE BLADE

I awoke after the sun was up with a headache that threatened to split my head in two. I was in my bed. I didn't remember how I'd gotten there. Someone was speaking to me, only I couldn't tell what was being said. I turned over and the light made my head hurt worse.

Betty sat on Lefty's bed. I blinked, thinking she was a mirage. She wasn't. She wore loose gray pants, a white shirt with the sleeves rolled up, and a red kerchief around her head, like Rosie the Riveter. She didn't know I was awake and she gazed out the window daydreaming, her lips moving, talking to herself. Her feet swayed back and forth just above the floor.

Her words started making sense to me. Something about the morning sun. Then she stopped speaking. I tried to sit up.

"I see you," she said without looking at me.

"Have you seen Nikolai?" I croaked.

"You were drunk."

"Is that what this is?"

She frowned. "Yes. Nikolai let me in."

I sat up too quickly and the side of my head started to explode. "What time is it?" I lay back down.

"Almost nine."

"How'd you get in?"

"I just told you."

"I thought you didn't want to talk to me."

She stood up abruptly, smiling. "Wash yourself and get dressed."

I hesitated to remove the sheets. Nikolai must have undressed me because I only had my undershorts on.

"Now you're shy? You think I haven't seen you without your shirt on before?"

I shrugged, got up slowly, and got dressed.

She turned her head away slightly and pretended not to watch.

"You'd better wash first," she said. "In case you hadn't noticed, you smell."

I hesitated, then walked over to the basin. She waited, patiently.

"We're going out," she said.

"Where?" I asked as I dried myself off.

"Out."

The morning sun was bright and the sky crystalline blue. The air was warm on my skin. Even though my head made me pay with every step I took, I enjoyed walking next to Betty.

We bought stale rolls and lemonade at a pushcart on the corner of Broadway and Twenty-third for a nickel, then hopped on the B trolley heading up Broadway.

"Look," Betty said, pointing across to the southbound

side where an unpainted all-white trolley lumbered down-town. "It's Car 555."

I nodded. The trolley we were on took its time heading uptown, stopping every couple of blocks as passengers got on and off. We were on one of the convertibles and its side panels were down, allowing a breeze to cool our legs as we click-clacked along the tracks.

We got off at Columbus Circle and wandered into Central Park, the outline of the Plaza Hotel at our backs. The long shadow of the Farthingses' estate on Fifth Avenue seemed to touch me from the other side of the park, chilling me.

I didn't know the park well and struggled at first to keep up. Merchants' Gate was crowded with sightseers and I had to push my way through. I followed Betty past the Heckscher Playground and the green-and-yellow umbrellas of the Tavern on the Green. Then she walked across a dry meadow and disappeared into a copse. I followed her into the twilight beneath the thick overhanging leaves. Mosquitoes pricked my ears. I heard her laugh but couldn't see her as my eyes adjusted to the shadows. Something splashed as if a stone had been dropped into water.

"Come on," her voice called to me.

I reached a clearing and found her sitting on a small patch of mossy grass at the edge of a lake. She was in shadow but the surface of the lake shimmered from the sun as if it were covered with diamonds.

"This is my favorite place," she said.

I sat down next to her. Neither of us spoke for a while.

"I'm originally from Chicago," she said finally, as if

making a decision. "A town called Lake Forest. They say it's going to be a big place someday. It's next to a college that my parents teach at. Well, my dad did until he was drafted."

"Where is he?"

"North Africa, last I heard. He's with Patton. My uncle died at Anzio."

"Lefty said war is a stupid thing, good only for murderers and patriots."

There was silence again.

"I don't know anything about you," she said. "And you don't know anything about me. Maybe we should start at the beginning?"

I nodded. She took my shoulders and lay me down to her lap.

She told me about her life, who she was and where she had been. How Percival Clangor had saved her from a dreary existence in a small college town. How her mother had always wanted to be an actress and was not allowed because it was, according to her father, "A wastrel's profession not fit even for a man." She said all the men in her family were in the European theatre of operations and that made her laugh. "I think they are patriots," she said, "stupid ones because they might get killed. But what else could they do? Someone has to stop Hitler." She spoke for a long time and I listened. When she was finished she leaned down and kissed me.

When she asked me about myself, I couldn't speak. I didn't know where to start. Then she asked me about Lefty and I told her everything I knew, from our first meeting to our last. The story poured out of me and I couldn't stop it.

"Lefty should have been my father," I said, saying out loud what I had known for so long.

"He was," she replied.

"I wish I had told him that."

"I think he knew."

She kissed me again and this time I kissed her back.

It was the kind of afternoon that you remember in a dream. We went to see Cary Grant in *Arsenic and Old Lace* at noon and I laughed until the top of my head felt like it was going to come off. I walked her to her apartment on Ninety-fourth Street and sat silently with her on her stoop, her hand in mine.

"What happened to your arm, Cid?" she asked finally.

"What do you mean?"

"I saw the marks, the fresh cuts. We've all noticed you've stopped taking your shirt off at class."

"It's nothing," I said, smiling.

She looked at me. "Is Nikolai doing this to you?"

Looking into her eyes I couldn't lie. "It's the way he teaches. We're using sharps."

"Real weapons?" Her voice raised in alarm.

"It's to prepare me for the competition. I have to be ready as if I'll be fighting a duel."

She squared herself to look at me and gripped my hand in both of hers. "But it's *not* a real duel. It's a competition."

"They're the same."

"One is life and death, and one is sport," she said softly.

"I only need one strike," I continued, letting her words deflect off me. "Head, heart, or lungs. One strike and it will all be over."

"What will be over?"

"Everything."

"Cid, you're scaring me. I don't like it when you talk this way."

For a moment Betty's voice faded and I saw Edward Farthings in the distance, his competition whites covered in red.

"I don't want you to fence with Nikolai anymore," she said, bringing me back to her stoop with a gentle touch of her fingers to my cheek.

"What?"

"Look what he's done to your arm. He got you drunk last night. You talk about a sport as if it's life or death combat. Nobody teaches that way. He could get you hurt worse than he already has. He could get you killed."

"Lefty used to say the same thing."

"Then you know I'm right."

"He won't kill me. And"—I hesitated for a moment, then went on—"when we fence with sharps I forget about the pain. It hurts where he touches me but it doesn't hurt here." I touched my heart.

She placed her head on my shoulder and drew close to me. I felt the heat of her body against mine.

"Nikolai's my teacher," I whispered into her hair. "He's all I have left."

"I don't want to fight," she said.

"I don't either."

"Will you at least stop using . . ."

"Sharps?"

She nodded.

I said nothing.

After a while she asked, "Why is the competition so important to you?"

"Because I'm going to face Edward Farthings."

She nodded. "What about Mr. Scarpetto?"

I waited a long time to answer. "We are not finished with each other yet. I owe them both for the beating he gave me and for what has happened to Tomik."

"Your friend Tomik is going to drag you into it, isn't he?"

"Tomik is my friend. You don't let your friends down."

"What about me? Am I your friend?"

"More, I think."

She laughed and looked up at me. "You think?"

"When can I, well . . . When can I see you again?" I asked.

"Class, you knucklehead. Or have you already forgotten that you're still teaching?"

I followed her with my eyes as she walked up to the door of her brownstone. A woman in a gray housedress stood there waiting for her, her hair in curlers, her arms folded across her chest. She scowled at me as Betty walked past. The door closed and the image of Edward Farthings in bloody whites reappeared. When I blinked, he vanished as if he'd never been there in the first place.

Thirty-Five
COUNTER-BEAT

"Tomik, you stupid ass," Scarps said, his voice filling the theatre. "You stupid prick of an ass."

Tomik's blade hung over my head in an arc, his head cut frozen above my parry five. We were in the middle of the *Robin Hood* choreography, halfway into class and already into a good sweat.

I turned to see the large form of Rick Scarpetto standing near the back row. Behind him was Edward Farthings, flanked by two young men whose faces looked familiar. They were mirror images of each other, their white hair close-cropped, the collars of their white shirts stained gray, their black suspenders sharply contrasting in two solid bands down their fronts. The gleam of brass knuckles shown across their left hands.

"Holy crap," Siggy said, "it's the Smith brothers."

"Fucking Cedric Wymann and Siggy Braun," one of them said.

I stepped toward the front of the stage, followed by Siggy and Tomik. A large hand landed on my shoulder. It was Harry Boles's.

"Who are these guys?" Harry asked quietly.

"Stay out of it," I said, not taking my eyes from Scarps's face.

"No, he won't," Betty's voice added. "This is our theatre and whoever they are, they're not welcome."

"Betty, Harry, keep everyone up here on the stage, please."

"Listening to a woman, huh, Cid," Scarps said. "What's her name?"

I jumped down to the floor still gripping my rapier. "Last time I met you with one of these, you went home crying like a baby."

Scarps's face turned into a scowl and he stepped forward, reaching with his hand behind him.

"Cid," Betty shouted.

"Richard," Edward said, stopping him, "this is neither the time nor the place."

Scarps stepped aside and Edward Farthings walked past him, stopping a few paces in front of me. Seeing him up close in the flesh was a surprise. He was handsome, his features angular, his hair a dirty blond and cut neatly short.

"Mr. Wymann," he said, examining his fingernails. "The last time we met, you attacked me from behind, without warning. I believe, at this point in time, we are even on that count." Scarps grinned and the Smith brothers nodded.

"Get out of this theatre," I said.

"I think," Edward said, looking up at me, "you are in no position to tell me anything."

"I think he is." Harry's voice came deeply from behind

me followed by a chorus of agreement. I glanced to either side and saw that the whole troupe, even Dean and Kovacs, stood at the edge of the stage, their weapons gleaming. Betty and Di had hastily thrown on their shirts but the rest were still bare chested.

Tomik and Siggy stepped up to either side of me.

Edward scanned the theatre slowly, seeming to take note of the broken seats, the sagging stage, the dusty lights above us. Finally his eyes settled on me again. "I've come for Tomik." He looked back over his shoulder and motioned with his head. From the darkness of the hallway came Mr. Kopecky, his chauffeur's uniform wrinkled from a day of driving, taller still than anyone else in the room.

"Tomik," he said, coming up behind Edward. "Get your things and come wit' us."

Tomik looked at me and back at his father, then shook his head.

"Get your things," Mr. Kopecky said again, pausing on each word.

"No," Tomik replied.

"I've done a lot for you and your family, Tomik," Edward said. "I would think about this before I made any rash decisions."

"I'm not carrying your bag anymore," Tomik said quietly.

"Tomik!" Mr. Kopecky shouted, stepping forward, raising his hand to strike. Di cried out behind us, and I stepped forward, too.

"Mr. Kopecky," Edward said, raising his hand to silence him. "There's no need for that here. Take your son, and we'll deal with this in private."

"Pappa," Tomik said, "I'm not going."

"It is Wymann's fault," Mr. Kopecky said turning from Tomik to me. "He is like his father. Ruins what he touches." Mr. Kopecky reached out with his large hand for Tomik's arm but Tomik threw it off. A look of surprise on Mr. Kopecky's face told me that this had never happened before.

"There's a beatin' waitin' for you when you get home," Scarps said.

I stepped between Mr. Kopecky and Tomik. "He said he's not coming. Now it's time for all of you to leave."

"Mr. Kopecky," Edward said, "get your son."

"When I was six," I said to Mr. Kopecky, "I saw you stand up to six men who came looking for you. You sent them running with a shotgun at your side."

"Mr. Kopecky, get your son," Edward's voice pushed Mr. Kopecky to take another step forward.

"Where is that man?" I asked.

"Gentlemen." Percival Clangor's voice echoed throughout the room. "To what do we owe this visit?" He entered from the backstage door, Betty at his side. They advanced to the space between us, making us all give way.

"Who's the bird in tights?" one of the Smith brothers asked.

"Shut up," Scarps cut him off. "Listen and watch."

"My name is Percival Clangor and this is my theatre." Percy threw out his arms to either side. "These young people are my troupe. Perhaps you are interested in investing in the arts? As you can see, the arts have been neglected in this time of war."

Edward laughed, shaking his head, then stopped. "Maybe. That's not a bad idea come to think of it, Mr. Clangor. But not right now. My name is Farthings, Edward Farthings, and I'm sorry to have disturbed you and your troupe. I've come to pick up something that has strayed from me, but it seems I was mistaken as to its location. Again, I'm sorry to have disturbed you." Edward bowed slightly and Percy returned the gesture. "Now, if you'll excuse me, we have a table waiting for us at the Stork Club."

Edward turned away from us and took two steps, then stopped. "Mr. Kopecky," he said, without turning around to face him. "You will throw Tomik's belongings out when you arrive at the residence and I believe my father will meet with you in the morning to discuss your future and the future of your family as part of the Farthings estate. Do you understand?"

Mr. Kopecky didn't move. Cords of muscle stood out on his neck and his face flushed red.

"Do you understand?"

"Come on, Pops," Scarps whispered.

Mr. Kopecky bowed his head. "Yes, Mr. Farthings," he said. "I understand." Without any further hesitation, he turned away and walked past Edward Farthings.

Edward's back remained to me but he didn't move. "You have a weapon at your side, Mr. Wymann. I wonder if you know how to use it?"

"We'll see how well I can use it at the competition on Saturday."

Edward turned around, the look of surprise on his face barely masked by his smile. "Now that is interesting. I shall look forward to teaching you a lesson there, if we should meet."

"Oh, we'll meet," I said. "You can be sure of that. Only thing we need to find out is who gives who the lesson."

✠

"I'm sorry, Mr. Clangor," I said as soon as they'd left.

"It's not Cid's fault," Tomik interrupted. "It's mine. I won't be back, so you won't see them again."

"What do you mean, you won't be back?" Harry Boles said.

"Were we actually going to fight them?" Pekarsky asked. "You know I'm not really a fighter. I'm an actor."

"And not a very good one at that," Dean said. "I could see your arm shaking from here."

"Sure you didn't piss yourself?" Kovacs added.

"Who were they?" Pekarsky asked. "And who was that big guy? Was he your father, Tomik?"

"That's enough talk." Percy raised his arms above his head. "Let's have some quiet. Everyone, put your weapons away, the class is over for the evening. Cid, come with me."

I looked at Siggy and Tomik. "Wait for me here," I said, then followed Percy into his office. Betty came in behind me.

Percy raised an eyebrow at her, but she folded her arms across her chest and refused to budge. "Leave and close the door," he said, pointing a finger at the open door. Looking first at him, then at me, she left and closed the door behind her.

I sat in the only other available chair.

"I don't care who those people were or why they were here," Percy said. "I don't want to see them here again. You have a checkered past, Mr. Wymann, and unorthodox methods of teaching. I have ignored both up until now because of Mr. Leftingsham and because you have had results, but I will not have my troupe and I will not have Betty in danger. Do not make me regret taking you on."

"I won't, Mr. Clangor."

"Good. Now get the hell out of here before I change my mind."

✛

"You'll stay with me," I said, as the three of us walked home.

Tomik shook his head.

"You can stay with me," Siggy said. "My mom would love to have you over."

Tomik shook his head again.

"There's no argument," I said. "I have an extra bed and you don't have to pay. Lefty paid up the room until I'm eighteen. He wrote it into his will. Besides, you wouldn't be in this mess if it wasn't for me."

"No," Tomik said.

"Then where you gonna stay?" Siggy asked, walking quickly to get in front of Tomik and look him in the eyes.

Tomik stopped.

"Why did you do it?" Siggy asked. "Why didn't you just go home with him?"

"I don't want to be like my father," Tomik said. "I don't want to carry another man's bags and fetch his things, and watch him eye my daughters."

"Stay at my place," I offered again.

This time Tomik looked at me and nodded. Lowering his head in defeat, and thrusting his hands into his pockets, he gave in. The next day, a bag of neatly folded clothes appeared in front of my door.

Thirty-Six
THE TOUCH

Friday evening, the night before the competition, Tomik told me he had to return home.

"No," I said. "You can borrow equipment from Nikolai, the same pieces you've been using this week. He won't mind—I've already asked him."

"It's been a week, Cid. I'll be in and out before anyone can see me. I need my own equipment."

"Then let me go with you."

He shook his head.

I let him go.

The next morning I walked into the unassuming lobby of the Hotel Pierre, at 795 Fifth Avenue, with Nikolai Varvarinski at my side and my equipment bag on my shoulder. Tomik had not returned the night before and my search for him in the morning had turned up no clues as to his whereabouts.

"Will show up at tournament," Nikolai said after I'd

returned from my search. "Now forget about boy and get brain into place. You go to ground of killing. Have no room for other things, only *head, heart*, and *lung*." He touched me with his index finger in each targeted area and repeated the words again.

The Hotel Pierre sat at the bottom of Millionaires' Row. With its ballroom and banquet halls it was a popular spot for high society's coming-out parties.

The sound of air conditioners and a touch of cool air greeted us as we entered the lobby. I tried to focus on the competition but my mind kept drifting, wondering what had happened to Tomik. Up at the second-floor banquet hall, I was struck as we entered by the smells of tobacco smoke, musty drapes, and vinegar—the cleanser fencers used to wipe touch-marks off their jackets. Arranged before Nikolai and me were perhaps two dozen young men near my age and older, and twice their number in attendants: fathers, brothers, fencing coaches, and a few sisters, mothers, and wives. Some of the men wore black tie and tails, a strange sight for so early in the morning. The women, young and old, wore the latest Dache and Schiaparelli from Park Avenue.

I saw Betty, Siggy, Harry, and Gertrude, their plain clothes in stark contrast to the finery of the others. They had taken a small group of chairs off to one side. They waved at me and I nodded in recognition. Siggy hadn't even considered fencing in the tournament. "I'm just learning," he'd said when I'd asked him. "I'll come to watch, and in case you need help."

"You are ready," Nikolai whispered into my ear and gave me a push forward.

Edward Farthings stood next to six men. One was in his fifties, with graying hair and a long dead cigar clenched between his teeth. He wore a finely creased gunmetal suit with a bloodred carnation in his lapel and black shoes that shone. He placed one hand on Edward's shoulder as if it were an afterthought, then checked the time on a steel-banded watch that snugly fit the wrist of his other hand.

The six men who stood behind father and son were a varied group. One's back was to us, but his white hair marked him as an older man. Three were Scarps and the Smith brothers, and two were large older men with thick necks, wearing tight, ill-fitting suits the color of evergreens. One of them I recognized as the man who, in addition to Scarps, had given me my beating so many months ago. He had a large scar that creased his cheek and crossed the bridge of his nose. He saw me first, before the others. His lips moved slightly and his partner turned in my direction, followed by Scarps and the others. Scarps's face was blank, his skin pale. His left eye twitched when he saw me.

I moved forward but Nikolai's hand stopped me. "You are found, that is all," he said softly. "Would happen now or later."

"The one with the scar," I said, "is the one who beat me."

Nikolai nodded.

Whispers seemed to tickle Edward's ear, too, making him scan the room slowly. Then his eyes found mine. His facial muscles struggled to contain a mixture of mirth and condescension. With a nod he pointed me out to his father. Mr. Farthings's eyes were cold. I could see his jaw tighten as he bit down onto his cigar and assessed me in a quick glance.

"Fear the father more than son," Nikolai said.

I nodded.

The sixth man in Edward's group turned around so we could finally see his face.

"Joska Gerevich," Nikolai said.

"The instructor from the Gotham Fencer's Club?"

"He is Master, not *een-struc-tor*."

I'd remembered the face, but little else. Joska Gerevich was the same age as Nikolai, but whereas Nikolai was heavy and balding, Joska was thin with wispy white hair. He wore a rumpled gray suit, an old-fashioned style from before the war that hung off his shoulders a size too large.

I looked at Nikolai, swaying next to me. He wore pants and his usual long-sleeved black shirt with the stretched-out collar.

"You know him from Russia?" I asked.

"Italy. Do not look more at them. Look at others and remember what I tell you."

"Look for patterns," I said. "Look for weakness."

"What more?"

"Head. Heart. Lungs."

"*Da.*" He shifted his hand so he could clap me on the back and propel me to a red, cloth-covered table, behind which sat two older men, their noses buried in paperwork. Both wore black suits with vests, their lapels adorned with fresh white carnations.

I reached into my pocket and took out my Amateur Fencers League of America documentation. It had arrived just after Lefty had died. I'd only taken it out of its envelope that morning. The larger of the two men took it, drawing the paper close to his eyes. Squinting, he pulled out a pair of wire-rimmed spectacles and scanned my documentation.

"Cedric Wymann," I said. "I would like to compete—"

"With whom are you affiliated?" the man interrupted, not looking away from the small print.

"I'm not affiliated with—"

"Come, come, Mr. . . . hmmm, Wymann? Which *club* are you affiliated with?"

Nikolai placed both of his hands on the papers in front of the men, who quickly leaned back and looked up. "Today is open competition?"

"Now, there is no need for this kind of—"

"Nikolai Varvarinski?" a wary voice broke in from my side.

"Joska Gerevich," Nikolai replied.

"Do you know this man and his—student?" the man behind the table asked.

"Yes." Joska looked from Nikolai to me. "He is your student, is he not?"

Nikolai nodded.

"But Mr. Gerevich—" the man at the table stammered.

"His teacher is Nikolai Varvarinski," Joska said. "That is enough. Put the name of boy onto your list."

Nikolai and Joska faced each other.

"You are drinking," Joska said.

"I am Russian," Nikolai replied.

"Will there be trouble today?"

Nikolai didn't respond.

"Will there be? I will not ask again."

"Let us see what will happen," Nikolai said and took in a big gulp of air as he straightened up and threw back his shoulders. He looked over at me. "Find chair to sit and go."

I looked at Nikolai and wondered if he would be able to stay out of trouble the way he'd promised me the night before.

The competition had been set up by the Gotham Fencer's Club and the competitors' pedigrees reflected that in their mix of old and new money. Edward Farthings and his father sat with two other fencers he seemed to know, and who I assumed were from his club. Two épée fencers from the Fencer's Club were also there, as well as fencers from schools like City College, Fordham, and Cornell. I seemed to be the only fencer there without an affiliation.

The room was set up around two long fencing strips that had been marked out with black tape on the wooden floor. There was a center line, two starting lines, warning lines, and an end line past which you could not retreat. Nikolai had marked them out on the rooftop for me and I'd memorized their places. "You fight in line," he'd said. "Forward or back. Not to side. Not to circle. Not to use hand to parry. Not allowed in competition." Five or six rows of chairs ran on either side of the strips, creating a tunnel within which we would fence. The competitors sat to either side in the first row, their supporters just behind them.

I heard chairs move behind us and Betty's hand touched my shoulder. I looked down at it, the lines of her fingers etched against the worn yellow of my competitive whites. Her fingers were beautiful. Then the world turned black and white and the edges started to flicker.

"Get away from him!" Nikolai shouted. "No women, no friends, no one to be near!" I heard his voice drift as if far away.

"Where's Tomik?" Siggy's voice asked.

"Gone," Nikolai answered. "Will be here soon."

I didn't even turn around to look at their faces. I was in the glade that Paul Gallico had described in Aldo Nadi's book and I was not going to step out until blood had been drawn.

A man with a gray vest stretched across his large belly stepped into the center of the strips, standing beneath a crystal chandelier. Slowly, the room quieted down. The man dabbed at his balding pate with a white handkerchief, then took out a pocket watch and checked it.

I was dressed in my knickers, which Nikolai had given me for the competition, and my jacket, which was unbuttoned across the left side of my chest.

The man closed his watch and addressed us all. "Welcome to the Gotham Fencer's Club's épée competition at the Hotel Pierre, sponsored most graciously by Mr. Edward Farthings, Sr. My name is Frederick David Alden." He cleared his throat, then explained the way the competition would work and who the judges would be. The judges all wore white carnations, as did all of the tournament's officials.

"Do not hold back," Nikolai said in my ear.

I watched the others, looking for weakness, looking for fear.

"You are to kill—"

I nodded.

"No one touch you. No one come close. Kill them one after other. Kill them with first touch."

I looked down at my weapon. At the tip of the blade, where the point would have been, was a small steel crown with three sharp points. The points were wired with dental floss and would soon be painted with red ink.

My first opponent wore bright white knickers and a coat that seemed to make his body glow. He used the popular French-grip épée, as did most of the contestants. I knew he would use finesse in his attacks. I would use force.

The match director stood between us while our judges stood to our sides. I saw only the young man in front of me, even as I saluted him, the audience, and the judges. We placed our masks on our heads and went into en garde.

I could almost hear Aldo Nadi's voice in my head: *Man is how he behaves sword in hand.*

"Fencers ready?" I heard the director ask.

I watched my opponent jerk his blade slightly from side to side, his fingers nervously adjusting their grip. His arm pulled in slightly, as if afraid to be too close to my blade.

Within the privacy of my wire mask, I smiled.

"Ready," we both replied.

"*Allez!*" the director said, and I launched myself at my opponent. He tried a stop-thrust to my arm but I anticipated the movement, dipped the tip of my blade under his, trapped his foible with my forte, and struck his chest. Every inch of my body was extended toward that point, every inch committed to the attack. My blade curled into a half circle and the tip caught first a fold of his jacket and then the skin underneath.

Judges' hands shot up.

"Halt!" shouted the director.

I pulled my blade away and stopped my forward momentum, catching myself at his side.

My opponent had already taken a step in retreat and my strike had caught him off balance. The force of the blow sent him to the floor, onto his back. I turned away and walked back to my position. A woman standing to my right in a canary-colored dress pressed her hand to her mouth. The fingers of her other hand pointed at my opponent. Heads shook slowly as faces turned in my direction.

I turned at my start line to face my opponent. He approached his line warily, the fingers of his free hand massaging the place where I had struck his chest. His white pants and jacket had smudges of dirt on them from where he'd landed. He no longer glowed.

The director drew a black X with a grease pencil on the red mark my tip had made. "Fencers ready?" he asked as he returned to his place between us.

"Ready," we replied.

My opponent stepped forward and extended his arm toward me. I saw the motion, beat down hard on his blade, and flèched, aiming my point high toward the space between his eyes. He came up in a counter-of-sixte but was too slow, and his head jerked back as the tip of my épée punched into his mask.

Judges' arms flew up.

"Halt!" rang across the room again.

I struck my opponent five times in our first bout—three in the chest and two in the head—and left him standing on the strip uncertain of why he'd ever taken up fencing in the first place. I took the second bout just as quickly to win two out of three. He never touched me.

"Heart, head, lung," Nikolai said when I sat down in front of him afterward. "Good." He threw a towel onto my head. The smell of vinegar washed over me as the defeated and the victorious around me used it to remove the red marks they had accumulated from their clothes.

Nikolai's shaking white finger pointed past my nose across the fencing strips to a thick young man with blond hair and a reddish face. He was talking to a man with silver hair who appeared to be his father. He glanced in my direction as I looked at him, lowering his head in a curt bow without ever taking his eyes from me. We stared at each other until his father pulled him away.

I watched Edward Farthings fence. He greeted his opponent with a backslap and a firm handshake, then took him apart. The strikes, when they came, were simple, efficient, and direct. Edward dotted his opponent's body with red ink. When the bout was over, he had barely broken a sweat.

The young blond man was my second opponent. Leeds, called "Young Mr. Leeds" by the director, shook hands warmly when we were called forward to begin and drew applause from the crowd when he was introduced. When the director called "*Allez!*" neither one of us moved. When I finally stepped forward, Leeds mirrored me almost exactly in his retreat, his movements assured. We moved back and forth as if we were two dance partners exchanging leads. Finally I engaged his blade in tierce as I took a large step forward, causing him to take an equally large step back. But my legs were longer and the single step allowed me to close the distance just enough to attack. I lunged, striking at Leeds's belly as he tried to press back against my blade. He parried, expecting the move, only I didn't stop to give him the chance to riposté. I remised to his chest and he followed me, but too late, and my attack struck home. Leeds raised his own hand to acknowledge the touch.

He's dead, I thought, then we began again.

Leeds attacked right away, extending his blade toward my arm and advancing swiftly. I gave ground with a small retreat, waited until he was close to touching me, then parried with a quick riposté to his chest.

The director called halt and I walked back to my start line, only I heard Nikolai's voice thunder from the side.

"What is this?"

I turned to face Leeds. He was looking at the director. I noticed the judges to either side of Leeds still had their hands up. Behind me my judges had their hands up, too.

Nikolai pushed chairs out of the way and staggered toward us. "This is outrage. No touch was scored! Look at shirt. No mark on shirt!"

"There was no touch!" I heard Siggy shout.

"Please take your seat, sir," the director shouted back.

I looked down at my jacket. There was no mark, at least none that I could see.

The judge standing next to Nikolai looked straight ahead and ignored him.

"There was parry, then riposté!" Nikolai said, pressing his face in front of the judge.

"Sir!" the man said, stepping away from Nikolai.

"Someone get this man away!" the director added, pointing at Nikolai.

I looked at Leeds and I could see him looking at me.

"Sit down, Nikolai," I said.

The shouting grew louder and the two men who had taken my papers at the front door suddenly appeared at Nikolai's side. They seemed uncomfortable, standing there and wringing their hands.

I grasped Nikolai's shoulder and pulled him toward me. "It doesn't matter," I said. "He's already dead."

Nikolai shook his head. Spittle clung to his bottom lip in white bubbles, and his eyes were unfocused. "He did not—"

"It doesn't matter." I pointed at Leeds. "He knows it and so do we. That's all that matters."

"Then he give point to you," Nikolai said. Two hands appeared hesitantly on Nikolai's shoulders.

"Get your hands off him," I said just loud enough for the two men to hear. They pulled their hands back as if they'd been stung. "Sit down," I said to Nikolai, then added in a softer voice, "Sit down, please."

Nikolai blinked twice. He wiped at the spit on his mouth with the back of his hand, then stared at the wet mark it left on his skin. His hand shook and he grasped it with his other. The judge, now standing with the two men from the front desk, whispered something to them that I could not hear.

"Please," I said again.

Nikolai grunted and returned to his seat.

I turned back toward the director and found him not a

foot from me with an outstretched hand and black grease pencil. He placed an X on my chest and returned to his position between us. Three more touches were called against me, three more X's placed on white canvas. After the last, Leeds took off his mask and walked toward me. The director asked him what he was doing but Leeds ignored him. He stepped up to me. I took off my mask, unsure of what he wanted to say.

"You've won," he said.

"Not by the judges' score."

"They're wrong. We both know it."

I nodded.

"Do you know the judges or the director?"

"I know Edward Farthings and we're not friends."

This seemed to amuse him. "The director's name is Harrington and the judges are Kinsey and Surefellow. Six months ago at Rutgers, they called points for Edward in my semifinal bout with him. Edward won, of course. I registered complaints with the Association and expect to follow up again after this." He took off his glove and strap. "We'll fence again, I think, just not today." He bowed to me and walked off the strip, the director's voice calling after him louder and louder to return or forfeit. That made me smile.

I walked over to the director of my bout. I stood in front of him but he didn't look at me. Instead he placed his hands behind his back and chose a place to the right of my head to stare at. "Mr. Leeds has forfeited, Mr. Wymann. You will pass on to the next round." He waited there for a moment, as if expecting a response. I looked at his face closely and took a moment to memorize its features.

"I won't forget who you are or what you did," I said.

He coughed into his hand as if he hadn't heard.

I walked back to my seat.

"This time you could have lost," Nikolai said to me as soon as I sat down next to him.

"I won on the first touch." It was all I could do not to look at my friends, to see their reaction to what had happened, but I needed my focus. Instead I looked back at the strips to see who was still fencing. Edward Farthings was finishing off his opponent. But there was a clear red mark and a black X on his arm.

Behind me a young woman spoke loudly to the man she was sitting next to. I turned slightly to get a glimpse of her. She wore a pale blue dress and white gloves. Her hands were cupped together on her knee above crossed legs sheathed in nylons that became more visible as her hemline crept upward. "Where is Edward's servant, the young man, Kopecky? He put on quite a show last competition."

"I think," the man said, "that Edward has gone too far with that association." He was maybe ten years older than she was and sat up stiff-backed in his black tux.

"He seemed *gentleman* enough," the woman replied.

"Evelyn, my dear mother says everyone in the world is divided into two classes, snobs and slobs."

"You think *we* are snobs?"

"Of course we are. We have to be."

The woman laughed, a high bell-like sound. It made me shiver. "And this man in front of us," she went on in a stage whisper. "I heard he's a Jew."

"His name's Cid Wymann," Betty's voice cut in.

"Only thing worse than the nouveaux riches," the woman replied, ignoring Betty, "are the immigrant Jews. My father says no one can live with them and they won't go away."

"I'll show you who won't go away—"

I turned around to see Harry lift Betty up out of her seat just as she launched herself at the woman. Betty clipped Harry a few on the ears, struggling with him as he carried her to another section far from other people. Gertie smoked contentedly with a large smile across her face. Siggy shifted two seats in order to sit next to the woman who had made Betty so upset.

"Hello, I'm Siggy Braun, and I'm a Jew, too," he said, extending his hand to her.

The woman stood up, her throat blushing scarlet, and left for another section of the gallery.

I turned back to follow the bouts on the strips, watching the matches as I rubbed the marks off my jacket. I did not see Joska Gerevich approach.

"You do well with your student," Gerevich said, speaking to Nikolai.

Nikolai grunted.

I looked up.

"You teach him Greco."

"Before, I teach Greco. Now, I teach Varvarinski."

"Italian style is finished—too much muscle, not enough finesse. It is all French now."

"Only need to kill, not to make pretty picture."

"Santelli has students. I have students. Nadi is gone. He is in Cali-fornia and making a school there."

This made Nikolai laugh.

"Your boy here," Mr. Farthings said, coming up from behind Gerevich, "is quite good with the blade. Isn't that so, Joseph?" Smoking a large cigar, Mr. Farthings smiled around it.

"Nikolai Varvarinski, Edward Farthings," Joska said by way of introduction, without turning around.

Nikolai stared past Joska at Mr. Farthings. "I know this man. I know son."

Mr. Farthings nodded. He took the cigar out of his mouth and blew smoke. "I bet you do. Did Joseph tell you I brought him here from Hungary? Did he tell you I own him—that I could send him back tomorrow? His family is very popular with the Communist Party these days."

"Why you not kill him, Joska? He deserve killing."

Mr. Farthings placed his cigar in his mouth again and breathed in. The tobacco turned orange-gold as he inhaled. "Where is your family, Mr. Varvarinski?"

"That is enough," Joska said.

"Be careful, Joseph. Don't overstep yourself. Your friend has gotten my attention."

"There was time when you would have killed him like cockroach grown too big for room," Nikolai whispered.

The final bout ended and the audience applauded.

"We should talk more," Mr. Farthings said, pointing the stub of his cigar at Nikolai. "Today or tomorrow, next week, next month. It doesn't matter when." He placed his hand on Joska's shoulder and pulled him along behind.

✛

Joseph Lunievicz

Mr. Frederick David Alden, the master of ceremonies, stepped to the center of the floor and, raising his hands, called for everyone's attention. He announced the semifinalists. They were Edward Farthings; a medium built, black-haired Hungarian named Kelleman; a tall, broad Englishman named Piel; and myself.

I was up first against Piel. I had seen some of his bout earlier and had overheard others talk of him. He was a pugilist and he fenced the way he probably boxed, with quick short jabs and powerful thrusts. His arms were strong and his main attack targeted the forearm in a rapid series of two to four strikes while he advanced.

I decided to draw him in and take him with my riposté.

"*Allez!*" the director said.

Piel stepped forward and feinted an attack to my forearm. The movement seemed to come in slow motion, but I knew it was lightning quick. His blade made a slicing sound as it cut through the air. He feinted again, trying to draw me out, but I retreated and waited. The third time he committed himself further and I feinted a stop-thrust. My blade went forward, forward—then he saw it and counter-parried. His riposté came back at full speed as the world returned to normal. I caught his blade as he committed to the attack and my riposté struck his forearm exactly where he had planned to hit me.

Judges' hands raised and the director called halt. I had drawn first blood, but I had not killed. A glance to the side showed me Nikolai sitting with his arms folded across his chest, shaking his head slowly.

We engaged again and I scored another touch on my

326

opponent's arm. He was single-minded in his attacks, re-peating the strike to my forearm over and over. Sometimes he caught my riposté and forced me back with a counterat-tack of his own. The bout went long. I scored two more, catching him each time with a parry and quick riposté. My fourth touch hit his chest and I breathed a sigh of relief as the director signaled that time had run out and the first bout was over.

Taking off our masks, Piel shook my hand and we changed sides. Piel used a towel to dry off while I ran my arm across my brow and hair. Dark patches shaded our arms and backs.

The moment the director said "*Allez!*" Piel attacked. He put everything into it, striking five then six times at my forearm, each attack following like a jackhammer. I held my ground and parried but could not riposté. In the final at-tack, he used a simple deceive and struck me in the chest.

I looked down at where the point had hit. A sharp pain radiated out from it. There was a red mark there—my first true red mark. It looked like blood. I raised my hand to sig-nal the touch but the judges had already registered the hit. The director drew an X through the mark. I felt the steady pressure of the grease pencil on my chest. *Now who is dead?* I thought. *Now who lies in the glade bleeding with a hole in his lung?*

Siggy's voice cut through to me. "It's only one, Cid. Get back at him!"

I could hear Nikolai's voice in my head, "It only take one." I knew I had to make sure there would not be another.

Our next exchange was long and fierce, a series of attacks and ripostés, he trying to disengage and me maintaining pressure on first one side of his blade, then the other; each of us trying to cause the other to make a slip. When I finally struck his chest, it was with such force that my blade broke.

There was an audible gasp from those watching. The broken tip, sharp and dangerous, had caught his jacket at the shoulder and torn it. There was no blood, but only because he'd been lucky. The director stopped the bout, inspected the jacket and the skin beneath.

A flashbulb popped to my right.

I turned to look and saw a man in his twenties with blond hair, the reddish cheeks and pug nose of an Irishman, and a prosthetic hand in the shape of a mechanical claw. The knees of his pants were threadbare and a battered black felt porkpie sat on his head. He had a pencil clasped in his hand and a notepad in his claw. Beside him stood a photographer, a kid in a short-sleeved shirt who flashed my picture as I looked at him. My eyes saw stars and I heard Nikolai curse him.

A new jacket and blade were fetched and we continued. No other points were scored against me.

Edward Farthings finished his bout at the same time I finished mine. His face was flushed as he took off his mask and shook hands with his opponent. Then he turned toward me. The flash popped again and reflected sharply off the mirrored wall. I closed my eyes. When I opened them, Farthings stood in front of me.

Click, pop, flash.

I covered my eyes with my hand. When I lowered it,

Farthings was gone. I looked behind me and saw him talking to the man with the metal hand.

I finished my bout with Kelleman quickly. His legs were shot and he was tired. I sat down and watched as Farthings struggled against Piel. Farthings was the better fencer that day, but I could tell that Piel, on a different day, could just as easily have taken him. I rubbed absently at the place on my chest where Piel had struck me.

"So you're the new hotshot, huh?" a voice asked me. A metal claw and pencil came into view and I turned toward the reporter. He pushed his hat onto the back of his head and sat down next to me. "Name's Flannagan, kid. What's yours?" He reached over with his good hand.

Nikolai stuck his head between us.

"Take it easy, buddy," Flannagan said. "I'm not doin' nothin' against the law. Just gettin' a story."

"One more pop, pop, pop, and I take camera to wall."

"Hey, Bartholemew," Flannagan called to the photographer.

"Whaaaaat?" the kid yelled back.

People nearby scowled in an attempt to silence us.

"Cut it out, will ya, Barty. I'm gettin' a new angle on this story." He leaned over toward me and bumped into Nikolai. "Hey. Would ya mind?"

"Hah," Nikolai said, then leaned back out of the way.

"What's up with the old guy?" he asked me quietly.

"His name is Nikolai Varvarinski and he's my teacher."

"Teacher, huh? Well it looks like he's done all right by you." He nodded toward Farthings. "All you got to do is go up against him. Shouldn't be too hard." He put his pencil behind his ear and took out a cigarette. It was amazing the control he had over his claw. Sitting back, he lit up and inhaled. "What are you doin' here, Wymann, right? That's your name?"

I nodded.

"You're like a devil with the sword, anybody can see that. But you're not like the rest of these guys. Look at you. The jacket and pants. You don't look flush to me." He leaned forward again. "And your friends, well, they don't look flush either."

"Got something against Jews?"

"Didn't say nothing about you being a Jew, but now that you mention it . . ." He didn't finish the thought but waited for me to.

I kept quiet.

"Nope," he gave in. "Can't say's I mind a Jew with a sword either, long as it's pointed at the social register."

Edward's bout ended. He'd beaten Piel, but had taken a number of hits in the process. The smell of vinegar washed over me as the crowd applauded and Edward took a bow.

Since Edward and I were the only undefeated fencers, our match would be the last of the tournament. I stood up to get ready when Edward Farthings called to everybody to quiet down.

"Perhaps it would be more interesting," Edward began, "before Mr. Wymann and I fence, if we could be treated to an exhibition?"

The crowd murmured softly.

"What have you in mind, Mr. Farthings?" Mr. Alden

asked, taking out his watch to check it against the clock on the far wall.

"Why not an exhibition from two of our esteemed teachers, Mr. Gerevich and Mr."—he turned toward me—"Varvarinski?"

Joska stepped forward. "This is not place for two old men to fight."

"Oh, but it is," Mr. Farthings said. "My son's idea is brilliant, don't you think? What an opportunity! Two men of an age and skill, such as you both."

"I will not—," Gerevich began.

"You will, Joseph," Mr. Farthings said, smiling. "If you don't, I'll have you on the first boat back to Russia in the morning."

"I am Hungarian."

"The fuck if I care."

The room grew quiet.

Mr. Alden seemed about to say something. His mouth opened, then closed.

"I will fight," Nikolai said from behind me.

"Nikolai," I said.

He placed a hand on my shoulder and drew himself forward, standing. A bottle fell over beneath the chair he had been sitting on. It clattered to the ground. "We fight to one hit." He swayed backward, then forward.

"You are drunk, Nikolai," Joska said.

"I am."

Joska looked at him, then nodded. Mr. Farthings blew out a large cloud of smoke.

I knew Nikolai could take care of himself, drunk or

sober. But I remembered the last time Nikolai had faced Gerevich when he had been drunk at the Fencer's Club. I could not allow him to be embarrassed in front of these people.

"If you are too tired to fence now—," I began, but Nikolai stopped me.

He leaned in toward me. "Have you not wanted to see me fight?" he asked softly.

"Not here, in front of these people."

"I will fence," he said loudly, turning away.

"Get them jackets," Edward said, snapping his fingers.

Nikolai laughed and pulled his shirt off over his head. The woman in the blue dress gasped. The one in canary screamed.

"Really, sir," the man next to her said, but only half-heartedly.

"Do not need jacket," Nikolai shouted.

"To take off shirt!" Harry Boles yelled. Betty and Gertrude added their laughter to the others. Nikolai ignored them all.

Piel offered his jacket to Joska. Joska shook his head slowly, took off his suit jacket, and tucked in his shirt. Each man picked up a weapon. Piel held out his mask, too, and Joska looked at Nikolai.

"I will not aim for head," Nikolai said.

Joska waved the mask away, too.

The announcer offered to direct the bout, but both men said no.

"Is not needed," Joska said. "We will know when match is done."

The floor cleared, leaving Joska Gerevich, in his white shirt, and Nikolai Varvarinski, naked from the waist up, in command of the floor.

I watched as the two men approached each other warily, their invitations low. Joska lifted his guard to sixte and Nikolai settled himself just out of striking distance. His body became still. Suddenly they did not seem like old men to me.

"For a drunk he's pretty—," a man behind me began but he was cut off by the fierceness of Joska's attack.

I couldn't follow the movements of their blades. It seemed to me that Joska drove Nikolai back with second intention attacks, and that Nikolai retreated, throwing out stop-thrusts that cut into Joska's movements. Near the edge of the circle of spectators Nikolai drew in a deep parry in quarte to his chest that almost touched his skin, then launched an attack of his own. Joska's riposté didn't stop Nikolai's forward motion. Leaning, his arm extended, Nikolai nearly sprinted forward across the path on which Joska had pushed him back only seconds before. Their blades rang together in a flurry of parries and ripostés. Back at the center of the floor Nikolai tripped and stumbled. Joska took advantage of his lowered guard and stop-thrust to his chest. Nikolai caught himself before he fell, hand parried the blade away from his chest, and struck Joska in the heart with the tip of his weapon.

They froze there for a moment, two old men captured in amber.

The camera flashed.

Mr. Alden stepped forward and cleared his throat.

Nikolai stumbled to one knee and dropped the tip of his blade from Joska's chest. Joska took a step back and raised his hand to signify the touch. There was blood on his shirt from the three prongs of the steel crown.

"But Mr. Gerevich," Mr. Alden said, stepping forward. "Mr. Varvarinski hand parried. We all saw it. The touch is invalid. Your attack would have hit. You are awarded the touch as penalty."

"Varvarinski use different rules," Joska replied, breathing hard. He offered his hand to Nikolai.

Nikolai looked up at Joska. He laughed and took the proffered hand.

"Your instructor is a cheat," Edward Farthings said loud enough for all to hear, his voice cracking on the last word.

Nikolai attempted to stand, then fell back onto the floor.

"He is a cheat and a drunk."

"You're lucky it's not fifty years ago, Edward," I said, stepping over to Nikolai. I helped him to his feet. "He would have challenged you to a duel and killed you." The Smith brothers closed their distance around me, but for some reason Scarps was staring at the door, ignoring me.

Edward laughed. "I think he will be challenged enough finding his way out of this hall. Perhaps you should follow him?"

"Are you afraid you'll lose to me in front of your friends?"

Edward's face hardened.

Smoke filled the space between us. "One more match for the day?" Mr. Farthings said. "Mr. Alden will direct?"

Mr. Alden nodded.

"And we'll have two judges? How 'bout Kinsey and Surefellow?" He turned away from me, ready to walk back to his seat.

"I don't think so," I said.

"What was that?" Mr. Farthings said, stopping in his place.

I spoke loud enough for all to hear. "I would like two other judges. Mr. Leeds will explain."

"I will, Mr. Farthings," Leeds said from behind me. "Mr. Wymann must be allowed to choose two others."

Mr. Farthings did not move. His fingers slowly closed around his cigar, crushing it. "Two others, then," he said finally, "any others." He threw the remains of his cigar onto the floor and stepped on it, then turned around and walked back to me.

"What are you going to do," I asked quietly as he came near, "send your men to cripple me the way your son did?"

"You've got balls," he said in a whisper. "You'd better hold on to them before someone cuts 'em off." He raised his voice and turned away from me. "Now let's finish this."

Nikolai had risen to his feet while we spoke, and before Mr. Farthings could fully turn away, he grabbed my glove from where it was tucked in my jacket and slapped Farthings across the face with it. "Coward," he said.

Farthings's two bodyguards raced forward, but he held up his hands to stop them. He turned toward Nikolai, rubbing the place on his cheek where the glove had struck. "Nobody does that to me and lives."

"I live," Nikolai said.

The camera flashed.

"You think you're still in Russia? You're in the United States of America, my friend. We do things different here."

"Bolsheviks kill my wife and child. Burn babies when it was dark. Came like thief and coward. How are things different?"

Farthings turned away. "Get the camera," he said to one of his men and walked back to his seat. His bodyguard took off after the newspapermen. Flannagan and Bartholomew ran for the door. There was a scuffle at the entrance to the hall and we all heard the sound of a camera being smashed against the floor.

"You can't stop a good story, Mr. Farthings," Flannagan shouted as he was pushed out the door.

I caught Siggy's eye. He was unsure what to do. His hands were clenched in fists. I shook my head slightly. But Siggy moved forward with Harry, Betty, and Gertrude, to the seats directly behind my equipment. Nikolai did not run them off this time and neither did I. If something was going to happen, it would be better if they were close.

The room settled and everyone arranged themselves for the final bout. Now there was no small talk to distract us. The room remained silent except for the squeaking of our rubber soles on the wooden floor. We saluted each other and donned our masks. The world flickered for me in black and white.

"*Allez!*" Mr. Alden said.

Edward came at me quickly, beating my blade aside and lunging toward my arm. I counter-parried and ripostéd to his forearm, sending him back out of reach. He swayed back and forth, almost bouncing on his feet with energy. The next time he swayed back, I thrust for his arm, parried his riposté, and lunged for his chest. When he parried, I recovered forward and lunged again for his belly.

"Remise!" Nikolai shouted.

Again Edward parried and retreated, and again I recovered forward and followed. He swept his blade low for my knee, trying to cut into my advance, and I stood straight instead, thrusting for his face. My blade knocked his head back, and the judges' arms shot into the air.

I didn't move. My breathing was short and fast. I took a deep breath and willed myself to relax my guard. Edward seemed frozen, unable to believe what had happened. I walked up to him and said in a voice meant only for him, "If this had been a real duel you would be a dead man." Then I turned my back on him. I knew there were four more touches to score in the bout, but for me the competition was over. I took off my helmet. The day washed through me, making me shiver. Betty shouted my name as she jumped up and down, hugging Gertrude. Siggy was clapping, and Harry's horse whistle pierced the air like a siren. Seeing them made my heart lift and brought a smile to my face for the first time that day. I had beaten Edward Farthings with one touch. There was nothing else to do. There was nothing else to be done. I'd spent so much time thinking about getting to this place that I hadn't thought about what I'd do after I'd reached it.

It was then I realized what had happened to me since Lefty took me from St. Agnes. I saw what he'd done for me. How he'd given me a life—one filled with friends, with a purpose, with a direction. It lay spread out before me, only I hadn't seen it before. Now it was clear as day. I'd thought of Lefty every day since he'd died, but at that moment, I couldn't remember when I'd thought of him last. I missed him but my heart didn't ache the way it had—as a matter of fact, it didn't ache at all.

Then I remembered that Tomik was still missing and that made the hairs on the back of my neck stand up straight. My smile disappeared.

To my right Scarps still stood, unmoving, waiting for something, his mouth hanging half open. His fingers twitched once, then twice. I followed his gaze toward the door.

He's done something, I thought. *He's done something to Tomik.* Why hadn't I seen it before? Then the door crashed opened.

Mr. Kopecky stood framed in the archway, an unconscious Tomik held in his arms. "Look what you did to my boy!" he shouted. "You break every finger. Now I break you!" Tomik's right hand was bandaged and there was a cut across his forehead that still bled.

I looked back at Scarps, who swallowed thickly, his hand rising to his throat. "It had to be done, Pops," he whispered.

"We're not finished, Wymann," Edward shouted and I turned just in time to parry a thrust at my lower back. I dropped my helmet as I turned and smacked the flat of my hand into Edward's mask, catching him off balance and knocking him to the floor.

Scarps turned toward me, as if noticing me for the first time. "Pops," he said, raising his voice, "it's all Wymann's fault. All of it." He reached for something behind his back just as one of the Smith brothers launched himself at me. Siggy tackled him before he could reach me, hitting him shoulder to hip, and slamming him into his brother. Chairs crumpled beneath them. By the front door I saw Mr. Kopecky throw one of Farthings's bodyguards across the room while the other leapt onto his back. But I couldn't see Tomik.

People were screaming, trying to get out of the way. Chairs scattered and people fell to the floor. Nikolai grabbed Mr. Alden by the collar, just as the two men at the front table grabbed his arms from behind.

"Wymann!" Scarps yelled as Siggy cleared the space between us.

I turned and raised my blade as he charged. I saw a glint of steel in his right hand. Something hit me in the back of my legs and I started to fall backward. Scarps ran onto my blade, bending its length double as I fell. He landed on top of me as my blade broke. The flash of silver in his hand moved toward my side and I couldn't stop it. My head hit the floor and I saw stars. Scarps landed on top of me and I heard the sickening sound of steel piercing cloth and flesh. Then something sharp ripped into my side.

Rick Scarpetto's face was inches from mine. Blood ran out of his mouth from a bitten tongue and lip. His breath came in short rasping gasps. Just behind his ear I could see the bloody, serrated tip of my broken blade rising up from his back.

"I had to do it, Wymann," he gasped. "Don't you see?" His right hand lifted up, pulling red-washed silver out of my side. He was about to plunge it back in when Nikolai grabbed it and plunged the blade down into Scarps's own belly. Then a large man landed on Nikolai's back and they both fell forward, on top of Scarps and me, sending me into the darkness.

Thirty-Seven
THE FIRST POSITION

They tell me I didn't kill Richard Scarpetto—that my broken blade did not do the fatal damage. It was a knife wound to his belly that angled up into his liver that instead finished him off—that and the fact that it took so long to get him to a hospital. The police say he fell on his own blade, the weapon embedding farther when Nikolai and Farthings's man landed on him.

The papers said it was a fencing accident.

I know better.

I'm sitting on a hospital bed for the second time this year and it's evening. The stitches in my side itch. There were forty-five. The doctor said I was lucky no vital organs were hit.

I've had many visitors—Betty and Gertrude, the whole troupe of the Ridolfo players, Siggy and his mother, and Tomik. Even Flannagan, the newspaper reporter, came by.

Joseph Lunievicz

"You've made an enemy of Farthings," he said to me, shaking his head and scratching it with his metal claw.

"I did that a long time ago," I said.

"You going to compete again?"

I nodded.

"Then I'll see you out with the hoi polloi, I think. Yes I do."

Tomik's father no longer works for Mr. Farthings and they've moved out of the estate on Millionaires' Row. There was an apartment open at the Amalgamated on the floor below where Siggy lives. Mr. Goldberg helped them to get in. Mr. Kopecky is not a Jew, but he knows when to say yes to a favor.

Siggy said he'd take care of Tomik while I was recuperating, make sure he stayed out of trouble. I told him it was probably hard to get into trouble when all of the fingers on your right hand were broken. Siggy's nose was broken by one of the Smith brothers. We're still not sure which one did it. He wears a piece of tape across the bridge of his nose like a badge of honor.

"I saw what happened," Betty said to me the other day. "It wasn't your fault that he was killed. You had to defend yourself."

I nodded, wondering if it was true. *You are just like your father,* Mr. Kopecky had said. Only this time I wondered which father he meant. Did he mean Theodore Wymann? Did he mean Winston Arnolf Leftingsham? Or perhaps he meant Nikolai Varvarinski or Abel Braun?

The blood of my family did run through me—the blood of my mother and my father, the blood of Mad Maddie and Winston Arnolf Leftingsham, the blood of people I'd never met but perhaps one day would. But I also knew then that the blood of others, whose blood I would never share, also ran through me in their words and in their deeds. *I am who I am*, I thought, *and that will have to do.*

"I'm glad you're alive," Betty said, holding me tightly. When she released me, she slapped me hard across the face. "Don't ever scare me like that again. You understand?"

I nodded, knowing it was a lie, but not wanting to argue with her. I didn't understand women and knew I probably never would. *I am who I am.*

"Percy says you've got a place in the troupe in the new season if you want, as choreographer of the fights. I told him he was a fool if he didn't offer you a part. What should I tell him?"

"Tell him yes," I said.

"Has Nikolai been to see you?"

"Not yet."

But I know I'll see him. Maybe when he's more sober he'll come by. And if he doesn't, I'll go to him. I know where he lives.

I've taped my father's picture of *The Spider, Master of Men* to the mirror in my room. Siggy brought it to me. "I didn't know he drew the Spider," Siggy said. "Did he do any of the covers?"

I shook my head.

Who did my father see in the man in the black hat, mask, and cape? I see my father beneath the mask, imprisoned, a character he could draw only in the privacy of his back room—a person he could never be. But his limitations are not mine. *I am who I am*, but I am not only him.

✦

It's past visiting hours. The lights are off. Curfew is on, and the city breathes out silently. I hear the creaking of Lefty's leg as he unhinges it and lays it on the ground next to the chair by my bed. He's sitting there, a smug smile lifting the lips on the good side of his mouth.

Did you think I would leave you forever? he asks.

I shake my head slowly. I can feel tears falling on my cheeks and my chest aches so badly I think it will split.

Look at me, he says and points to his leg and arm. They grow out of his torso and fill his empty shirt arm and pant leg. He starts to laugh and the flesh of his face heals, revealing a handsome man with a toothy grin. He places both of his feet on my bed next to me. I can feel them press against my calf. He folds his arms across his chest. *Now you are whole in this world, Cedric, and I am whole in the next. That is as it should be.*

Thank you, I say as I close my eyes. Thank you.

Glossary of Fencing Terms

bind – To take your opponent's blade with your blade using the strong part (the forte) of your blade against the weak part (the foible) of his. When you bind your opponent's blade, you move it away from its defensive position so that you can then attack the open space left behind.

blood gutter – Also called "the fuller." This is the groove that runs almost the length of the blade where it was believed the blood would flow.' It's also said to be used to decrease suction on the blade when withdrawing it from a body. In actuality, its most important function is to decrease the weight of the blade without losing blade strength.

en garde – The basic fencing stance from which all movement starts and ends. The sword arm is bent at the elbow with the blade tip pointing at your opponent. The back arm is bent and the fingers hang loosely near the ear. The legs are bent with the back foot pointing to the side and the front foot pointing toward your opponent.

épée – A heavy thrusting weapon and one of the three modern fencing weapons. It is the closest to the traditional dueling weapon of the 18th and 19th centuries. The target in épée is the whole body, from toes to head and fingers. Unlike foil and saber, there are no 'right-of-way' rules as to who can strike and when. In épée, the first person to hit with his point gets credit for the touch. You score with the point of the weapon only. The hilt and guard are bigger to protect the hand and the blade is thicker and stiffer than on either foil or saber.

first position – The stance you take before en garde. The heels are together, with the back foot pointing to the side and the front foot toward the opponent. Legs and arms are straight, the arms angled down toward the floor, with the sword point aimed in front of and slightly toward your opponent as an extension of the arm. You salute your opponent and judges from first position.

flèche – French for arrow. You leap off the front foot, strike at your opponent, and run past him. A running attack.

foible – The upper or weakest part of the blade. In épée, you attack with the point at the tip of the foible. In rapier and saber, you attack with the edge of the foible (which is supposed to be razor sharp) or the tip.

foil – A light thrusting weapon and one of the three modern fencing weapons. The target is only the torso and doesn't include the arms, legs, or head. There are "right-of-way" rules that govern who can strike and when. The blade is thin, bendable, and can only score with the point.

forte – The lower and stronger part of the blade. You parry and bind with the forte of the blade.

French grip – A traditional hilt with a slightly curved grip and a large pommel. The grip is the part of the sword you hold in your hand when you fence. The two original main styles were French and Italian grips.

glissades – An attack that glides along your opponent's blade, controlling it and pushing it out of the way as you strike.

Italian grip – A traditional hilt with finger rings and a crossbar. Not used very often these days, having been replaced by the more modern pistol grip. The grip is the part of the sword you hold in your hand when you fence. The two original main styles were French and Italian grips.

parry – To deflect your opponent's blade away from you so that you are not hit. There are parries to protect each part of the body in épée; they are similar to the parries in foil but, because the whole body is a target, they cover a larger area. Note that these assume a right-handed fencer.
  • A parry of 2 or seconde (point down, palm down)

and a parry of 8 or octave (point down, palm up) protect the right hip and leg.

- A parry of 3 or tierce (point up, palm down) and a parry of 6 or sixte (point up, palm up) protect the right torso, arm and head.
- A parry of 4 or quarte (point up, palm up) protects the left torso, arm and head.
- A parry of 7 or septime (point down, palm up) and a parry of 1 or prime (point down, palm down) protect the lower left side of the body.

passatta back and forward – Passatta is Italian for pass. A rapid and large movement forward or back. It is larger than an advance or a retreat. The back foot from en garde passes forward past the front foot. The front foot then moves forward to en garde in the recovery forward. In the passatta back, the front foot moves all the way back past the back foot.

rapier – The weapon of the 15th, 16th, and 17th centuries that had an edge and a point. A meter or more in length, it usually had a complex hilt to protect the hand. It was the weapon of Shakespeare's time. Transitional rapiers of the early 17th century used the point more and the edge less, eventually becoming the smallsword of the 18th and 19th centuries, and finally the épée and foil of modern times.

remise – Immediate replacement of an attack that either missed or was parried with another attack without withdrawing the arm. An attack followed by an attack.

riposté – A counterattack made immediately after a successful parry.

stop-thrust – A counterattack that thrusts into your opponent's attack.

thrust – An attack made with the point.

touch - To score a point; to touch the opponent with the point of the blade.

Acknowledgments

Writing this book has been a real dream come true for me as a writer. It could not have been written and found its way into print without the help of a number of people. Special thanks go to my agent, Joanne Brownstein at Brandt & Hochman Literary Agents, Inc., for her editorial help and for seeing something in the work that told her not to give up.

Special thanks go to three fellow writers who helped again and again saying "Yes" to one more read through and editing job: Michael Malone, Rachel Kranz, and Tim Coleman.

Thanks to the other writers in the Pentameters writers' group including Aury Wallington, David Freeland, and Chris Gullo, who pitched in on various versions of the book. Thanks to Jonathan Pecarsky for the idea to turn this novel into a young adult book.

And special thanks to the publisher Evelyn Fazio for her support and belief in the story of a boy from Queens who picks up a sword.

As a book of historical fiction, set in a time and place where real people lived and breathed, it also took a lot of research to get the important details right. *The WPA Guide to New York City* (the Federal Writers Project guide to 1930s New York) was essential to my work.

Special thanks to my father, Bill Lober, and my father-in-law, Vince Vicente, for the long talks about their experiences growing up in the 1930s and 40s, which added texture to Cid's story.

I am indebted to Joe Daly, a true master of fence, both with the épée and the stage rapier—all I know about stage combat I learned from him.

Joe Brodeth, another fencing master and teacher, generously gave his time to help me with the details of how competitive fencing was done "back in the day."

The New York Public Library was an invaluable resource to camp out in and read all those *New York Times* editions on microfiche.

The Ragdale Writer's retreat in Lake Forest, Illinois, afforded me the time in four extended stays to think about Cid while I walked and watched the snow fall.

The New York City I wrote about in this book is mostly true; the main characters and their actions are fiction. Any inaccuracies, intentional or unintentional, in time and place are completely the fault of this author.

Last but not least thanks must go to my wife, Karen, who has always believed in me, even when I did not believe in myself. She has waited almost as long for this as I have.